New York Times bests

...d and three sor
boys, and currently o..
somes in her home, she realises the most valuable
asset a woman has for coping with men is a sense of
humour. Not to mention a large trash bag and a pair
of tongs.

Writing as Sherrilyn Kenyon and Kinley MacGregor,
she is the bestselling and award-winning author of
several series, including The Dark-Hunters®.

Visit Sherrilyn Kenyon's award-winning website at
www.dark-hunter.com.

Knight of Darkness

Sherrilyn Kenyon
writing as
Kinley MacGregor

PIATKUS

PIATKUS

First published in Great Britain in 2008 by Piatkus Books
This paperback edition published in 2008 by Piatkus Books
First published in the US in 2006 by Avon,
An Imprint of HarperCollins Publishers, New York

A CIP catalogue record for this book
is available from the British Library

ISBN 978-0-7499-3873-4

Papers used by Piatkus are natural, recyclable products made from
wood grown in sustainable forests and certified in accordance with
the rules of the Forest Stewardship Council

Typeset in Times by
Action Publishing Technology Ltd, Gloucester
Printed and bound by Clays Ltd, Bungay, Suffolk

Piatkus Books
An imprint of
Little, Brown Book Group
100 Victoria Embankment
London EC4Y 0DY

An Hachette Livre UK Company

www.piatkus.co.uk

Knight of
Darkness

Prologue

It has been said by the wise that in the heart of every man there lies a noble beast who seeks to do what is right. But before he becomes a man, he is a child. A boy. In the best of circumstances, that child is conceived in love, and he is nurtured so that he can grow to manhood to be noble and kind, and fulfill his destiny.

And then there are others. Those who are conceived in darkness and deceit. Those who are suckled on bitterness and hatred. These are not noble beasts. They are fierce and angry.

They are feral lions bent on the destruction of all.

These men grow to resent those around them. Not by choice, but because whenever they dared to reach out to anyone for comfort, they were met with more anger and hostility. With scorn and brutality. It is all they know. All they've ever learned.

These men are what they're exposed to. For good.

For bad.

For evil.

How do I know? I'm one of those of beasts. Meant to be a son of light, I was born of the darkest arts. Torn between the two, I've never known peace or succor. Never known a gentle touch. Malice. Cruelty. Rage. Those are what nurtured me into what I am today. Not noble, but definitely a beast. One who stalks this life in search of those like me who walk the path of evil so that I can expose them for what they really are. And once they are known to us, it is by my hand that they die.

I am fortitude. I am sinister.

Most of all, I am hatred. It is what nourishes me more than mother's milk ever could.

I would have it no other way. For it is that darkest part of my soul that allows me to do what I must. But whether I work for the betterment of mankind or the betterment of myself is anyone's guess.

Even my own.

Chapter One

'There's a traitor among us.'

With a completely stoic expression, Varian duFey looked up from the desk where he was wasting time on a Sudoku puzzle to meet Merlin's worried gaze. As always, she was dressed in a long white medieval styled gown that was trimmed in gold, while her pale flaxen hair fell around her shoulders and down her back like a mantle of silk. Unlike the Merlin who'd served King Arthur, Aquila Penmerlin was lithe and young, with a beauty that was only surpassed by her intelligence and magick.

Scratching his chin, Varian merely arched a single brow at her agitated demeanor. 'No shit, Sherlock. There's always a traitor among us.'

Closing the distance between them, she cradled his chin in her hand and forced him to look up at her. Those cold blue eyes bored into him, and by the sharp turn of her perfectly shaped lips he could tell she didn't find his words amusing. Before he could move, she waved her hand in a circle before his face, causing a mist to form a ball in the air. As the mist swirled, it began to reveal an image.

It showed a man in his mid twenties lying facedown

in a pool of his own blood ... only the blood wasn't red, it was a dark sickly gray ... as was everything in the picture. That told him that the body wasn't in the world of man or in Avalon. It was on the 'other' side – the one that was controlled by unrelenting evil.

Beautiful, just beautiful. He could see right where this was heading ... straight down a shitty road that ended with him getting screwed over.

Again.

He must truly be a masochist, otherwise, he'd get up right now, tell her to shove it, and leave.

If only it were that easy.

Varian narrowed his gaze on the man's body. Dressed in the chain-mail armor and dark surcoat that were common for mid twelfth-century England, the dead man had one arm outstretched toward an old stone building as if he'd been reaching for help when he'd died. Not that anyone in that particular realm would ever stoop to help someone, at least not unless an obscene amount of money had changed hands.

But that wasn't what disturbed Varian, nor did he care that it was obvious from the bruises and cuts that the man had been severely beaten and tortured before death had spared him. What made his heart stop beating was the sight of where the knight's armor had been torn free of his left shoulder blade to reveal the tattoo of a dragon encircled by fire rising out of a goblet. There were only a handful of men who bore that mark, and their names were a very carefully guarded secret. More than that, they were men who'd been imbued with extremely strong magick. That alone should have kept the dead man safe from whatever had killed him.

'A grail knight?'

Merlin nodded as she released him and stepped

back. 'Tarynce of Essex. Morgen's MODs seized him before I could dispatch aid. They dragged him from his home in medieval England through the veil into Glastonbury, where they killed him.'

Little wonder that. He personaly knew several of Morgen's minions of death, and they were a hardy bunch who lived for the opportunity to kill anything. To be unleashed against an original knight of the Round Table was something they would sell their own mothers for. There was nothing they loved more than to bathe in the blood of their enemies ... or their friends either for that matter.

'Did they learn anything from him?' he asked Merlin.

The worry returned to her brow. 'I don't know. No one does, except the MODs or Morgen. That's why I need you.'

How he hated those words. He'd long grown tired of being Merlin's tool. She was forever asking him to ferret out traitors and information from the other side. And when the traitor needed executing, that, too, was his job. Honestly, he wanted to absolve himself from these distasteful tasks. He was tired of being caught between Merlin and Morgen. 'You don't need me for this.'

'Yes, I do. From the way his armor was torn from his shoulder, it appears they knew to look for the mark. Someone had to tell them of it, and if Morgen has learned that, then she knows how to identify the remaining grail knights. We are all in danger, Varian. *You* are in danger.'

He had to stamp down an extremely sarcastic 'duh' at her dire tone. He was always in danger from someone or something. So what? Even now, he lived among his enemies, and they made no bones about the

5

fact that none of them would mourn his death.

'You can't scare me, Merlin,' he said quietly. 'I'm too old for ghost stories, and I really don't give a rat's ass about Morgen or her flock. If they want to come for me, notify the undertaker. He'll need to stock up on body bags.'

'Then you don't care that the rest of the grail knights are to be slaughtered like animals?'

He met her question with one of his own. 'Should I?'

She shook her head at him. 'As fellow members of the Round Table, they're your brothers.'

Yeah, right. None of them had any more care for him than he had for them. If the tables were turned, they'd hand him over without a second thought. 'Tell that to them.'

Merlin reached out a kind hand to touch his forearm. She alone knew that kindness was one of the few things that could render him weak. He'd had so little experience with it that it baffled him, and he never knew how to react.

'Please, Varian. For me. You're the only one I trust to go inside Glastonbury and look around for information. I have a traitor who told Morgen about that tattoo and Tarynce. Only you can find out what the MODs learned before they executed him. Not to mention someone needs to bring his body home for a proper burial. It's the least we can do for one of our own.'

How easy she made it sound, but Glastonbury was no place for a man like him. Then again, maybe it was. Back before Arthur had fallen under Mordred's sword, Glastonbury and its abbey had been places of beauty. Now they existed in a nether realm between Avalon and Camelot.

Nothing with any kind of decency lived there. Nothing. It was hell, and he'd rather have his nostrils

6

slit than ever step foot in there again.

But before he could tell her that, the door to the lounge room opened to admit three men. Like him, they were remnants of King Arthur's Round Table. Ademar, Garyth, and the aptly named Bors, who was, in fact, extremely boring. Bors's father had been a cousin to Varian's. Side by side, their fathers had once fought. Unfortunately, that brotherhood was lost on their sons who couldn't stand each other.

'I see you've found our traitor, Merlin,' Ademar sneered as he raked Varian with a lethal glare. He had slicked-back brown hair and sharp, pinched features that reminded Varian of a mouse. At five-six, the knight carried himself as if he were equal to a giant's height. And had the skill to back that arrogance, which he didn't.

Only three inches taller than Ademar, Garyth was stout, with beady brown eyes and dark brown hair. He moved to stand closer to Varian so that he could make his disdain known – not that Varian hadn't known Garyth hated him. He'd have to be completely stupid to miss that. 'Like father like son.'

That stung, but not for the reasons Garyth thought. It wasn't Lancelot's treachery that bothered Varian. It'd been his father's cruelty.

Varian leaned back in his chair and crossed his arms over his chest as he offered the men a blank stare. 'If you wish to pick a fight with me, don your armor and meet me in the list. I don't need words to goad me to kick your asses. Hell, I won't even use my powers to beat you. Be good to get blood on my hands again.'

'Varian,' Merlin said sternly as she moved back a step. 'We don't need trouble while we have a critical situation brewing. There are only five grail knights left. If Morgen learns the location of the grail . . .'

She didn't finish her sentence. There was no need.

Without the bloodline, there would be no one to stand before Morgen and defeat her. The grail held secrets and a primordial power so great that it would render the person who commanded it indestructible. That was why it, unlike the other sacred objects Arthur had used to rule Britain, had more than one protector to hide it.

Each one of the grail knights held a direct tie to the power that had created the grail and each of them was entrusted with a single clue that could lead to its hiding place. No one of this earth knew where the grail was hidden.

No one.

But if Morgen gained the single clue from each of the six knights, then she would have the grail's location. And Varian had seen enough of her magick to know exactly what that would mean to the world.

Why do I care?

He had no idea, but the pathetic truth was that he did. Glancing up at Merlin, he projected his next thought to her alone. *I need to know who I protect.*

Sadness darkened her eyes. *You know I can't tell you that. It's not that I don't trust you, Varian, but should you fall into Morgen's hands, it is best that only I know the identities of the surviving grail knights.*

She was right. If Morgen were to torture him, he couldn't guarantee that he wouldn't betray them to get her to stop. He'd made selling out friends and allies his life's ambition.

Fine. Getting up, he closed his Sudoku book.

'That's right,' Ademar said, twisting his lips. 'Slink back into whatever hole you climbed out of.'

Merlin tensed. 'Ademar, you should be grateful that I still hold sway over Varian. But if you continue this, I won't rein him in. Woe to you should he ever be unleashed.'

Ademar scoffed. 'I don't fear demonspawn. I destroy them.'

Varian laughed at that as he paused beside the knight who barely reached his shoulder. He took a deep breath so that he could smell the man's fear and sweat. 'The prideful only boast to cover their cowardice. You may not fear demonspawn, Addy, but you *do* fear me.'

Ademar started for him, only to have Bors pull him back. Tall and lean, Bors had features very similar to Varian's. 'He's not worth it, brother.'

The humor fled Varian as he met his cousin's gaze. They were family. But more than that, they were enemies. And bitter ones at that.

'It's true, Addy,' Varian said with a note of amusement. 'Attacking me isn't worth your life, and that is the price I'd demand for it.' He turned to look at Merlin. 'I'll go and do your bidding, Merlin. But my patience and willingness to be your lapdog is stretching perilously thin.'

'Understood, Varian. But know that you have my gratitude.'

Her gratitude and their scorn. That just made him feel all warm and toasty inside. But then he couldn't blame them for hating him. He'd been born cursed. The son of Arthur's most beloved knight and the son of Arthur's most bitter enemy. Unlike the others, he had blood loyalty to both sides of this conflict. And it was a loyalty both sides didn't hesitate to abuse.

He paused at the door to look back at Merlin. 'You know there is one good thing in all this.'

Merlin gave him a puzzled stare. 'And that is?'

Varian indicated Ademar with a jerk of his chin. 'At least my mother didn't give me a name that sounded like a bad candy bar.' He stepped through and shut the door an instant before a dagger embedded itself right where his head had been.

He stared at the tip of the dagger, which had pierced all the way through the wood, and gave a sinister laugh. Honestly, he wasn't his father's son so much as he was his mother's. There was nothing in life he enjoyed more than taunting others. Nothing he liked more than feeling the blood of his enemies coating his hands – but not before he'd had ample time to torture them.

Kindness, compassion – The Lords of Avalon could shove that up their collective asses.

Battle, mayhem, insults. Those were his business, and he thrived on them.

Varian waved his hand over his clothes, changing them from his black shirt and jeans to the medieval attire that was needed to venture to the abbey. His dark brown leather jerkin was heavy, but not nearly as much as the mail shirt that whispered metallically against his skin.

He pulled into place the studded black leather vambrace that held a metal inset to protect his forearm from a sword strike and rested his hand against the hilt of his sword. To search this out, he'd have to go into the Glastonbury Abbey itself.

On the human side of the veil, the abbey was nothing but ruins. Behind the veil, it was still thriving, only there was no godliness in that place. It was unholy. It was also a neutral zone where no magick would work.

No one was really sure why. But Varian suspected that it had to do with the fact that when Camelot and Avalon had been pulled out of the mortal realm into the one of the fey, Glastonbury was supposed to have been left untouched – as ignorant of the defection of the two places as the rest of the world. Instead, the magick had accidentally seeped over into their village, sucking them out along with the positive and negative magick that made up Avalon and Camelot.

Now he was heading into a place where his magick was useless – which was probably why the MODs had killed Tarynce there. It was one of the few places where the grail knight would have been without his magick to fight off his attackers.

In Glastonbury only the skill of Varian's sword arm could help him. That and his willingness to ruthlessly kill anyone who annoyed him.

Oh yeah, it was good to be evil . . .

11

Chapter Two

Glastonbury Abbey was a cesspit of human filth and debauchery. But back in the day when Avalon and Camelot had been part of the human world, it'd been a marvel of engineering and beauty. The ribbed vaulting of the nave had been painted bright colors and gilded until it shone like the very sun. The stained-glass windows had been a riot of color that caught every ray of sunshine before spilling it in brilliant rainbows against the stone floors.

People had journeyed from all over just for a chance to see it. The monks who'd called it home had taken great care to keep up its beauty. Their voices had once rung out in a capella chants like an angelic choir.

But that was then.

Now it existed in a shadowy realm where there was no color at all, only shades of dismal gray. And it had been brought here by sheer accident.

In the original plan, only Camelot and Avalon were supposed to have been taken behind the veil to conceal them from the world of mankind in order to protect that world from the evil that had infected this one. But Damé Fortune wasn't always kind, and Glastonbury, along with her prestigious abbey, had been taken behind the veil, too.

Unaware of what was happening on that fateful night when Avalon and Camelot were concealed, numerous men and women had been caught in the middle of this battle and been trapped here, out of time. In the human world, their families had assumed they'd run off or died. But in this world, they still lived through the centuries and remembered a time when their world had been vast and they could leave Glastonbury or Camelot as they pleased.

But that was lost to them.

Banned by accident from the realm of Avalon, their only choice now was to live in Glastonbury or to venture into the lands of Camelot, which were fraught with evil beings who lived only to torture and kill those foolish enough to approach them.

For obvious reason, the occupants of Glastonbury chose to stay in the limited neutral zone. Yet with every passing year, their neutrality dwindled, and the inhabitants were beginning to look more and more like the twisted souls who called Camelot home. It was a shame really. At one time, they'd been mostly decent people. But then, in times of war, it was always the innocent who suffered most, and in this war, they were the innocent bystanders who'd been caught between the two most powerful forces on earth.

If one stood in the northernmost tower of the abbey or the Tor, they could glimpse the division of the lands. To the left was the curtain of light and color that delineated Avalon. To the right was the dark gray world that was Morgen's Camelot.

It should be easy to cross the line of demarcation. But looks were definitely deceiving. To the soulless and damned beings who lived in Camelot, the light of

Avalon was truly painful. It burned so much that only a small handful of them could bear it.

For those who lived in Avalon, the darkness was something to fear. It was said that any who dared to venture to it would be consumed by it. To live in darkness was to surrender all that was good inside you. The Dark was a vicious mistress who demanded the sacrifice of morals and decency.

And in the middle of those two lands was this one. Banished to eternal night, there was no color here, any more than there was in Camelot. The sky fluctuated from black to a drab gray. Days blurred together as the townsfolk tried to find any solace from their fate that they could.

But there wasn't much to be had.

And just like the inhabitants of Camelot, they, too, despised those who lived in Avalon.

At one time Merewyn of Mercia had lived in the realm of the light. Not in Avalon itself, for that was something she'd never even known existed. No, she'd lived in the land of Mercia as a princess. More beautiful even than Helen of Troy, she'd been the most sought after girl of her time and had been forced to watch men kill one another just for a chance to see her smile.

She'd hated every minute of it. And when her father had told her that the time had come for her to marry a man who saw nothing more than her beauty, she'd summoned one of the creatures that called the darkness home. With magick best left untouched, she'd conjured one of the Adoni – an elfin race so cruel that even demons feared them.

In the light of a full moon, Merewyn had made a bargain that had haunted her ever since. She'd traded her beauty for freedom, or so she thought. A sore bargain that, for Merewyn had had no idea of the repercussions that would come.

Now she was in the abbey, hidden behind a wall with her mistress – the very being who'd stolen her beauty and enslaved her.

She ached to know what they were doing here in the bar, but didn't dare ask. Her mistress didn't tolerate questions. Then again, her mistress tolerated very little.

With an envious eye, she stared at her mistress's long, curly, blond hair. All of the Adoni were beautiful, but even by their exceptional standards Narishka stood out. Petite and curvy, she was what every man dreamed of touching and what every woman dreamed of being. Except for the blackness of her soul, which was only matched by that of her heart.

'Get me more wine, worm.'

Merewyn blinked at the unexpected order. That delayed reaction cost her as Narishka backhanded her.

'Are you deaf as well as ugly, chit? Move!'

Her cheek stinging, Merewyn grabbed the goblet from in front of Narishka and scurried away before her mistress struck her again. She hated her limping gait that was caused by one leg being shorter than the other – an accident that had happened the only time she'd ever tried to escape her cruel mistress.

She glanced back through the wall to see if Narishka was watching her, but she couldn't tell. The wall completely concealed Narishka's presence.

'Watch where you're going, hag!'

She stiffened at the harsh words of the knight she'd almost brushed against in her haste. 'Beg pardon, sir.'

Still he shoved her away from him, into the back of another man. Turning, the man cursed and screwed his features up in distaste as he saw her hideously pockmarked face and matted hair.

'Get off me, you heinous gorgon.'

Then he, too, shoved her away, into a table where a group of men were dicing. This time her collision caused drink to spill all over the man whose arm she bumped. Cursing, he rose from his chair, twisting a circular dagger on his index finger as he glared his hatred at her.

Merewyn tensed in expectation of the dagger slicing through her body. But just as he would have plunged it into her, he was spun about to confront another man. One who held her attacker's hand and dagger so that they were harmless.

Her jaw went slack. Not from fear, but from speechless awe. The newcomer was tall and lean with the greenest eyes she'd ever seen in her life. As clear as a scrying crystal, they seemed to glow from a face that was so perfectly sculpted he should be Adoni. Indeed, he had the lethal manner of that race, but no Adoni would ever bother saving something like her.

His curly black hair brushed against his shoulders in a haphazard manner that said he wasn't one to be overly concerned with his looks – as did the whiskers that darkened his tanned cheeks and accentuated the slight cleft in his chin.

Without a word, he used his studded vambrace to twist the dagger from her would-be attacker's hand and knocked him back. The man staggered against the table, then rushed toward her savior. But before he could reach him, another man shoved him away.

'That's Varian duFey you're attacking, Hugh. Think long and hard.'

Merewyn snapped her jaw shut at the name that was legendary among the evil beings who called Camelot home. It was said he was demonspawn who lived on the blood of his enemies. That he'd sold his soul to the devil or Tuatha Dé Danann so that no man would ever be able to defeat him in battle. That he'd killed his own brother just so that he could learn Adoni magick and feed his own powers. But even worse, it was said that he knew magick so black that even Morgen feared him.

Those were only a few of the numerous stories that told of his insatiable cruelty.

And by the evil twist of his lips as he watched Hugh like a man eyeing a fly he intended to kill, she could believe every one.

'What's the matter, Hugh?' Varian taunted in a deep resonant tone that went down her spine like warm velvet. 'You only attack those who can't fight back? What say you try to carve me a little?'

Hatred flared in Hugh's eyes, but he knew better than to respond. Rumor claimed Varian duFey used the entrails of his victims as laces for his boots and armor. He was one of the few beings who could walk between Avalon and Camelot because neither Merlin nor Morgen dared to confront him.

Hugh spat on the ground before he sheathed his dagger at his waist and retook his seat.

Varian glanced around at the others, who were frozen in tense stances. And as his gaze fell to each one, they looked away nervously before they returned to what they'd been doing. That alone spoke volumes about the man's skill and powers.

She saw the satisfaction in Varian's crystal green eyes before he bent to pick up the goblet she'd dropped on the floor.

To her complete shock, he handed it to her, and if she didn't know better, she'd swear his face actually softened as his gaze met hers. Still, she noted the pity

17

in his eyes as he saw how deformed she was. 'You'd best be on your way, lass. A little more carefully this time.'

The single word that acknowledged her as a woman and not a hag went through her with a giddy rush. It'd been centuries since any man had looked at her with anything other than complete disgust in his gaze. Countless centuries since one had called her anything other than 'hag,' 'crone,' or some other insult.

Bowing to him, she quickly scurried away to complete her errand. But she couldn't resist a quick glance back to where he was making his way toward the bartender. He'd already forgotten her, but she would never forget him or the kindness he'd shown her.

Varian took a stance at the end of the bar with his back against the wall. A force of habit that came from having so many people around him who'd rather slide a knife into his spine than speak to him. He liked to keep his eye on the crowd at all times.

And speaking of, he found his gaze traveling over the angry patrons to find the gnarled crone he'd saved. She walked with a limping gait and was hunched over with a large hump on her back. Her black hair was matted and unkempt. But it was her face that bore the tragedy of her life. Scarred by the pox, she had a lazy eye and an overly large nose. Her lips were twisted and swollen, and given to so much moisture that she was constantly having to wipe them on the back of her hand. If not for the fact that she was here in Glastonbury and was so obsequious, he'd think her one of the twisted graylings who served Morgen.

Poor thing to be stuck here with people who were so concerned with their own bitterness that they had no pity to spare for anyone else.

'What are you doing here?'

Varian looked back at Dafyn, who eyed him with malice . . . and that cut him soul deep. Centuries ago, Dafyn, who was a large, stout man with round, whiskered jowls, had owned a small tavern in Glastonbury. And as he raked Varian with a sneer, Varian remembered the first day they'd met. Varian had been seven, and his mother had just abandoned him on his father's doorstep. Neither parent had wanted him, so he'd decided to run away and strike out on his own.

He'd only made it as far as the tavern when, exhausted from his long hike from the castle to town, he'd sat down just beside the door. Dafyn had seen him panting there and asked him what he was doing. As soon as Varian had explained, he'd offered him work. 'Well, if you're to be on your own, lad, you'll be needing coin. I have floors that need be swept, and I could definitely use a taster to make sure my bread is the best in town before I serve it to clients. What say you work for me?'

Thinking that his life was about to improve greatly, Varian had gratefully accepted.

Of course his father had found him a few hours later. He'd boxed Varian's ears for leaving and forced him back to Camelot against his will. But as Varian had grown to manhood, he'd often found himself back in the tavern, spending time with Dafyn.

Until the night the veil had come down and Dafyn had discovered himself trapped on this side while his family was still in the human world. The pain, grief, and bitterness of that had ruined a good man, and now Dafyn, like all the others here, would kill him if he had a chance.

Varian opened the small leather purse at his waist

and pulled out twenty gold marks. 'There was a man murdered outside the abbey last night.'

Dafyn curled his lip as he took the coin and pocketed it. 'There's always a murder here. So what?'

'This was one of the Lords of Avalon.'

'And again I say so what?'

Varian ground his teeth before he pulled out more gold pieces and placed them on the bar in front of Dafyn. 'Nothing happens in or near the abbey that you don't know about it. Tell me who killed him.'

Dafyn's brown eyes actually lightened a bit as he scraped the pile of coins from the counter and put them in his pocket. 'Bracken was leading them.'

That name actually gave Varian pause. Bracken was one of the more lethal MODs Morgen commanded – though the term 'commanded' was used loosely since the MODs had eaten their last master, the god Balor. They more or less had a tenuous contract with Morgen of 'we'll serve you only so long as you keep the gods from killing us and don't annoy us too much.' At the end of the day, there was no doubt that they could kill her easily enough, but the last thing the MODs wanted was to be turned out to face the wrath of the entire Tuatha Dé Danann. That particular group of Celtic gods were known for their viciousness.

And Bracken's involvement didn't bode well for Varian since he'd be the one questioning the demon who didn't like to be questioned at all.

Suddenly, Dafyn's gaze went over Varian's shoulder and narrowed.

A fissure of power rippled up Varian's spine, and even though magick was neutralized in the abbey – which was why Dafyn had moved his tavern within its walls – he knew the person approaching him was extremely 'gifted.' And it was a mark of power he recognized immediately as Dafyn made himself scarce.

'Hi, mum,' he said before he turned to look at her over his shoulder.

Narishka was still as beautiful as any twenty-year-old human woman. Being an immortal Adoni definitely had its advantages. Her golden blond hair was worn in braids that she had coiled around the crown of her head in an intricate design and fell in loops about her shoulders. Her flowing black gown barely covered her ample assets as she offered him a cold smile. 'Welcome home, Varian.'

He reached behind the counter to grab a jug and goblet before he poured himself a potent drink. 'This is hardly my home.'

'Ah yes, you prefer to make your bed with our enemies.'

He snorted at that before he tasted the rancid mead that burned through him like fire. 'You threw me out, remember?'

'A strategic miscalculation on my part.'

'Hmm . . .' he said, not believing that for a moment as he set his goblet down. His mother never made those kinds of mistakes.

Tilting his head to one side, he frowned as he saw the twisted crone in his mother's shadow.

His mother noticed his distraction instantly. 'Thank you for saving my servant. I would hate to have her any more mangled.'

He glanced back at his mother's cold gaze. 'Then perhaps you should free her.'

'Perhaps I should . . .'

He didn't miss the calculating gleam that came into her eyes. 'So why are you here, mum?'

She feigned an innocent pout. 'Can't I simply be missing my boy?'

21

He actually choked on the mead at the ludicrousness of that statement. It took him a few seconds of coughing to clear his windpipe. 'And just how many centuries has it taken for you to discover this deeply buried maternal instinct? Oh wait, I better get a jackhammer to cut through the granite so we can find it, huh?'

She tsked at him. 'I have missed you, Varian.' She reached out to touch his cheek.

Varian quickly stepped back. His accusation hadn't been light. Never once in his life had his mother ever touched him with affection. And unless she'd seriously snapped a wheel, he doubted she was going to change now.

'Fine,' she snapped, realizing he wasn't so stupid. 'Morgen and I want you on our side.'

'Yeah. Of course you do. But it's a few centuries too late, mum. You two witches should have used your powers to see that little Varian wouldn't come back to the flock. Ever. You told me on the day you left me at Camelot that you had more important things to do than play nursemaid to an unruly brat.'

'What I did was regrettable—'

He had to stifle laughter at that. The only reason it was regrettable to her was the sheer fact that he'd grown into one of the most powerful sorcerers in Merlin's corps.

'But I *am* your mother. And I have watched you all these centuries as your powers have grown. I've been quite proud of you. Well, not proud that you fight for that bitch and thwart Morgen's plans, but proud that you don't hesitate to kill those who get in your way. You are evil at heart, just like us. I've seen it myself, and it has given me hope. Come home, Varian. Morgen will reward you mightily. You can have all the coin you wish. You can have the most beautiful women – even virgins. Though it will probably take some searching to find those at Camelot, but ... Whatever it takes to win you over, we will gladly cede.'

'I wouldn't go back to Camelot for all the riches of this world and the others combined. I need no help with women, and I personally like what I do. So, no offense and with all due sincerity, sod off, mum.'

She gave him an arch stare. 'You like being used by Merlin? Being sent out to do the jobs that the other Lords of Avalon won't soil their hands with? Is that truly what you want? They don't even say thank you for it. Instead they hate you.'

It was true, but it changed nothing. 'So instead you'd have me serve Morgen, killing indiscriminately? Still hated and still worthless? Really, mum, what do you take me for? Morgen has killers aplenty. Why am *I* so important that you make this offer to me now?'

'Because we *need* you. Merlin trusts you as she trusts no one else.'

He narrowed his eyes at that statement, which told him much. 'So what exactly did you learn from Tarynce's torture?'

Completely unabashed by what they'd done to the poor man, she actually answered. 'There are other grail knights. Five more to be precise. We must have their names.'

'And why would I ever give them to you?'

'You could be the right hand of Morgen herself, Varian. With the grail, she would need nothing else. For you, she'd even kill the new king. Say the word, and Arador is dead. You can be his replacement.'

Oh boy! Let him sign up for that ... not. 'Until she finds a way to resurrect Mordred, then I'll be as dead as Arador.'

'She wouldn't do that.'

Yeah, right. 'This is Morgen we're speaking of. Morgen who threw the entire universe out of order for her own selfish gain, murdered her own brother and who has no love or respect for any living creature. Uh-huh. You would really trust her?'

She lashed out and grabbed his arm in a grip so tight, it managed to hurt even through the armor. 'Morgen wants that grail, and I have promised it to her. If you will not serve us, then we *will* kill you.'

'Good luck trying.'

Her eyes flamed to red as her grip tightened even more. Cursing, she let go of him. 'We will get you, Varian. One way or another. You can mark those words in stone.' And then she tried to zap herself out of the room.

Varian laughed at the stunned look on her face. 'Your magick doesn't work here, mum. Remember?'

She let out a fierce screech before she turned on her heel and made her way toward the door with her servant behind her. Varian would have enjoyed the sight of her anger but for the fact that he knew her brain was already concocting some way to fuck him over.

Yeah, it was always good to be him.

Sighing, he grabbed the jug and poured another drink. He still had a body to take back to Merlin. But at least he now knew who to contact for more information about Tarynce's death ... and he knew that Morgen had learned one of their most carefully guarded secrets. There was more than one knight who hid the grail.

And with that, Morgen now wanted him to help her take over and destroy the world. Which meant she wouldn't rest until she either killed or converted him.

The latter would never happen, so that left him with Morgen throwing everything she could at him. Night and day. Day and night. Eternally.

Letting out a sigh, he knocked back the drink and shook his head as it numbed every taste bud in his mouth.

Yee-haw, this was just starting to make his bright day even better. All he needed now was for Bracken to gouge out his eyes and swallow them.

Chapter Three

Narishka came through the wall of Morgen's chambers with the air around her crackling from her fury and her powers. As was typical, Morgen was naked, entwined on her bed with her latest paramour. An evil Adoni like herself, Brevalaer was a trained courtesan and thus far had lasted longer than any of Morgen's previous lovers.

With no embarrassment whatsoever, Narishka approached the dais where the large, carved bed rested and parted the bloodred silk curtains. Morgen lay with one hand entwined in Brevalaer's dark hair while his head was buried deep between her spread legs. Morgen's large breasts were covered by a sheer red gown that Brevalaer had pushed up to pool at her waist so that he could attend to his business.

His tanned, rippling body was every bit as bare, but unfortunately Narishka could only see his well-shaped buttocks and back. How she wished she could join them, but unlike Morgen, she believed in business before pleasure.

'A moment, my queen?' Narishka asked.

Morgen turned her head toward her slowly, but she didn't stop Brevalaer. Little wonder that. It was said that his tongue held more magick than the whole of the fey court. 'What?' she asked irritably.

'Merlin did just as we thought. She sent Varian to Glastonbury to investigate.'

Morgen sucked her breath in sharply as if Brevalaer had found a particularly pleasing spot or rhythm. 'Did you speak to him?'

'Yes and as I predicted, he refused completely.'

Brevalaer started to pull away to give them space only to have Morgen grip his black hair fiercely. 'You stop now, and I'll cut your tongue out.'

His face completely stoic, he dipped his head and immediately went back to pleasing his mistress.

Morgen glared at her. 'You're his mother. What will it take to get him on our side?'

Narishka shook her head. It was a question she'd been asking herself repeatedly. 'I have no idea. He's grotesquely abnormal, which is why I sent him to live with Lancelot when he was a child. I've never understood him. He's not motivated by greed, lust, or anything else that makes sense. If he has a weakness, I don't know it.'

Morgen shifted slightly, giving Brevalaer more access to her body. 'We have to have him. You know that. Given what the MODs learned from whatever his name was before they killed him, we can pretty much guess that Galahad and Percival are grail knights, but neither of them will ever be foolish enough to fall into our hands. We need someone who can get near them and strike from behind.'

'I know.'

Morgen drummed her fingers against Brevalaer's head as her eyes narrowed threateningly. 'There has to be something that entices him. Something he reacts to without fail.'

27

Narishka paused at those words as she remembered the little fat mouse trailing behind her. Turning her head, she saw the girl still there, her eyes cast to the floor, her body as still as a statue's.

Merewyn. She'd been the only thing that her son had reacted to. He'd saved her from being struck, and in that instant, she knew his weakness. 'Pity.'

'Yes,' Morgen agreed irritably, 'it is a pity.'

'No,' she said, turning back toward her mistress. 'His weakness is pity.' One corner of her mouth lifted up as she turned around to stare at Merewyn. 'I think I know exactly what we need to do to win him over.'

Cradling Tarynce's body in his arms, Varian entered the tombs of Avalon. It was a small crypt that was kept beneath the castle. There were only a handful of sarcophagi here. Bors's father rested to his right, and to his left was Guinevere's father, along with several other knights who'd died fighting beside Arthur at Camlann. Varian's father was buried at his own home, Joyous Gard, while Guinevere's grave was kept secret so that none of the surviving knights would desecrate it out of meanness.

And then there was Arthur . . .

That sarcophagus was in the center of the room. It held the gilded image of a knight on top that he knew for a fact wasn't true to the king. The stone face carved there looked passionless and cold, two things Arthur had never been. True to the legend, he'd been larger than life. The kind of man who earned the respect of everyone who'd been fortunate enough to meet him. At least until the end, when everything had fallen apart. But even then, Arthur had faced the tragedy of his life with kingly grace. He'd fought bitterly to the end. Not for himself, but for his people.

And Varian had sworn to him that he would spend his life protecting those who couldn't protect themselves. That he would model himself after the only man he'd ever respected or loved and do his best to keep Arthur's dream alive.

The sarcophagus was plain except for the gold that Bors and Galahad had insisted on in direct contradiction to Arthur's wishes.

'*I need no fancy crate for my remains. Spend the gold on those who are still living. Where I'll be, for better or worse, it'll do me no good. But if it'll feed one hungry child, it'll be much better spent than on a dead man's grave.*'

Arthur truly had been a great man.

Clearing his throat against the knot that suddenly appeared to choke him, Varian took Tarynce to a small table that was against the far wall and laid the body on it. He took a moment to drape the man's arms over his chest so that he looked as peaceful as possible. Then he whispered a small prayer for the man's soul before he closed Tarynce's eyes one last time.

'Merlin?' he said quietly, knowing she could hear him. 'I've returned.'

The air beside him stirred an instant before she appeared. 'That didn't take long.'

He stepped away from the body. 'The information wasn't well guarded. I know the name of his executioner and from my mother's own lips, I know that they've learned other grail knights exist.'

She sucked her breath in sharply at that as she stepped back as if to leave. 'I will send word to them.'

'No,' he said sternly.

'Why not?'

'My mother and Morgen both know the good guy playbook. You start notifying the others, and they'll

29

follow your messengers right to their doorsteps. It's probably why my mother told me so easily. I'm sure she's waiting for us to move so they can, too.'

Still Merlin wasn't appeased. 'We have to warn them. They need to know.'

'Not yet. Besides, once word of Tarynce's death spreads beyond the walls of Avalon, they'll know to be on guard. Morgen has no names at this point although I'm sure she can figure out a couple of them, same as me. But the rest should be safe ... at least for the time being. Let me talk to Bracken and see what else I can learn before you alert anyone.'

She actually gaped at his words. 'The *demon* Bracken?'

He had no idea why she was surprised. 'It's why you wanted me on this assignment, isn't it?'

Shaking her head, she reached for him. 'Varian—'

He moved back, out of reach. 'It's all right, Merlin. Dealing with assholes is my specialty.'

'Assholes are one thing. Insane demons are another.'

He snorted at that. 'Maybe in your book. In mine they're the same. Both cowardly bastards who come at my back.' He had much more important things to worry about than Bracken. But as he neared the exit for the tomb, he paused as unfounded pain washed through him. 'Just promise me one thing, Merlin.'

'And that is?'

He glanced to the brutalized body of the fallen knight and remembered the last time he'd brought a body home from Morgen's abuse. 'If I die, make sure I'm cremated. I don't want Morgen putting me on display for the others.'

She gave him a gimlet stare as if she understood the nightmare he still had of his father's death. He might not have loved or respected his father, but no man deserved to die the way Lancelot had.

'I promise.'

Nodding, he made his way from the tomb out into the light of the courtyard. The air here was sweet, scented by apples and lilac, the light sublime and warm against his skin. This was Avalon. A perfect paradise that had once existed on earth. But he also knew the darker side that lived here in the sanctity of this place.

Maybe he was being stupid by fighting his mother and her wants. Maybe he should switch his allegiance. Really, would there be a difference?

An image of the hapless crone in the abbey being bandied between the men flashed in his mind. Along with the sight of her gratitude when he'd picked up the goblet and handed it to her. She was the reason why he fought alongside Merlin. His life had sucked, but it shouldn't be that way for others. Arthur had taught him to let go of the bitterness and embrace a better way. If he could spare one kid his childhood, then it was worth fighting this battle between his mother and himself.

The strong should never prey on the weak.

His conviction set, he changed his clothes yet again from the leather to his black armor. It was scant protection from the demon's magick, but at least it would protect him from Bracken's daggers, swords, or claws.

Merewyn stood before the mirror in complete shock. For centuries, she'd avoided anything that could cast a reflection. But now . . .

Now she bore the face that she'd been born to. Gone were the scars and the twisted body of the crone. She now stood upright with no hump, no pain. She was beautiful.

Unable to believe it, she cupped her face in her

hands and kept waiting for Narishka to take it away from her again.

'What have you done, child?'

She turned to find Magda standing behind her. Old and gnarled, she'd been one of the few people who had befriended Merewyn during her centuries here. 'I made a pact with Narishka. I do one last service for her, and she's going to let me go.'

Magda scoffed. 'Have you lost your mind? She never makes such bargains.'

It was true. Her current fate had come from just such a bargain gone wrong. The original terms had been for her to remain ugly only for the cycle of the moon. But Narishka had failed to tell her that here in Camelot there was no moon cycle at all, and so she'd been trapped for eternity.

Until now.

Now she had the one chance she'd waited for.

'I told you, Magda, that one day I would get my beauty back, and I have.'

'At what cost?'

Varian's service to Morgen. She had three weeks to turn him to their side. Three weeks. If she failed, Narishka would return her to the hag's form and spend eternity punishing her for her failure. But if she succeeded, she would be allowed to go free. Not as a hag, but as the woman she'd been born to be.

'Don't worry about the cost.'

Magda shook her head. 'I'm not the one who should be worried, child. That would be you.' The old woman drew closer to her so that she could touch the long, silken tresses of her black hair as if to prove to herself that it was real. 'Is this why you struggled so hard to survive all these centuries?'

Merewyn didn't respond. Instead, she remembered

a conversation they'd had long ago.

'*Give up hope, child. This is your fate. You're one of us now. Grayling in form, you will never again be the beautiful woman you were.*'

'*I can't give up hope, Magda. It's all I have. I was stupid once, but I know that someday I'll have the chance to be free. Should I die, then I'll have lived only as a fool. I don't want that to be my life. I want to be my own person again. Not a twisted crone, but a woman.*'

'*You're a fool, Merewyn. There is nothing but misery here. Learn to embrace it and don't wish for more. You'll only be disappointed if you do.*'

She'd refused to believe it, and now here she was, restored.

Magda narrowed her beady eyes on her. 'And whose life have you sold for the beauty you have now?'

A slice of fear pierced her. 'How did you know?'

'There could be nothing else that would make the mistress put you back as you were. So who will you destroy to be beautiful?'

'Varian duFey,' she said quietly, then louder added, 'But he's a monster, and we both know it. Tell me, have you ever heard anyone say anything good about him?'

Magda's eyes turned dull. 'Only you.'

Merewyn looked away as pain filled her. It was true, he'd been kind to her. But one act of kindness couldn't erase all the cruelty he'd committed in his lifetime. All the lives he'd taken. He was the son of Narishka. His father had destroyed the brotherhood of Arthur's Round Table and ultimately ruined everyone's life. And the two of them had bred a child equally as vicious.

What she was doing was a service to the world.

Shaking her head with a disgusted sigh, Magda made her way back toward the door.

'I don't want to hear it,' Merewyn called to her as she started to leave. 'You've done your own share of mischief and cruelty at Morgen's behest.'

'True,' she said quietly. 'But I'm not now, nor have I ever been human. I lack your conscience and your conviction. Tell me, Merewyn, once you've done this, will you still be able to look at yourself in the mirror, knowing that your beauty was bought in someone else's blood?'

The centuries of brutal abuse she'd suffered here went through her like a hot lance. Men such as Varian had spat on her and beaten her for no other reason than because she was ugly. They'd never shown her compassion or mercy. She wouldn't go back to that. Not now. Not ever. She wanted to be human again, and she would do whatever it took to make that happen.

'Yes,' she said confidently.

Again Magda shook her head at her. 'And here I thought you were the only human in Camelot. 'Tis a pity I misjudged you so.'

Merewyn curled her lip as the woman left her alone. 'You're just jealous that you're trapped here while I've been given a chance to earn my freedom.'

Nothing but silence answered her, but it didn't matter. She knew the truth. There were no decent people left in this world. None. So what if she turned Varian over to Morgen? It wasn't like they planned to kill him. They only wanted him to serve in their court. There was no harm in that. At least he had family here. And he had beauty, the one thing the inhabitants of Camelot valued above everything.

No, she wasn't hurting Varian. She was only

34

helping herself. There was nothing wrong with that. Nothing.

Closing his eyes, Varian took himself from Avalon to the dark back halls of Camelot. He was one of the few who could travel between the two realms who was actually willing to do it. Not that he particularly enjoyed this. Since his mother was the right hand of Morgen, their most-despised queen, and his father had been Arthur's right-hand champion, it left the inhabitants of Camelot a little . . . shall we say, abrupt with him.

There wasn't a creature here who wouldn't love to carve his heart from his chest secretly. And the key word was 'secretly.' None of them would ever come from the front.

So with his hand on his sword, he walked slowly down the hallway with the gait of a predator. Every shadow could contain an enemy. Every whisper could be one of the braver fools coming at his back. He kept his head bent down and searched the darkness with his peripheral sight while he listened carefully for any tell-tale sound.

As he neared the torches on the walls that were held in brackets made to look like blackened arms, they lit themselves, then extinguished once he'd passed. The smell of the rush lights was pungent and thick in the air and it was stirred by his movements.

Varian cocked his head as he felt a whisper behind him that could only come from one of the sharoc – a shadow fey that was renowned for its cruelty and mischief. He gripped the sword hilt, ready to draw it instantly as he continued on his way, waiting for the attack.

But the sharoc pulled back . . . no doubt going to

report his presence to his mother or Morgen.

Let it. Varian had other matters with which to concern himself. He headed down the turret stairs that led to the underground floor. On the north tower, this area was reserved for the dungeon and Morgen's torture chambers.

On the southern tower where he was, it was the domain of the MODs. 'MOD,' pronounced mode, was an acronym for Morgen's minions of death. At one time, they'd been servants for the Celtic god of death, Balor. Confined to the underworld by their master, they'd been the scavengers sent to battlefields to kill and torture any who turned coward and fled.

It was rumored that they were originally the beloved children of the Celtic gods Dagda and the Morrigen. But they fell from favor when they sided with the Milesians in an ancient war against their father Dagda. As Dagda was driven by his enemies into the underworld, he'd cursed his children to be servants there under the direction of Balor.

Balor wasn't one of the more benevolent gods. Vicious and cold, he'd been the one to teach the MODs many of their more brutal ways.

His cruelty to them was what had ultimately led to their turning on him and killing him by ripping out his single eye. Legend said it was his grandson Lugh who'd done the actual murder, but that'd been a lie perpetuated by the gods who didn't want it to be common knowledge that Balor's servants had that kind of power.

Under a death warrant that'd been issued by the entire Tuatha Dé Danann group of gods, the MODs had been hunted to virtual extinction until Morgen had offered them refuge in her shadowy realm. Now they all lived with a tenuous pact that Varian kept waiting to see end with Morgen's untimely death.

Unfortunately, that hadn't happened yet.

Varian pushed open the heavy iron door that led to the MODs' quarters. Since they weren't exactly civilized and disdained even the dim light that was found here, they'd decided to live beneath Camelot, in a cold, damp hole. The stone walls oozed some effervescent green muck that smelled like rotten limes. And in true MOD form, they lived in a commune environment. Bracken was the only one of them who had private quarters. The rest fed, slept, ate, and fornicated out in the open.

There were probably a hundred of them strewn about the open area, but only a small handful even bothered to look at him as they went about their business, which included eating the flesh of Adoni victims scattered about the floor.

His stomach turned at the sight and the smell of it. One of the MOD females looked up with a speculative gleam in her eyes as he walked past. He gave her a look to let her know that he wouldn't die easily.

More to the point, he wouldn't die alone.

Licking her bloodied lips, she returned to her 'dinner.'

All in all, he had to give the MODs credit. Like the Adoni, they were beautiful. Golden and fair with wings that were black and amber, they were more akin to the angels attributed to heaven. Though their magick wasn't as great as the Adoni, they still held enough of it to make them formidable enemies, and what they lacked in esoteric power they more than made up for in raw physical strength.

Varian paused as he rounded the corner that led straight to Bracken's room. He'd expected to meet the demon lord on his own terms. What he hadn't expected was to meet Bracken while the demon was nuzzling Varian's mother.

That action was wrong on so many levels that he couldn't quite sort out which one disturbed him most. One thing was certain, he'd never call that bastard Dad.

'Am I interrupting?'

Bracken pulled back from his mother's neck before he raked Varian with a sneer. 'You are ever a pain in my ass.'

'Good. I've spent the whole of my life aspiring to hemorrhoid status. Nice to know I've finally attained it.'

Bracken's black eyes flashed red at the same time his mouth opened like a snake's to show a row of jagged teeth. His skin mottled from tawny to reptilian brown, then as soon as it appeared, he brought his anger under control and returned to his more aesthetic being.

Varian still couldn't keep his lip from curling at the fact that his mother could cuddle up to something so repugnant. 'Nice trick. Bet you're hell on the other contestants at a freak party contest, huh?'

Bracken would have attacked him had his mother not put herself between them.

'He's only trying to get under your skin, Bracken. Ignore him.'

Bracken's eyes flickered in the dim light. 'If you want to keep him breathing, Narishka, you'd best get him out of my domain.'

Varian eyed him without fear. 'Tell me what I want to know, and I'll be out of here so fast, I'll leave a vapor trail.'

'And that is?'

His mother answered before he could even open his

mouth. 'He wants to know what the grail knight told you before you killed him.'

How nice of his mother to help him for once. Not that it mattered. Bracken laughed at her words. 'He didn't say much. Pietra tore his tongue out after he refused to tell her his clue.'

In a very fucked-up sort of way, it was nice to know that the fine art of torturing someone for information was lost on the MODs.

Varian forced himself not to react even though inside he ached dearly for the poor unsuspecting man who'd been up against Morgen's pets. The fact that MODs held no compassion for anyone was what had enabled them to turn on their own parents. 'How did you capture him?'

One corner of Bracken's mouth quirked up. 'I can't be giving away our secrets, turncoat. If I did, you might know how to keep us from dragging you off one night while you sleep.'

Varian gave a low, lethal laugh. 'I would pay you to try. Just one night, you and me.'

Bracken's mouth flashed back and forth again, letting Varian know that the demon was salivating for the chance. Which meant someone, most likely his mother or Morgen, was holding the demon back.

His mother stepped closer, placing her hands on his breastplate. 'Come, Varian. You visit me so seldom that I don't want to waste our time down here with the MODs.'

He started to correct her about the fact that this wasn't a mother-son visit. But she knew as well as he did that he hadn't come to spend time with Mommie Dearest. He allowed her to turn him around and lead him back the way he'd come, which made him wonder what she wanted with him. Normally, whenever he visited Camelot, she left him completely alone.

Neither of them spoke as they left the underground chamber and headed back upstairs.

'I'm beginning to get nervous, mum,' he said, as she opened the door to the third floor and led him into a narrow hallway.

'Why would you be nervous, love? I've already told you that we want you on our side. I merely have someone I'd like for you to meet.'

He froze in the middle of the hallway as her words went through him like acid. 'And you also told me that you'd see me dead, which makes me wonder if this person is the one you'd have kill me.'

She laughed lightly. 'No.' She pulled at his arm, but he refused to take another step.

It was time for him to return to Avalon. 'I've learned what I wanted to know. I'm leaving now.' Yet before he could move, he felt her snap something onto his wrist.

He looked down at the small gold bracelet that was heavily etched with the fey words – *Era di crynium bey. Freedom is an illusion*.

It didn't hurt, but he couldn't figure out why she'd placed it there. 'What is this?'

There was an odd serenity to her face that scared him more than an entire raiding party of MODs. 'That is your shackle, dear boy.'

'Shackle for what?'

She stepped forward to whisper, 'You can no longer travel through the veils. You're stuck here, Varian. More than that, your magick is neutralized so long as the bracelet is on your wrist.'

He tried to flash himself out of here, but true to her words, nothing happened. 'What the hell?'

'You *will* join us, Varian.'

'Never,' he said from between clenched teeth.

And before he could move, his mother clapped her hands. A group of male Adoni appeared.

'Take him,' she said coldly.

Varian struck out at them, but since their magick wasn't negated, he was fighting a losing battle, and he knew it. He succeeded in knocking several of them back and splitting their lips. In the end, however, he was outnumbered.

One minute he was in the hallway and the next, he was in the bowels of the northern tower. The cell was small and cramped. Even though he continued to fight, they clapped a chain on each wrist and chained his arms to opposite walls so that he was standing in the room with his arms spread wide.

There was no missing the satisfied gleam in his mother's eyes. 'Peel his armor off.'

'Love you, too, mum.'

She didn't respond as they tried, only to learn it was held in place by the spell he'd put on it in Avalon. Since his magick was now missing, he couldn't have taken it off if he'd wanted to. 'It won't come off.'

She narrowed her eyes on him as she crossed the floor and tried to remove it herself.

'I'm not *that* stupid, mum.'

Shrieking, she struck him hard against his back, forcing him forward so that his arms were wrenched by the chains. She turned to the others. 'Fine, then, fetch us two mandrakes and sledgehammers.'

Varian forced himself not to react to that. He had to give her credit. Even in armor, a sledgehammer would hurt. Given the fact that it would be wielded by a mandrake – a half-human, half-dragon fey creature, it would hurt a lot.

He locked gazes with her, but there was no compassion to be found there. Not that he'd expected it. No

Adoni had ever possessed an ounce of maternal instinct. It just wasn't in their genes.

'You might as well kill me now, mum. I won't join you.'

She ran a cold finger down his cheek and eyed him as if measuring his strength. 'You say that now, Varian. Let's see what you say in a few hours.'

'I will still say it.'

The door opened to show him two large, stout mandrakes. As was typical of their breed, they were extremely tall and well muscled. Their silver eyes flashed with eagerness as they took the sledgehammers out of the hands of the servants who came in behind them.

Varian pulled against the chains and tried to use his magick to get out of this, but it was useless.

His mother tsked. 'Words are so easy to say. Now, let's have a go at that conviction of yours.'

And as the first mandrake slammed his hammer down on Varian's shoulder and he felt it all the way to the marrow of his bones, he knew this was going to be a seriously long day.

Chapter Four

'Are you ready, chit?'

Merewyn looked away from the mirror at the sound of Narishka's voice. She'd been mentally preparing herself for this for hours. Her job was to seduce Varian, which, given how randy the Adoni were as a rule, seemed an easy enough task.

The only part that gave her pause was the fact that she'd never been touched by any man. Her father had kept her carefully sequestered as a child, and once Narishka had turned her ugly, her father had cast her out, and no man would look at her, never mind touch her.

But that didn't matter. Her virginity was a small price to pay for freedom.

'I'm ready.'

'Good.' Narishka motioned her to follow. 'Now remember, you have to weaken him. He's strong. Too damned strong, honestly. I doubt we'll get him to break without you. Your goal is to be nice to him. Take him food and water.'

Merewyn paused at the unexpected order. 'Am I not supposed to do more than that, mistress?'

'No.'

Still, she was baffled. 'I thought you wanted me to seduce him.'

Her brow furrowed in aggravation, Narishka turned on her with an impatience that would normally result in a vicious slap. But her mistress must have feared marring her face. 'That is seducing him, chit. Trust me.'

Trust her? That would never happen.

But as she started after her mistress again, she was greatly relieved by this turn of events. When Narishka had said 'seduce,' she'd naturally assumed intercourse. This bargain was looking better and better.

Merewyn frowned as they started down the back stairs that led to the dungeons. Fear shot through her as the hallway narrowed, and she could hear the screams and pleas of those being tortured.

Was Narishka lying to her? Servants who came down here seldom returned, and the last thing she wanted was to die in one of Morgen's torture rooms. 'Why are we going this way?'

Narishka raised her arm as if to strike her, then caught herself. 'Relax, simpkin. This is where we're keeping him for the time being.'

That didn't make sense to her. If they wanted someone to join their ranks, wouldn't they be kind to him? 'You're torturing him?'

Narishka gave her a look that asked, what do you think?

Merewyn cringed as she caught a whiff of the stench of blood, fear, sweat, and decaying remains. She pressed the back of her hand to her nose to keep from choking on it as she tried to understand the woman who seemed immune to the nastiness of this place.

The fey Adoni continued down the stairs and into the bowels of the dungeon without any visible signs of being disturbed by the men and women who begged her for mercy as she passed their rooms.

Merewyn only wished she was equally as cold. But the truth was each and every cry went down her spine like a lash. If she could, she'd free them all.

This is your fate if you fail . . .

And that cemented her determination. Just like them, no one would ever come to her aid. No one would care. She'd be left here alone to die. Painfully. Cruelly. There was no compassion in this world. People would only help others if they could profit by the aid, and she had nothing to offer anyone.

It was why she had to escape this place.

Trying her best to ignore the others, she focused on Narishka. 'I thought you wanted Varian on your side.'

'We do, and I know my son well enough to know that he won't be bribed.'

So they thought torture would work? Were they mad?

Foolish question that. She'd lived here long enough to know that they didn't think of kindness. Ever. It was all but alien to them.

Narishka finally paused beside an old oak door that was held by thick black iron hinges. She manifested a tray of food and water, then handed it to Merewyn. 'Just feed him and leave. That's all you have to do,' she whispered.

Narishka pulled open the door.

Merewyn took one step inside, then froze in place. The horror of what she saw made her stomach turn. Varian was slumped over as two chains on opposite walls held him on his feet with his arms spread wide. He couldn't even kneel to rest himself, not without the chains pulling at his arms and hurting him more.

His long, black hair fell forward, obscuring the

handsome face she'd seen in the abbey. His black armor was dented and twisted, but what disturbed her most was the blood that was pooled at his feet. As she watched, more blood dripped at sickening intervals from his downcast head to the floor below.

What had they done to him? He was a far cry from the proud, powerful man she'd met in the tavern. He seemed more human now. Vulnerable. Yet for all the pain, she could feel his anger reaching out to her. He wanted blood for what they'd done to him. It was a sentiment she fully understood.

And all thoughts of herself fled as she slowly approached him.

Varian heard the soft rustle of a woman's gait. Assuming it was his mother come to ask him again to convert, he didn't bother looking up. Honestly, he hurt too much to breathe, never mind move. Besides, the last thing he wanted was to see his mother's face again. At least not unless it was while he was choking the life out of her treacherous body.

He wanted to lie down so badly that he could taste it, but the chains kept him from it. Every breath, every heartbeat made his crushed armor bite into his flesh. In spite of the bracelet, he'd discovered that he had enough magick to remove the armor, but that would have been stupid beyond stupid.

Not to mention it would get him killed. Unfortunately, though, not until after they'd stepped up the torture to a mind-blowing level.

He felt a gentle hand on his head an instant before it brushed the hair back from his face. It was so tender that for a moment it actually weakened him. It was the kind of caress he'd ached for all his life.

But no one ever touched him like that.

Prepared to spit the blood in his mouth at his mother

or Morgen, he lifted his head to confront whoever dared touch him.

Shock riveted him as all of his anger fled. It wasn't either of them.

Instead, it was the most beautiful woman he'd ever seen. Her long, dark brown hair fell in soft ringlets all the way to her waist. Her face was small and oval, with brown eyes tinged with amber that slanted up like a cat's. Her lips were full and inviting.

But it was her pained expression that seared him as she gently used a cloth to wipe at the blood on his brow and cheek.

'They told me to feed you,' she breathed in a soft, dulcet tone that was tinged by an old Anglo-Saxon accent.

He laughed at that. 'Why bother?'

'To keep up your strength.'

'So they can torture me more? Forgive me if I'd rather die of starvation.'

Merewyn was surprised by his dark humor. How could he make a joke now? She frowned at the damage they'd done to him. His brow was split and bleeding. His lips swollen and purple, but not nearly as much as his left eye, which he could no longer open at all. There was no trace left of his handsomeness. Indeed, he looked more like her when she'd been a crone.

She couldn't imagine how much pain he'd have to be in. Her own beatings had hurt so badly at times that she hadn't even been able to move afterward, and none of them had left her this bloodied or swollen. How could he even be conscious? During her centuries at Camelot, she'd seen a great deal of horror and numerous atrocities, but never anything like this, and the fact that it was his own mother who had done such was incomprehensible to her.

Her heart aching for him, she carefully wiped away the blood from his mouth, then picked up a small bite of garlic-roasted venison and held it to his lips. Given his earlier comment about starving, she half expected him to spit it at her or refuse. Instead, he dutifully parted his lips and allowed her to place the meat on his tongue.

Varian wasn't sure why he was allowing her to feed him at all as the salty meat burned the cuts on his lips and his loosened teeth. Yet he couldn't seem to help himself. He was afraid that if he refused, she'd leave him, and he was strangely enjoying her pampering, such as it was. No one had ever been so kind to him, especially not when he was weak like this. All the people he'd known, including his father and brother, had only attacked him more whenever he was down.

Her touch was gentle and warm, and it soothed him on a level that was frightening.

But what surprised him most was the fact that she wasn't a miren, mandrake, Adoni, or sharoc. There was no magick to this woman whatsoever. No power.

She was human. Completely.

How was that possible?

He winced as he swallowed the meat down his bruised, parched throat. 'Why are you here?'

She looked back at the tray of food on the floor. 'To feed you.'

'No,' he said quietly. 'How can a human be here in Camelot?'

Her eyes turned dark and sad. 'By great foolishness on my part.'

It was then he understood. And when she met his searching gaze, he knew exactly what had happened to her. 'You made a pact with an Adoni.'

She nodded glumly.

48

To his shock, Varian actually felt for her and whatever stupidity had possessed her to make her bargain. The Adoni never fulfilled their promises, unless they involved pain and torture. No human should ever be at their mercy. 'How long have you been here?'

'A few hundred years.' There were tears in her eyes that she didn't allow to fall as she wiped more blood from his brow. 'Early on, I kept thinking that I would eventually die of old age and leave here. But they wouldn't even allow me that. So here I am, eternally at their mercy.'

'I'm sorry.'

She frowned at him as if she found his words as hard to believe as he did. Yet he truly meant them. 'Why should you be sorry? I'm not the one chained to the walls.'

She did have a point. 'True, but eventually, I'll get out of here and kill them.'

She looked doubtful as she fed him more venison.

Varian carefully chewed and swallowed before he spoke again. 'Do you have a name, lass?'

'Merewyn.'

It was a beautiful name that fit her ethereal grace. In the fey Adoni language, a merewyn was a sea witch. A tempting mer-creature that would grab unsuspecting sailors from their boats and drag them down to the bottom of the sea and trap them there to serve them until they grew tired of the man's presence or form. Then the merewyns would feed them to the sharks.

Perhaps that was a fitting name for a woman like her.

'Would you care for wine?' she asked softly.

'Please.'

She lifted the cup to his lips, then tilted it a bit too much. The wine ran into his mouth, stinging his cuts and causing him to gasp at the new pain. He choked.

She pulled the cup away and quickly wiped his lips with her towel. 'Forgive me. I'm so sorry. I didn't mean to do that.'

Varian closed his eyes. Even through the agony of his body her touch soothed him. How could he feel anything other than the pain of his beating? It didn't make sense, and yet somehow he did. Somehow she touched him through it all, and that honestly scared him.

As she fed him a piece of bread, he caught a whiff of her sweet skin. She smelled of rosewater and lilac and it made him wonder what it would be like to lay his head in the crook of her neck and just inhale her fragrance.

What it would be like to touch her smooth, soft skin. Taste her mouth and have someone so kind ... so human, in his bed.

But then he knew better than to even think that. No matter how much he might wish otherwise, he was Adoni. Conceived by deception and sold for one woman's vanity. It wasn't for him to have a human. He didn't deserve such comfort. All he deserved was hatred and scorn.

Angered at the thought of her kindness and at the fact that she was weakening him, he pulled back. 'Leave me.'

Merewyn was stunned by his harsh words. 'What?'

He pinned her with an icy glare that cut straight through her. 'Leave,' he growled in a tone so guttural, he reminded her of a gargoyle.

'Merewyn?'

She flinched at the sound of his mother's voice. She didn't want to leave him alone to their cruelty again. How could she? No one deserved this.

'Did you hear me, scab?' Narishka snarled.

Still she hesitated even though she knew she'd most likely be beaten for it. She didn't want them to renew their cruelty to a man who was so obviously suffering. Her stomach tight at the thought of what more they'd do, she took a moment to clean his swollen face one last time.

Varian met Merewyn's gaze and saw the compassion and regret that filled her. She gently wiped his mouth before she released him.

He had to clamp his swollen jaw shut to keep from calling her back. How ironic, their cruelty hadn't once moved him to tears or pleading, but the thought of her leaving him almost did. It was why she had to go.

Weakness was death to a creature like him. Strength. Solitude. Those were what he needed to live and thrive.

And when she paused at the door with the tray held in her hands to look back at him, it was all he could do not to beg for mercy.

Instead, he glared at her, hoping . . . no, praying that she didn't return. He couldn't afford it. Closing his eyes, he let the pain take him away from any solace. Let it seep through him until it was all he felt. It allowed his magick to grow in strength, but it still wasn't enough to get him out of this. Not yet. But with any luck, if they kept beating him, it would.

Then he would show his mother exactly what she'd bargained for. He would happily give her a taste of his hell-born powers.

Merewyn felt a single tear slide down her cheek as Varian dipped his head again so that he was looking at the floor while his dark hair hid his features from her. Wiping the moisture away, she hated the thought of what else they'd do to him. His face was so misshapen, and his eyes had been filled with utter agony. But that wasn't her business. She'd done what her mistress required.

Stiffening her spine, she walked through the door and closed it tight, then glanced at Narishka, who appeared proud of her accomplishment.

'Will you continue his torture now?' she asked, as the tray dissolved out of her hands.

Narishka shook her head. 'We'll let him heal a bit. Right now he's so sore that he's most likely numb to any more pain. Besides, he's got enough magick left to make himself feel better.' She stopped as if considering that thought for a moment. 'I wonder why it is that my spell didn't remove all of his powers? Perhaps I should have made it stronger. Although I gave it enough of a charge that it should have depleted even the Kerrigan. Amazing really. I guess I underestimated his strength. No more of that, eh?'

Merewyn was aghast at Narishka's coldness, but she made sure she didn't show it. She wanted to ask her how she could do such a thing, but she already knew the answer. Narishka was evil to the center of her dark soul. She didn't care for anyone. Really. If Morgen were to fall from power tomorrow, Narishka would just as easily serve another. So long as she could spew her venomous cruelty, she was happy. She didn't care who it was against or even who she aligned herself with.

Narishka looked at her and tsked. 'We'll have to hide you for a bit.'

'Hide me?'

'Yes. To look as you do now is to invite nothing but trouble from the others. And the fact that you're a virgin ... too tempting. There are many dark spells that call for the sacrifice of beautiful virgins. It would

52

do me no good to have you sliced open right now for someone's play for power. And it would take me too long to replace you with another human. So, hiding it shall be.'

Before Merewyn could even open her mouth to speak, she found herself alone in a windowless, doorless room. 'Mistress!' she called, but no one answered.

She felt her way around in the darkness, only to learn she was in a very small, empty room with no blanket, pillow, or anything else. Once again, she was at Narishka's mercy, and she hated it.

Shrieking, she slammed her hand against the black wall as her eyes strained to see something. Anything. But it was hopeless. Narishka had left her with nothing.

That lying bitch!

Merewyn slid to the floor as her ragged emotions tore through her. Anger, hurt, hopelessness. Yet underneath that, she realized that as bad as this was, she was still better off than Varian. At least she wasn't chained to the wall for their cruel pleasure.

And with that came a wave of despair so large that it rolled over her and left her breathless.

'There's no way out,' she whispered, her chest aching with the truth. Magda had been right. Narishka had no intention of letting her leave. Ever. She was going to die here. Somehow that bitch would trick her again and keep her in this land of viciousness.

'No, she won't,' she swore to the darkness with angry conviction. She was smarter now than she'd been as a girl in Mercia. Having lived with Narishka all these centuries, she'd learned much from her mistress. She knew this game, and by all that was holy, or not, she was going to win her freedom. No matter what it took, she would leave this place and never look back. She didn't care who she had to sacrifice or what she had to do.

'I won't ever be a fool again.'

Chapter Five

Two days later

'It's no good, my lady. So long as his armor's in place, there's not much else we can do to him.'

Varian took pride in the scream of frustration his mother let out at the mandrake's words.

She coldcocked the mandrake hard enough to send him straight to the ground before she raked her nails down Varian's swollen cheek. He hissed from the pain but refused to make any other sound in response.

Her eyes snapping fire, she turned on the other mandrake, who cringed in fear of what she'd do to him. Cupping himself, he took three steps back and had to stop as he collided with the wall. It was enough to make Varian laugh.

Which only made her angrier. 'Fetch a crowbar, jaws of life, can opener, I don't care what you have to do, I want that armor off him!' she ordered the one standing mandrake.

The dark-haired mandrake nodded quickly before he ran from the room and Narishka's reach while the blond mandrake was still in a fetal position in the corner, cupping himself.

Varian spat the blood from his mouth onto the floor. 'What's the matter, mum? Is my torture getting to you?'

She backhanded him.

He laughed at her anger. 'You know. They're right with their saying. There's nothing sweeter than the loving touch of a mother.'

She grabbed the sledgehammer from the floor where the immobilized mandrake had dropped it and slammed it into his stomach with enough force to lift him off his feet. Varian felt the blow all the way to his bones as his body was jarred by it. Still he refused to cry out or beg for mercy even though it was all he could do to breathe he hurt so badly. Every gasp, every bone. All he wanted was for this to stop.

His mother shrieked again. 'Why won't you bend?'

Because it was what everyone expected of him. His father, his brother, every warrior in Avalon. Hell, even Arthur had expected him to side with his mother and Morgen at some point. There were times when Merlin, too, looked at him as if she were waiting for him to turn.

But he would never do that.

Even if his own conviction wasn't so set, the fact that everyone expected it would be enough to keep him on the path of light.

He would never prove them right by joining ranks with the Adoni and Morgen.

Varian hissed as he felt something biting into his back as a grayling tried to pry the armor free. 'It's like it's skin or something, my lady.'

His mother cursed him as she realized he was correct. That's exactly what his armor was, and it was why it hurt so badly whenever they tried to remove it.

Her cheeks mottled by her fury, she threw the sledgehammer into the corner. 'There has to be a spell to weaken this. Mandrake, grayling, withdraw!'

They quickly left him alone with his mother. She buried her hand in his hair and jerked his head up until he was looking at her. He could taste the blood that was running from his lips and nose, smell the sweat of his body from the hours of grueling torture.

Her eyes were dark with curiosity, and they lacked any compassion for him. 'Why would you rather I beat you than simply do what I ask?'

He gave her a taunting smile. 'Because it is ever my goal to piss you off.'

She snapped his head back before she let go of his hair. 'Why I bargained for you, I'll never know.'

'Simple, mum. You wanted a bouncing baby boy to love and take care of you in your old age.'

She sneered at him. 'I should have drowned you when you were born.'

And he returned that gesture with the same degree of disgust. 'I should have been so lucky.'

That got him a nice slap in the face before she stalked out of the room and left him there to hang. Literally.

Varian let out a slow, tired breath as he stared at the fresh and dried blood on the floor. His blood. It made him wonder what his father had gone through at Morgen's hands before she'd killed him, too. Not that he cared. It was more morbid curiosity than anything.

'What did you do?'

He glanced up at Merewyn's soft voice as she stood in the doorway with a look of abject horror on her beautiful face. 'Bled mostly. Why?'

She grimaced at the sight of his face as she drew nearer. He could only imagine what he must look like to her. Not that it mattered. He wasn't exactly in the mood to woo a woman anyway. Rather, he was basically worthless.

What else is new?

Still, he knew it wrong to look forward to her visits. Especially since he knew who and what she really was, and yet he couldn't stop himself from wanting to see her every day. She was the only bright spot his mother had allowed him . . . which was his mother's intent.

Merewyn placed her tray on the floor before she picked up the cool cloth and held it against the worst of the cuts on Varian's face. Four rows of jagged welts went from his temple to chin. It looked as if one of the mandrakes had drawn his claw down his face. She couldn't help but ache at the sight of it.

He sucked his breath in sharply at the touch of the cloth that must have stung deeply. 'I don't need your kindness, Merewyn.'

'You need someone's. Perhaps your own might do you some good.'

'Is that supposed to make sense?'

'Yes,' she said sharply. For some reason, his stubbornness angered her. Why wouldn't he just do what they wanted and end this? 'Give them what they want so you can go free.'

He snorted at that, then grimaced as if a sharp pain had gone through him. 'Would you sell out someone for your freedom?'

She looked down at his words, unable to respond. The answer made her feel ill. 'They're going to kill you, Varian.'

His face was stoic as those vibrant green eyes captured her gaze. They held a passion and fire that was fathomless and surprising given his current situation. 'We all die, one way or another. It's how we live that matters.'

Even so, she didn't understand what allowed him to stand strong against such brutality. 'What matters to you so much that you would endure this pain for it?'

He didn't respond.

'Tell me?' she asked as she moved the cloth to wipe away the blood from his lips. 'Is it friendship?'

'No.'

'Love?'

He gave a bitter laugh at that. 'I don't even know what that is.'

'Then what?' She pulled back to stare at him. 'What is so dear to you that this' – she gestured at his mangled body – 'is trivial in comparison?'

'I don't know,' he said in a quiet tone.

She shook her head in disbelief, then narrowed her eyes at him. 'You don't know, and yet you bleed for it?'

He gave her a gimlet stare that froze her to the spot. 'Is there not something you would bleed for?'

'No,' she said fervently. 'Nothing. Why should I? No one would ever bleed for me.'

One corner of his mouth turned up in a mocking smile. 'Then we're the same, you and I.'

'How so?'

'No one would ever bleed for me either.'

Was that supposed to make sense? 'Then why suffer this?'

Again she was stung by the intensity of emotions that shone so brightly in his eyes. 'Because I won't be what my father was. I won't turn against my oath. Not for anything.'

She didn't agree with him, but at least that made some sense. 'Then you bleed for honor.'

'I have no honor.'

'Then you bleed for nothing.'

'And you would bleed for nothing, either.'

She dropped the cloth and clenched her hands in frustration at him. 'Don't twist my words around.

That's not what I meant.'

'I know.'

Unable to stand the scrutiny of his gaze and the sting of her own conscience, she started for the door.

'Merewyn, wait.'

She paused at his voice and turned to face him again. 'Yes?'

His gaze was sharp as if he were measuring her worth before he answered. 'I . . .' He glanced to the floor as his voice broke off.

'You?' she prompted.

Once again he met her gaze and held it. 'I need a favor, if you don't mind.'

A favor. There was something no one had asked her for in centuries. Here in Camelot they only ordered her about. Favors were for fools. Surely Varian of all people knew that.

But her curiosity got the better of her, and she wanted to know what a man like this would ask of her. 'What is this favor?'

'Could you loosen the laces of my breastplate so that I could breathe a little easier?'

Merewyn hesitated. She knew from Narishka that her Adoni mistress had been trying for days to get his armor from him with no success. Varian had kept it well in place and taunted her with it. 'You would trust me?'

'No. But I can't loosen it myself and I know better than to ask my mother for help.'

He was certainly right about that, and if she removed it from him, Narishka would reward her. Greatly. Maybe she'd even release her early . . .

Merewyn took a step forward, then paused again as she imagined the sight of her removing his armor and leaving him bare for their torture. They would be even more merciless, and he would have no protection from them at all.

None.

Do it! Narishka would be pleased beyond measure.

She saw herself as she'd been in Mercia ... dressed in a beautiful gown with noblemen vying for a smile from her. In her mind, she imagined the world she'd left behind. The beauty. The warmth.

The color.

Here the only color to be found was bloodred.

And eyes so green, they practically glowed.

Merewyn winced at that. She glanced to the blood at Varian's feet and hated herself for what she was about to do. Her spine stiff, she lifted her head. 'I can't.'

He frowned at her. 'Why not?'

She hesitated a moment before she did something she hadn't done in centuries. She told the honest truth even though it would cause her harm. 'Because I might remove it if I did.' And with that, she left the room.

Varian stared at the closed door for endless minutes as Merewyn's words echoed in his ears. So she wasn't completely trustworthy.

At least she had the temerity to admit it, and she hadn't hurt him. That was actually a first. Not that he would have allowed her to loosen his armor anyway. He'd just wanted to know what she'd say.

If she'd try to remove it.

Perhaps she wasn't his foe after all. Or perhaps she'd seen it for the test it'd been and was smarter than that. There was never anyone to really trust. He knew that. Everyone he'd ever let inside his defenses had only used it as a chance to hurt him. His father, Galahad, Dafyn, even Merlin.

And speaking of the latter, he'd been trapped here

for days now, and no one had been sent from Avalon to check on his health. If he were anyone else, Merlin would have been calling down every double agent she had to help the member in trouble.

But none of them were worth jeopardizing for him.

That was all right though. He didn't want to be in debt to anyone else. This was just another day in his life. Another humiliation.

Another pain in his ass ... back, shoulder ... hell even his eyelids hurt.

Closing his eyes, he did what he'd always done when his life sucked, he dreamed himself away from here. He imagined a place of solitude and peace.

More than that, he could feel the gentle touch of a woman's hand on his cheek. She'd always been face-less and formless in the past, but not this time.

This time she had long dark hair that fell in ringlets to her waist, and she held beautiful amber-tinged eyes that called him insane for enduring this.

And for once she had a name. One he dare not trust.

Dreams were ever evil. More men had fallen because of them than anything else, and he certainly wasn't stupid enough for that.

Sucking his breath in, he summoned his magick and used it to knock out as many of the dents in his armor as he could before his mother's spell weakened his power again and left him with nothing.

Tomorrow he would get rid of Merewyn and her kindness. That was the first step. The next would be to gain his freedom.

Or at the very least, his death.

Chapter Six

Merewyn wanted to run as far away from here as she could get, and yet as she neared the end of the hallway, she realized that she had nowhere to go. No place to hide in this land where Narishka and her minions wouldn't find her and bring her back. There was no way out of Camelot without extremely strong magick, power, or a merlin's key – things she didn't possess.

The only place to go would be Glastonbury, where the cruel inhabitants would take glee in handing her over to her mistress.

And if you keep going, Narishka will beat you for it. An image of Varian's bloodied body went through her mind. They needed him alive. She, personally, wasn't that lucky. There was nothing Narishka needed her for. She would be beaten and tortured until she died.

When Narishka had found her after she'd fallen from a rooftop during her one escape attempt, she'd told Merewyn that if Merewyn ever tried to run away again, she'd feast on her entrails, then bring her back from the dead as a mindless ghoul.

Flinching with that thought, she reversed course and returned to the dismal room where the stench of blood and sweat permeated the stagnant air. Blood coated the links and metal cuffs that kept Varian chained to the walls and on his feet. She was certain he hadn't slept in days. Hadn't sat or been off his bruised legs for even a moment.

Yet he said nothing about the abuse. He merely took the beatings in stride as if he somehow deserved them.

As she neared him, he lifted his head and pinned her with a stare so malevolent that for once she saw the resemblance between mother and son.

'So you've returned,' he said dryly.

She gestured toward her tray at his feet. 'I forgot my things.'

He raised a doubting brow that all but called her a liar. Merewyn moved closer to him so that she could take her tray.

He didn't speak until after she'd bent down for it. 'I know who you are.'

She snorted at the words he whispered in an ominous tone. 'Of course you do. I've already told you my name.'

'No,' he said, his voice thick and dry. 'I know you're the deformed woman I saved from a beating in Glastonbury.'

Those whispered words froze her to the spot. She couldn't breathe or move. Surely it was a game he played with her. There was no way he could know that. Deciding to brazen this out by not letting him know that he'd guessed correctly, she forced herself to put the cloth on the tray.

'I don't know what you're talking about.' She tilted her head back to meet his probing stare.

There was no reprieve or mercy in those glowing green eyes. They burned her with intelligence and unholy power. It was as if he could see straight into her soul, and it sent a shiver down her spine.

'Of course you do. I'm not a fool, Merewyn. I knew the moment I saw your eyes who and what you were. My mother changed everything about you except for that. Your eyes will always give you away.'

A need to close them consumed her, but she didn't so much as blink. She wouldn't give him the satisfaction of knowing he'd gotten to her.

'I know my mother, lass. The question is, do you?'

The tray forgotten, she rose to her feet to confront his hostile glare. She refused to let him judge her when she was only doing what she had to, to survive in this hell. 'What is that supposed to mean?'

He licked the blood away from his lips before he spoke again. 'Whatever bargain you made with her to be beautiful, I assure you it won't work. She won't leave you with that beauty, trust me. She'll take absolute pleasure in stripping it from you and listening to you cry out from the pain of seeing it gone.'

That was her worst fear, and it held her throat in an iron grip that radiated through her entire body. She didn't want to be ugly anymore. She didn't want to be spat at, despised, and mocked for ugliness.

She only wanted to fit in and be seen as something other than a monster.

Still, he gave neither her fear nor conscience reprieve. 'You're going to die, Merewyn. Without a doubt.'

'Narishka won't kill me.' Those words were bitter on her tongue, and having said it aloud to him only added to her conviction that Varian spoke the truth.

'You're lying to yourself if you believe that.'

Merewyn shook her head, and she forced herself to believe her own lie. 'I've been with her far more centuries than you have. I know her better than you.'

'Do you?' he asked with a cold, humorless laugh.

'Here, let me guess at how all of this has played out. She told you to come in here and be nice to me. To bring me food and water, and bathe my brow, so that I would be tempted by your beauty and weakened by your kindness. Your task is to talk to me of goodness and to show me mercy so that I will be bonded to you and grow to like you – that has been her plan from the moment she started beating me. But it won't work. I'm not weakening even in the slightest degree. And when my mother grows bored from trying to pry my armor off, she's going to bring you in here to stand before me and hold a knife to your throat. She'll press it so close to your beautiful neck that it'll prick your skin until a bead of your blood coats the blade. You'll most likely be crying as you realize that your fate is in the hands of a woman who couldn't care less about you. Then she's going to give me a choice – join her and Morgen or watch you die by her hand.'

Merewyn didn't move or even breathe as the image he painted with his words hung heavy and clear in her mind. She could even feel the coldness of the blade. See the twisted delight in Narishka's eyes as she demanded Varian join them.

Varian gave her a look that pierced her straight to the heart, and when he spoke, his voice held the full weight of his intent. 'When that moment comes, I *won't* save you.'

Her mind screamed a silent denial. Surely she hadn't come this far and survived so much cruelty to die as he said. Not even Damé Fortune would be that mean. 'I don't believe you.' Varian was on the side of good. Such men as this didn't let innocent people die. Not when they could stop it.

'Oh you better believe me, little girl,' he said, curling his lip. 'Better *you* should die than those who

66

protect the grail from Morgen. Just as I'm willing to die for my conviction, I'm willing to see you dead for it, too. That is a promise.'

She swallowed at his sinister tone, and she didn't doubt it for a second.

'If you want to live with that beauty you've bargained for, then you'd best run.'

How easy he made that sound. Didn't he think that she wanted to? 'And where am I to go? There's no place for someone like me to hide from your mother. Her powers are absolute ... she even captured you who claim to know her so well. She would seek me out and kill me instantly just for causing her to leave her chambers.'

'Then you are doomed.'

She clenched her teeth against the wave of hopeless, bitter pain that consumed her. 'I already know that.' And it was true. She'd damned herself the moment she'd sought out the old hag in the Mercian woods and paid her to summon an Adoni for her so that she wouldn't be forced to marry a man who couldn't see anything more than her beauty.

There was no going back now.

Yet as she stared at the mangled man before her, she realized just what she'd become here in Camelot. Magda had been right. She was no longer human. She'd allowed Narishka to take everything from her.

Everything.

Even her humanity.

She was completely worthless now.

But then, she'd never been strong. All her life in Mercia, she'd been spoiled and vain. Stupid. A young girl so caught up in her own world that she'd thrown her entire life away rather than marry the man her father had chosen. She'd foolishly dreamed of love and happiness. At that time, she'd thought herself worthy of it.

And now, instead of bargaining herself, she'd sold out another person for her own selfish gain. She looked at Varian's bloodied face, at the places on his wrists where the iron cuffs had chafed and bruised him.

'*Will you be able to look in the mirror knowing your beauty was bought in blood?*'

She knew the truth.

Hanging her head, she removed her tray from the floor and started to leave. But before she did, she turned back to look at Varian. His beautiful hair was matted by tangles and blood. His handsome face distorted by bruises. Still, he stood strong even while in pain. Still, he managed to appear powerful and certain when inside he had to be tired and dying. He was such an idiot to fight them when it was obvious he couldn't win.

Or ... maybe he knew something they didn't. Maybe, just maybe, he was his mother's match.

That thought led her to another, which gave her the first bit of hope she'd had in a long time.

Don't do it, Merewyn. Don't!

But the words were out of her mouth before she could stop them. 'If I were to free you, would you take me away from this place?'

He gave a bitter laugh as if he found the idea every bit as preposterous as her inner voice did. 'You can't free me from here.'

Even so, she was undaunted. 'What if I could?'

He met her gaze levelly, and the ice in his eyes chilled her. 'You get me out of here, and I will make sure that no Adoni ever lays a hand to you again. Ever.'

'How do I know I can trust you to keep your word?'

'I swear it on the soul of Arthur himself.' He said those words with such heartfelt conviction that she did the impossible. She believed him.

'Very well. I will trust you to keep that oath, and I will free you anon.'

Varian watched as she left him alone once more. He knew better than to put any faith in her. What could she, a mere servant, do?

You will die here.

Clenching the chains in his hands, he pulled against them with every ounce of his strength. His body throbbed and burned in protest as he tried something he knew was futile. Still, he had to attempt it. It'd never been in his nature not to fight.

Anger swelled inside him as he was forced to relax and hang limply from the chains.

Weary, but not defeated, he hung his head and closed his eyes to summon something soothing to ease him from the pain and despair he felt. Normally he envisioned a small, quiet cottage on top of a hill, where he was free to sit and read while a bright sun peeped in through the open windows, and the gentle breeze carried the scent of honeysuckle and birdsong.

Today that dream eluded him. Instead of his cottage on the hill, he saw the winsome smile of a woman he knew he couldn't trust at all. The winsome smile of a woman who'd traded his life so that she could have her beauty . . .

Merewyn left her tray in a small alcove, then stealthily made her way through the winding gray corridors of Camelot. What she was doing was so foolish that she couldn't believe her gall, and yet what choice did she have?

Varian was right. His mother would never let her go.

And no matter how much she wanted to believe otherwise, she had no doubt that he would sacrifice her without hesitation. Just as he'd said.

This was the only way she knew to save her life.

Her heart hammering, she paused outside a large, black door that dwarfed her small frame and rapped quickly on the cold wood.

'Come in.' The voice was deep and masculine.

Merewyn hesitated until she remembered the fact that the man inside couldn't really see anything whenever he was in human form. He wouldn't know she was any different than what she'd always been.

Holding that thought close, she opened the door and stepped inside the small bedroom that belonged to the mandrake named Blaise, who sat by his fire in repose. He had his hands resting on his taut stomach, with his legs stretched out before him as if he'd been napping. Tall and leanly muscled, with long white blond hair, he'd once been the personal servant of the former king of Camelot, Kerrigan.

But Kerrigan had turned against Morgen a little over a year ago and had joined ranks with the Lords of Avalon. Blaise had been with him in the fight until he'd managed to free himself from the king's clutches. Then Blaise had returned to Camelot to report Kerrigan's treachery to Morgen.

At least that was the story Blaise told.

Merewyn knew better. There was much more to the mandrake's return than he let on. Narishka might have taken her beauty, but she hadn't taken her intelligence or her intuition. 'Forgive me for disturbing you, my lord.'

He cocked his head at an odd angle as if he were trying to see her with those light violet eyes that shimmered with color. His white hair was pulled back into a long braid that fell over his shoulder, to his waist. Though he claimed albinism, he had deep tawny skin and a face so ruggedly handsome that every Adoni here had quested for his body ... at least for one night. She, herself, had never failed to notice his beauty, but it was his gentle regard toward her that had attracted her most. 'Merewyn?'

'Aye.'

'Does your lady need something?'

In all these centuries past, she'd never ventured into his chambers for any other reason. The two of them had only passed each other by as they ran about on errands for their masters. Their meetings had been brief and usually consisted of her relaying a message from Narishka to Kerrigan.

One way or another that ended today.

She had no guarantee that Blaise would help her in this, but he was the only hope she had. 'I need a favor from you.'

He arched his brows in surprise. 'A favor from me?'

'You would be the only person in this room besides myself. So that means you are the only you I could be speaking to, correct?'

A lopsided smile curved his lips. 'Sarcasm? That's new for you, isn't it?'

Not really. She'd always been that way, but usually she kept such comments to herself. 'Please, I haven't much time. There is one here who needs help.'

His expression sobered instantly as he straightened up in his chair. 'You know as well as I do what helping someone gets you here in Camelot.'

Closing the door, she moved across the room until she stood close to Blaise. She lowered her voice so that no one outside the room could overhear them. 'I do. But if something isn't done, Varian will die.'

71

His expression turned to stone as if he were trying to hide his emotions from her. 'Varian? duFey?'

'The same.'

'What concern is his life to me?'

'I should think his life is extremely important to you.'

'And why is that? Why do you come to me about the life of a man everyone claims is worthless?'

She swallowed before she answered truthfully. 'Because you're the only one here I can trust. You are the only one, besides Magda, who has ever shown any kindness toward me. For that reason, I believe you can and will help me.'

He tilted his head back as if he were using his powers to sense the air around them. 'How do I know this isn't a trap?'

'I don't betray my friends.'

He snorted at that. 'Since when am I one of your friends?'

She reached to touch his left shoulder blade and pressed her hand against a spot she knew had meaning for him. 'You have always been counted as a friend. For many, many years.'

Recognition darkened his gaze as he swiftly caught her meaning. 'Why do you want to help Varian?'

'He will help me escape, too, if I find a way to free him.'

Blaise narrowed his eyes in a way that made her wonder if he could actually see her after all. 'Is that the only reason?'

'Aye.'

Her arm fell from him as he rose to his feet. 'Then come, we'd best hurry before Narishka learns what we're about and decides to roast us for it.'

Merewyn took a deep breath in relief even though

they were far from safe. At least she'd made it this far, and Blaise had agreed to help her. It was more than she'd had before. 'He's in the dungeon.'

Blaise gave her a stare that said 'you think?' before he took her hand and flashed them from his room to where Varian waited in chains.

Luckily, the room was still empty.

'Damn,' Blaise said under his breath as he squinted toward Varian. 'Even half-blind, I can see that they made one hell of a mess of you.'

Varian jerked his head up. Disbelief was etched firmly on his face. 'What are you doing here?'

'Come to save your rotten ass. What else?'

Varian's gaze went to her.

'I told you I could get you out.'

He scoffed at her bold words. 'I'm not out of here yet. And neither are you.'

Blaise moved forward to stand by Varian's side. He took one of the thick black chains in his hands and tried to pull it apart. 'Whose magick binds you?'

'My mother's.'

Blaise made a face of disgust. 'Can you combine your powers with mine to break it?'

'I'm not sure. She's using a dampening spell on me that is seriously putting a crimp on what I can do.'

Blaise cursed. 'No wonder you look like shit.'

'Yeah, well, you're not exactly date material yourself, buddy.'

'Could you two hurry,' Merewyn snapped at them. 'While the bantering is semientertaining, we do have a bit of a dilemma here that will become severe should someone discover us.'

'She has a point,' Varian said.

Blaise grimaced before he cupped the metal cuff on Varian's left wrist. 'All right, on three, two . . . one.'

The men closed their eyes as Blaise strained to pull the cuff apart.

A sharp light flashed from the two of them and pierced the room an instant before the cuff broke free. Varian staggered and would have fallen to the floor had Blaise not caught him.

'Here,' Blaise said, setting him back on his feet. He moved to cup Varian's face between his hands as he whispered quietly in Mandrake. '*Asklas gardala varra deya.*'

Hissing, Varian jerked back as if pain was shooting through his body. The sound intensified as an eerie yellow glow moved slowly over his body. As it did so, his wounds healed, and his armor undented itself until, once more, he was whole and healed.

Varian let out a deep, relieved breath. His eyes were filled with gratitude.

Blaise patted him on the shoulder an instant before he moved to the other cuff. 'Again. Three, two ... one.'

The cuff broke away.

Varian closed his eyes and rubbed his arms. 'Thank you, Blaise.'

Merewyn couldn't move as she was struck by how handsome Varian was. His face had been so misshapen for so long that she'd honestly forgotten just how incredibly perfect his features were. His black hair hung in waves that only emphasized the strength of his sculpted jaw, which bore a week's work of whiskers.

Blaise hesitated before he dropped the cuff to the floor. 'Are you okay, V?'

He nodded. 'Yeah. Just a little disoriented from your healing.'

Blaise frowned as he looked him over. 'What did they do, leave you in pain while you were alone, then heal you right before they beat on you some more?'

Varian nodded.

Merewyn cringed. She hadn't even thought about that cruelty.

'Did you tell them anything?' Blaise asked quietly.

'Tell them what? That I'm an asshole? I think they already know that.'

Merewyn would have laughed, but she froze as she heard someone outside the room. It was definitely the sound of approaching footsteps. 'Someone's coming,' she whispered to the men.

'You two better get going,' Blaise said before he vanished from the room.

'Blaise!' Varian hissed quietly. When the mandrake didn't respond, he set off into a long string of curses.

Merewyn was baffled by his anger. 'Can't you use your powers to take us out of here?'

He jerked at a small gold bracelet on his wrist. 'Not at the moment. No.'

Merewyn felt the blood drain from her face as she looked about for a place to flee or hide.

There wasn't one. The room was completely empty except for the chains ... and them.

The footsteps came closer until they stopped just before the door. Terrified, she looked up at Varian who put himself between her and it. But he was every bit as defenseless as she was. He didn't even have his magick.

They were dead!

A key rattled in the lock.

She clutched at Varian's arm, which kept her behind his back as the door was slowly pushed open.

Chapter Seven

Varian tensed, ready to fight as the door creaked open. A heartbeat before he saw who was entering, the room went black. Completely black as he felt himself falling into an abyss. Instinctively he tightened his grip on Merewyn, seeking to protect her as best he could.

When next he blinked, he found himself standing in a small bedroom somewhere in the castle, while Merewyn's tight grip restricted the blood flow in his arm.

He turned to find Blaise scowling at him. 'Cutting it a bit close, weren't you?'

He released a long aggravated breath before he twisted his wrist away from Merewyn. 'Not as close as you did. What the hell's wrong with you?'

'Me? You're the one who's half-Adoni. Why didn't you get out of there when I left?'

He held up his wrist with the band on it to show the two of them. 'Remember what I said? My mother is still restricting my powers. I can't travel anywhere with my magick so long as I have this on.'

'Then you better find a way either to pry it off or lose the hand, bud.'

'Is that a problem?' Merewyn asked. 'Can't Blaise get us out of here?'

'Yes,' Varian said automatically. He knew for a fact that the mandrake had come and gone between the realms in the past.

'No,' Blaise corrected.

No? The word echoed in Varian's head as he envisioned himself strangling the mandrake.

'What do you mean, 'no'?'

'I can't get you guys out of here either. I don't have a key to open the portal.'

Varian's features turned stony and dark. Murderous. 'Where's your key, Blaise?'

'I left it with Kerrigan because some people like your mother were getting a bit suspicious of me after I came back here. Had one of their snoops found it anywhere in my vicinity, my scaly hide would have been picked clean.'

Oh this was just too perfect. Varian felt suddenly ill as he realized that they were completely screwed. 'You've got to be kidding me.'

He looked at Merewyn, who appeared to be grappling with the matter a bit more calmly. At least she didn't look like she wanted to strangle Blaise. 'So there's no way for us to leave here?'

'Nope,' Blaise said. 'Not unless Varian frees his powers and zaps us out.'

If only.

Merewyn held her hand to her head as if she were getting a vicious headache. 'Then it was all for nothing. I risked my life, and now it's over. Narishka is going to kill me!'

Varian shook his head. 'It's not over yet.'

She turned on him with a murderous glint in her amber eyes. Even though he hated to admit it, she was breathtaking with the heat of anger in her cheeks. Her eyes snapped fire at him, and it singed him to the deepest part of his manhood. 'Of course it is. Where are we to go that they won't find us?'

He glanced out the small window that overlooked the valley at the far end of Camelot. 'Val Sans Retour.'

Both Merewyn and Blaise gaped at him. 'The Valley of No Return?' Merewyn asked incredulously. 'You'd have us go there?'

Varian couldn't help taunting her. 'You got a better idea?'

She growled at him in a way that shouldn't be adorable and yet strangely it was. 'In case you haven't noticed, simpkin. No one, and I mean, *no one* returns from that godforsaken place. Hence the name.'

Blaise folded his arms across his chest. 'I have to agree with her, Varian.'

He gave the mandrake a droll stare. 'No, you don't. Besides, how do you know they die there? If you had a chance to put this place behind you and live somewhere else, would you come back?'

Blaise thought about it a second before he turned toward Merewyn. 'He does have a point.'

Merewyn glared at them both. 'That still leaves me trapped here in this realm . . . with' – she raked Varian with a cold stare – 'you. No offense, I'd rather take my chances with your mother.'

Blaise laughed low in his throat. 'And that insult's gotta hurt.'

Varian narrowed his eyes at the mandrake. 'I don't need your blow-by-blow, Cosell. In case you hadn't noticed, I'm right here.'

Suddenly, a loud bell began chiming. It thundered painfully through the air.

Blaise covered his sensitive ears. 'It appears they

know you're gone.'

Varian couldn't help cringing himself as the sound reverberated through the room. He could actually feel it in his bones. No doubt the gargoyles were being activated by now to help Morgen and Narishka search the castle. They didn't have long before his mother located them.

He turned toward Blaise. 'Look, there's something weird about that Valley.'

Blaise gave him a duh stare. 'Yes, and we all know it. It's enchanted by Morgen.'

That wasn't what Varian meant. 'And it backs up to Avalon. I'm willing to bet that if you make it through the valley, much like Glastonbury, you can walk through to our side.'

Merewyn's face turned pale at his words. 'I can't go there.'

'Yes, you can. The barrier is only to keep out evil. You're not evil, Merewyn. You're just foolish.'

As he intended, that snapped her out of her fearful panic. 'And what does that make you?'

'Stupid and evil, both of which are tempered enough that I can walk through the barrier and not turn to dust.' He winked at her before turning his attention to Blaise. 'Take us to the opening of the valley.'

Blaise appeared less than enthused about the order.

But it was Merewyn who protested. 'And what if I don't want to go?'

'You have to make a choice. Me or my mother.'

By her face, he could tell she hated her options. He didn't know why he enjoyed teasing her – it wasn't really in his nature, and yet for some reason he liked to nettle her.

She let out an exasperated breath. 'I suppose you're the lesser evil.'

'Not really.' He met Blaise's curious stare. 'You need to get us to the valley,' he repeated.

Blaise's face was doubtful. 'That's easier said than done. If they see us, I'm through as a double agent. They'll know beyond a shadow of a doubt that I'm working with Merlin. No offense, but I've spent too many centuries spying in Camelot to just throw that away now.'

'Don't you think they're going to know you're on our side when they find us in your room? They're not dumb enough to think Merewyn brought me here, and they know I couldn't have freed myself.'

'Good point. But we still have the problem of them seeing us while we flee.'

Varian closed his eyes and summoned what magick he could. It wasn't much, but it should be enough to provide them with some cover. He whispered the words that would unleash the breath of the dragons who'd once made Camelot home. They were the forefathers of the mandrake people. A stronger, more primitive race, the dragons had lacked the magical abilities of their progeny. A magick that had come as a result of the dragons breeding with the fey until the last of their pure breed had died and left the halfbreeds such as Blaise and the rest.

It was said that the elders of their breed slumbered in the ground beneath the castle. And one of the first tricks any sorcerer learned was how to awaken the dragons for a brief time. It was that spell Varian used now.

As he chanted, the dragons' breath came up from the ground in great bursts of steam until the area outside was thick with swirling gray fog.

'All right,' Blaise said as he shifted from human into his own dragon form.

Varian frowned as his scales turned from their bright green to a shadowy silver and black. 'What are you doing?'

'Just in case I get seen, I plan to look like Maddor. Best-case scenario, they'll think I'm him and kill him. At the worst, they'll know it wasn't him and won't know who to blame, so my butt will be safe. Now, climb on, kids.'

Varian helped Merewyn on first before he climbed up in front of her. He felt the pressure of her against his back, but with the armor on, he couldn't feel her, which was probably a good thing. She wrapped her slender arms around his waist and slid herself close to his spine. The delicate pallor of her arms struck him. But not nearly as much as her hands, which were ill kempt and raw. She wasn't a lady. She was a servant who his mother hadn't hesitated to abuse, and for that he felt a strange pang of guilt.

There were times when he absolutely hated his mother, and this was definitely one of them. However, he had much more important things to think about at the moment.

'We're ready,' he said to Blaise.

Blaise dropped from the window, spread out his silvery black wings, and took flight over the treacherous landscape. The steep dive actually took Varian's breath as the open air washed against his face and whipped his hair.

He'd never particularly cared for this form of travel. For one thing, mandrakes could be unpredictable. For another, it meant relying on someone else for his safety, and trust had never come easily to Varian. But at the moment, he was too grateful to be free of pain to question it.

Blaise's sides heaved under Varian's legs as the

mandrake headed for the valley as quickly as possible.

'Varian?'

He turned his head at Merewyn's call as she tightened her grip around his waist. Looking over his shoulder at her, he saw the gargoyles in flight behind them, gaining speed. So much for the dragon's breath. But then it hadn't reached up this high.

'We've been spotted,' he shouted to Blaise.

Blaise looked back, then picked up speed as he headed toward the gray snowcapped mountains. Varian sighed in aggravation. A sword was useless against the gargoyles ... as was Blaise's dragon-fyre. The only thing that could kill them would be a sorcerer's blast which he couldn't do so long as he wore the bracelet.

Damn.

'Feint left, then dodge right and swoop toward the trees,' Merewyn called.

'What?' Varian asked.

'Trust me. Gargoyles can't distinguish color, only movement. If Blaise flies around the dark gray trees, the color of his scales will blend in, and so long as the breeze is moving the leaves, they won't be able to tell which is Blaise and which is the forest.'

Varian frowned. 'Is that true?'

'Only one way to find out.' Blaise headed for the trees as Merewyn had suggested. Sure enough, the gargoyles slowed down.

Varian smiled at the sight of their confusion. 'I never knew that.'

'Me either,' Blaise said in his raspy dragon's voice.

'Neither of you have ever had to hide from them,' she whispered in his ear. 'Now be quiet so that they can't pinpoint us by sound.'

Varian did as she said, while Blaise kept low to the tree line. He covered her hand with his as he wondered how many times she'd been forced to hide from the gargoyles that she'd learned this nifty trick.

Her plan was working, at least until Varian heard the sound of approaching wings. There was only one thing that could cause that. 'Mandrakes,' he breathed. Unlike the gargoyles, they weren't blind to color. Or much else. Even Blaise's eyesight was crystal clear and sharp in dragon form.

They were also incredibly smart and highly predatorial.

'Hold on,' Blaise said in a deep, raspy tone.

No sooner had Varian tightened his hold on Blaise and Merewyn on his waist than the mandrake let out a belch of fire, lowered his head, and dove at the trees. Varian had a bad feeling about his intention.

And it turned out to be correct as they slammed through the trees. The branches and leaves lacerated their bodies as Blaise headed straight for the ground.

They landed with a roll that sent Varian and Merewyn flying from Blaise's spine. Acting on pure instinct, Varian rolled with her, trying to keep her from being any more bruised than was necessary. Something that was much easier said than done.

When they finally came to rest on a small clump of prickly gray grass, she lay atop him, her legs spread over his hips with her gown riding high on her thighs, her soft black hair falling into his face. Varian drew a sharp breath as a wave of misplaced desire stabbed him hard in the groin. Desire that wasn't helped by that fact that her cheeks were flush, her breathing heavy. She looked extremely sexy with her hair and clothes mussed. Her lips parted.

As if she sensed his thoughts, she scurried off him and pushed the hem of her gown over her bared legs. Damn shame, that.

83

Still dazed by the heat in his groin, Varian was much slower to rise as he listened to the dragons circling in the sky above them. Their war cries rang out as fire blazed through the dense trees, setting aflame many of them as the dragons tried to pinpoint their location.

'You'll have to run for the valley from here,' Blaise rasped as he staggered a bit in dragon form. 'I'll try and draw them off in the other direction.'

'Can't you flash us to the valley like you did from the dungeon to your room?' Merewyn asked.

Varian answered for him. 'He's a mandrake, Merewyn, not a sorcerer. Without something to boost them, his powers aren't strong enough to carry both of us that distance and drop us in the valley safely. If he tries, we could end up in splintered pieces.'

Blaise nodded in agreement.

Varian patted the dragon's side in gratitude. 'Thanks, Blaise.'

The dragon inclined his head to him before he took flight again and headed back toward Camelot.

Varian started to summon a horse, then stopped himself as he remembered that he couldn't. He pulled angrily at the bracelet, which didn't give at all. 'I've got to get this damned thing off my arm.'

Merewyn stepped forward. 'Give us a look at it.' Her touch was featherlight and delicate – like the brush of a fairy's wing. Even though her hands weren't smooth, they were still soft and gentle. Hands that had tenderly wiped the blood from his face and given him water and food while his mother had tortured him.

Hands that he felt a strange desire to nibble with his teeth and tease with his tongue. And with that thought came the question of what she would taste like. Her lips would have to be even softer . . .

Stop it, Varian. He needed to stay focused on the task at hand, not on the woman he was with. But the Adoni in him was fascinated by her. It was the curse of his mother's race that they were part incubus. There had never been an Adoni born who didn't have a hefty sexual appetite. One that was hard to satiate. Though Varian tried to leash that part of himself, it wasn't always easy.

And right now, with her touching him, it was all he could do not to dip his head and seize those moist, sweet lips.

Her brow furrowed, Merewyn tugged at the bracelet until she had no choice but to admit defeat. 'I truly hate your mother.'

He actually felt her withdrawal from his arm like a physical ache. 'If you were looking for me to defend her, you'd be sadly disappointed. At the moment she doesn't rank high on my list of favorite people either.' He moved farther away from her so that he could clear his head. 'C'mon, we need to get going before they find us.'

Merewyn took a moment to close her eyes and get her bearings before she followed after him. Why was she putting her life in his hands? He was the son of her worst enemy, and he bore a reputation for cruelty that was only surpassed by his mother and Morgen. They were being chased by an army of dragons and gargoyles who wouldn't hesitate to kill them ... well, her they would kill. Him, they'd just capture.

I am the greatest idiot ever born. But there was no way back from this. She'd cast her dice, and now she had to live with the consequences whatever they might be.

And that terrified her.

'What do you think is in the valley?' she asked

Varian, as they trudged through the thick woods.

'My guess is a lot of pissed off men.'

She rolled her eyes at his acerbic tone. It was a well-known fact that Morgen banished all of her old lovers to the valley once they ceased to please her. 'Why do you think she does that?'

'Does what?'

'Banishes her lovers there. Why not just kill them?'

He gave a cold laugh. 'She's twisted. No doubt she sees it as a fate worse than death for them.'

That still didn't make sense to her. 'Yes, but wouldn't she be afraid they might find a way out of their prison and come for her?'

He paused to look at her. 'I don't think Morgen truly fears anything, do you?'

'No. She is a bit arrogant that way.'

Merewyn watched as Varian held a branch out of her way so that she could pass quickly through the overgrown path. And as she did so, she wondered about this man she'd joined her fate to. What made him so different from his mother? From the rest of the Adoni she'd met? Unlike them, and unlike what she'd heard of him, he didn't seem to take pleasure in hurting others.

Rather he seemed much more quiet and sedate – something that was completely at odds with the aura of power that clung to him.

'Were you one of the knights who quested for the grail?' she asked.

'No.'

'Why not?'

He shrugged as he led her through the forest. 'Only the pure of heart could touch it. I knew that wasn't me, so I stayed behind where I could help protect Arthur's throne from Mordred and Morgen.'

That made sense to her. 'Your brother Galahad is the one who found it, yes?'

His expression froze for the tiniest bit of a heartbeat, but it was long enough to let her know that she'd struck a nerve with that question. 'Galahad started for it, but Percival beat him to it. He was the one who brought the grail to Arthur.'

Merewyn's breath faltered as she tried to imagine that moment when they'd first seen it. Like everyone else, she had no idea what it looked like, but she would love to know. 'Did you get to see the grail?'

He didn't answer.

'Varian?'

His entire body was tense, but not angry. 'The Lords of Avalon never speak of the grail. Its power is too great for that. But to answer your question, no. I only saw the container that Percival put it into as he carried it through the hall to Arthur's throne.'

She could just imagine the applause and joy that had greeted Percival and Galahad when they returned with their precious charge. From Narishka and others at court, she knew the legends of the two men only because they would often read the tales of Arthur's knights, then mock them.

Still, she believed what was written. Surely they were everything they were supposed to be. Golden and fair, seeking only to help those who needed it. Men who fought for a noble cause. Men who knew nothing of cruelty or maliciousness. How she would love to meet someone like that. Just once.

'Are Percival and Galahad as glorious as everyone proclaims?'

'They are good and decent men.' But there was something in his tone that belied his words.

'You don't like them.'

'I liked Percival a lot more before he touched the grail and was changed by it.'

'And your brother?'

He ducked under a branch. 'We need to move faster.'

Merewyn frowned at his admonition. There was something almost angry underlying his demeanor now. 'You're changing the subject. Why?'

He paused to give her a heated stare. 'I don't discuss my family with strangers. No offense.'

'You certainly haven't hesitated to discuss your mother with me.'

'That's because you personally know the great evil herself. The rest are off-limits.'

She opened her mouth to respond, only to have him grab her roughly by the arms and push her to the ground. She was angry until she realized he was covering her with his body at the same time a large shadow passed overhead.

The mandrakes were circling again.

'Not a sound,' he breathed in her ear.

Grateful he'd seen them before they'd been spotted, Merewyn held her breath as she waited for the mandrakes to discover their location. Varian's weight was oppressive against her body, but she didn't dare move even the slightest bit for fear of giving their position away. He shifted ever so slightly on top of her as if he realized he was hurting her.

That action, coupled with his newfound position, sent an odd wave of heat through her. There was something extremely intimate about this even though they weren't being tender with one another. And as she lay there, looking up at him, she wondered what it would be like to have a kiss from him.

Even though she was a virgin, she'd been in

Camelot long enough to know every sexual position ever invented. The men and women there didn't really care who watched them while they sought to please themselves. Sometimes, they didn't even bother to find a partner. Rather, they'd touch themselves and smile wickedly while others watched.

It was something she'd only tried once, but like everyone else, her twisted body had repelled her so much that she'd figured either it was overrated or she was too inexperienced to understand how she was supposed to touch herself for pleasure.

Now she wondered what it would be like to share her body with Varian. If he were anything like the rest of his mother's people, he would be not only an experienced lover but an extremely skilled one, too.

Biting her lip, it was all she could do not to rub herself against him.

Their gazes met, and time seemed to be suspended as they stared at one another. She saw a deep hunger in those green eyes, and she wondered if her own eyes betrayed her lust. Did he know what she was thinking?

He shifted ever so slightly, and as he did so, his cold armor brushed against her swollen breasts, wringing a low moan from her. She wasn't sure which one of them was the most surprised by the sound. Heat scalded her cheeks, but he didn't say anything as he broke away from her gaze to search the sky above them.

I am so embarrassed. Just let them find me and kill me.

She wasn't that fortunate. Instead, she was tortured more by his close proximity.

By the time he moved from her completely, her legs were numb from his weight. Even so, she didn't mind. There was a part of her that missed the sensation of him pressing against her.

He helped her to her feet.

They'd only taken two steps when something very soft grazed against her cheek. It was as if something had kissed her. She'd never felt anything like it before.

'Stun darts,' Varian snarled, pulling her against a tree with him. He shielded her body with his as the feathered darts began raining down all around them. They came so fiercely that they made a loud swishing noise as they shot through the trees and foliage.

She bit back a cry as one of them landed in her arm. Pain shot from her shoulder to her wrist as it rendered the limb completely numb almost instantly. The toxin spread through her entire body in only a few seconds, numbing every part of her.

Her arms hung limply at her sides, and her legs buckled while she struggled to breathe. It felt like something huge was lying on her chest, preventing her from breathing. Panic seized her as she feared her lungs and heart would freeze, too.

'Calm down,' Varian said as he scooped her up in his arms. 'Stop trying to fight it and just breathe normally.'

She did as he said, and it did become a bit easier.

In all honesty, she expected Varian to leave her on the ground and escape them. She would have done that to him.

Instead, he cradled her to his chest before a helm appeared on his head, completely obscuring his face and shielding him from the darts. He held her close as if she were precious to him before he started forward again.

It was so strange to be completely cognizant of everything around her and yet be unable to move even the slightest bit. She was utterly helpless. She couldn't even speak.

'Don't worry,' he said, his voice muffled by the helm. 'They're just trying to slow us down.'

Trying? From where she was sitting, they seemed to be succeeding.

Varian cut around a tree, then came to an abrupt stop. It wasn't until he set her down to lie on the ground and her head lolled sideways that she saw why. There was a short, round kobold eyeing them through the trees. A cursed race of fey, the kobolds were more akin to trolls than their more fair cousins. Hairy, twisted creatures who could be kind or evil depending on their moods, the kobolds were best avoided.

Merewyn couldn't tell if the creature was male or female. But it had bright blue eyes that were large in its round face. Unmoving, it stared at Varian.

'Friend or foe?' Varian asked.

The kobold licked its lips as if it were eyeing a piece of meat it intended to devour. 'That depends.'

'On?'

'What ye be looking like without that helm. If ye be a fair creature, the Rosebold means you no harm. But if you're not, you'll . . .' Her words broke off as three darts struck her. She fell to the ground, every bit as frozen as Merewyn was.

Varian wasted no time pulling the sword from the kobold's body and strapping it to his side. 'Sorry,' he said in a tone that belied his words. 'But I appreciate the sword.'

He turned and picked Merewyn up from the ground before he started forward again. 'We don't have much farther,' he assured her. 'Over the next hill and we'll be at the opening of the valley.'

Merewyn helplessly watched as more darts rained down from the sky. Luckily they glanced off Varian's armor. She, on the other hand, wasn't so fortunate, as several more found her. At the rate she was going, she would be a permanent pincushion. Something that wasn't helped by the fact that she was starting to drool on herself.

I might as well be cursed again!

How she hated this. But Varian didn't comment on the fact she was disgusting as he struggled to save both their lives. There was no scorn in his eyes as he looked down from time to time to assure himself that she was still breathing.

The only part of this that remained in their favor was the fact that the mandrakes were still airborne, though to be honest, she wasn't sure why.

That changed when they topped the hill he'd spoken of and she saw the open meadow that separated the forest from the valley.

That was bad. Worse was the black, boiling water in the moat that surrounded the valley, and worst of all, there had to be at least fifteen mandrakes in the air, circling above the meadow as if they knew what Varian planned.

Varian paused as he surveyed the distance over the exposed ground and the dark water that lapped angrily against jagged gray rocks. He'd never been to the Val Sans Retour before. Now he understood why no one came back from it.

Just getting into it would probably kill them. But what choice did they have? Either Camelot or Glastonbury was certain death for them both.

The valley was only probable death.

Panting from his sprinting, he could feel the sweat streaming down his back and face. Taste it on his lips. His muscles strained from the effort of carrying Merewyn. Even though she was slight of frame, he didn't possess his full strength. True, Blaise had healed his injuries, but he hadn't been able to take away Varian's exhaustion. Or the fact that it'd been countless days since Varian had been able to sit down and rest.

Now his exhaustion hit him full force. All he wanted to do was find a nice, quiet place to sleep until his head and body ceased to ache.

He looked down at Merewyn and considered leaving her here for the others. If he could run uninhibited, he might be able to make it to the moat . . .

'*We are the champions of the weak. Because we are strong, we fight for those who can't.*' Arthur's words haunted him. His king had drilled morals into his head at every turn.

Merewyn had trusted him to see her to safety. She'd exposed herself to his mother's cruelty to free him.

Now it all looked to be in vain.

Think Varian, think . . .

They were so close he could taste it. If only he had his magick. Then it would be easy to summon cover or shield. Hell, he'd be able to flash them into the valley or better yet, home to Avalon. But he didn't have it . . .

Suddenly, there was a loud thrashing behind him. He turned to see the gargoyles stomping through the brush, looking for them. They were getting closer by the second. He looked up and saw the dragons eyeing the meadow, waiting for him to break cover and cross it.

He couldn't go back.

He couldn't go forward.

What was left?

'We are so screwed.'

Merewyn saw the panic in Varian's eyes through the slit in his helm as she heard his whispered words. She had to give him credit, he was still trying to save her. It wasn't his fault it was hopeless.

93

At least he'd tried. It was more than anyone else had ever done for her.

He actually gave her a kind look before he spoke again. 'Well, I don't know about you, sprite, but I'm not going down without giving it all I've got, and since you can't move or speak, you're in it with me whether you want to be or not.'

How she wished she could tell him how much those words meant to her. The knowledge that he wasn't going to abandon her to the others actually brought tears to her eyes.

'If you know any prayers, this would be a good time to start in with them.'

His arms tightened around her before he ran head-long for the meadow.

The sound of angry dragon cries filled the air. Merewyn's head rolled back so that she had a clear view of the mandrakes flying above them. They circled and swooped, breathing fire as they dove.

Varian dodged, turned, and ran. Still his grip on her never wavered or weakened.

She watched the sky as two of the dragons flew at Varian's back. She wanted desperately to warn him of their silent approach, but her voice was as frozen as the rest of her. All Merewyn could do was watch in horror as they came in fast and deadly with their talons flashing, their eyes cold with maniacal victory.

The dragons raced each other to get to them first. Both silvery gray in color, their iridescent scales flashed in the dim light as they shoved each other.

As if he could sense them, Varian ducked the claws of the first one to reach them, then rolled on the ground with her. But before he could regain his hold on her or rise, the second dragon scooped them both up in its talons.

94

Chapter Eight

Varian snarled as he struggled to get to his sword and free it. It was no use.

'Stop fighting me.'

He froze at the sound of Blaise's raspy dragon's voice. It was the last sound he'd expected to hear. 'I thought we were on our own.'

'Looks like we're all stupid, huh?'

No sooner were the words out of Blaise's mouth than the other mandrakes attacked.

Blaise tucked them up under his large body as he veered away from the others and glided over the black water. Varian thought they would safely fly over the valley to the other side until he heard a feral curse from Blaise. A heartbeat later they came crashing down on the opposite bank.

Varian let out his own curse as his armor bit into him. He lay a few feet from Blaise and Merewyn while the dragons still circled on the other side of the moat. Strangely enough, none of them were crossing the water to attack them where they were.

How odd.

He rolled over and scowled at Blaise. 'You know, a softer landing would have been nice.'

Blaise changed from his dragon form back into a naked man. It was only then that Varian realized Blaise had been injured in the fall. His nose and mouth were bleeding profusely, and he gasped as if his body was aching as much as Varian's. There were large bruises already forming on his left rib cage and another on his left thigh.

Varian pulled the helm from his head before he went to kneel beside Blaise to check on his injuries. Blaise summoned clothes for his body as he cradled one arm against his chest.

'You okay, bud?'

Blaise coughed, then flinched. 'It's just a flesh wound,' he said in a voice that was reminiscent of the black knight in *Monty Python's Holy Grail*.

Varian rolled his eyes. 'You're not funny.' He went to check on Merewyn.

'Not trying to be.' Blaise pushed himself up slowly before he wiped the blood away from his face with the back of his hand.

Varian quickly skimmed her body with his hands, but he didn't feel anything that was broken. What he did feel were soft, warm curves that set fire to his blood and brought a wicked image of her naked and entwined around his body. A dark blush stained her cheeks as if she knew his exact thoughts. He felt the heat rise in his own.

He was blushing? *Him?*

Varian couldn't recall a time in his life, ever, that he'd blushed, and it certainly wasn't from touching a woman's body. He'd always been certain and confident in those skills. What the hell was wrong with him?

'Is she all right?' Blaise asked, distracting him from his awkwardness.

'I think so. They hit her with stun darts.'

Blaise shook his head. 'Damn dragons. They have no couth. I tried to get them to go toward Glastonbury, but they weren't so stupid. They doubled back here to find you.'

Varian gave Blaise a measuring stare as he tried to understand him. 'Why did you come back?'

He shrugged with an unwarranted nonchalance. With his actions, Blaise had signed his own death warrant. He would never be able to return to Camelot now. If any of Morgen's corps ever caught sight of him again, they'd attack without question.

'I knew you two didn't stand a chance without me.'

Varian felt a strange stab in his middle as unfamiliar feelings washed over him. He was so unused to kindness, and yet that had been all either Merewyn or Blaise had shown him. Honestly, he wasn't sure how to respond. 'Thank you' seemed extremely inadequate given the fact that the two of them had just thrown their lives away to help him escape.

So he responded with what he knew best, an aggravated tone. 'You know, you could have carried us all the way to the other side of the valley before you dropped us.'

Blaise snorted. 'Yeah, not bloody likely.' He pointed up at the mandrakes in the sky who still hadn't crossed the water to attack them. '*No* dragon flies over this place. And now I know why. I slammed into something rock solid, which is why we're all lying here now.'

'What do you mean?'

Blaise pointed up toward the other dragons who were hovering but making no attempt to come after them. 'There's something here. No one knows what. Popular belief says it's a holdover from the magick that was used to create this prison. My guess is it's intentional magick that keeps the valley's inhabitants inside

97

so that they're trapped without any hope of escape.'

He let out a sound of disgust. 'I would have taken you guys back the other way, but there were too many dragons and gargoyles for that. I'm good, but with the numbers they have, they'd have eaten us alive in a few minutes.'

Varian didn't speak as he watched the gargoyles and dragons turn back even though they were in plain sight of them. He vaguely recalled when the valley had been created. Though Morgen denied it, this whole place had been created to confine the burgeoning sorceress. Instead, she'd escaped the trap Emrys Penmerlin had laid for her and had used it ever since as a punishment for those who irritated her.

He looked at Blaise. 'Once they're gone, you can fly us out of here, or at the very least turn into a dragon and jump back over the moat.'

'You would think so, wouldn't you?'

'What's that supposed to mean?'

Blaise pushed himself up from the ground. 'I'm not in human form right now out of choice, V. Something made me change, and it's hiding my light under a bushel so to speak. I was able to summon clothes, but I can't shapeshift. It, whatever *it* is, won't let me use that magick.'

That figured. What next? At the rate they were losing magick, the two of them would be human by morning. Something that was a scary thought given the fact that neither of them had any idea what was waiting for them in this place. It would be nice if they could actually fight back.

Varian sighed before he picked Merewyn up. 'I'll bet that right about now you're thinking you should have left me chained to that wall.'

'No,' she said, the word slurred. 'Thank you.'

That gratitude surprised him. Personally, he'd be cursing himself for botching this so badly if he were she. In his opinion, she had every right to call him a few choice names.

Varian inclined his head to her as he carried her toward Blaise, who stood on the edge of the water. 'So what now?'

Blaise shrugged as he glanced about the black-and-silver landscape. 'I suppose we have no choice but to carry out your original plan. Make our way through the valley to the other side.'

As Varian started for the forest, Blaise bent over and picked up a jagged rock from the ground. He hurled it toward the moat.

Just before it reached the water, the rock bounced back and almost took Blaise's head off. The mandrake dove at the ground as Varian had to step back with Merewyn to keep them from being hit, too.

'Do you mind?' Varian asked in an angry tone. 'I don't exactly have my typical reflexes while I'm carrying her.'

'Sorry. But I was really afraid of that, and I just had to know for certain. We can't go back the way we came. I only hope that whatever is there as a shield, isn't on the back side of this place, too.'

The mandrake had a vicious point. If that field or whatever it was, surrounded the valley on all sides, they were completely screwed and trapped here.

How ironic.

One of the things Morgen wanted most would be forever beyond her reach. It strangely served her right. But it didn't do a damned thing for him.

Varian stared at the twisted black trees behind them that held no foliage at all. They went on for leagues and were tangled with thorny black vines. Black moss and brush clung to the trees and thorns, growing over the slim pathway. The grass under their feet was a sickly gray that matched the angry sky, which looked like it was ready to start soaking them at any moment.

Legend had always said that the valley was green and lush . . . Yeah, right.

This place looked even more inhospitable than Camelot, and given how disgusting that was, it said something. 'Was this really my idea?'

Blaise nodded. 'Yeah.'

'And you two were dumb enough to listen to me? I'm an idiot.'

The mandrake gave him a lopsided grin as he joined him. 'Notice I'm not arguing.'

'That's because you're an even bigger idiot than I am. You're the one who followed me here.'

Blaise shook his head before he gestured toward Merewyn. 'Let me carry her. I know you have to be tired, and I'm not sure I can heal anything at the moment given how oddly my magick is acting.'

Varian hesitated, and he wasn't sure why. His entire body ached, and yet he didn't want to let go of her. There was a strange comfort in keeping her close to him. But that was ridiculous. He needed to get whatever rest he could. 'Do you mind?' he asked her.

'No.' The word was still slurred from the effects of the stun darts. But at least she had her voice again.

Varian forced himself to hand her over to Blaise, then took a moment to enjoy the freedom of movement again. It'd been a while since he'd been able to do something as simple as move his arms and walk without pain.

Picking up his helm from the ground, he paused as he caught sight of Blaise heading toward the small, dark path that led deeper into the valley. He held

Merewyn against his chest with her head cradled against his shoulder while he comforted her with words of encouragement that actually made her smile and thank him. Something about their actions reminded him of two friends speaking together.

A vicious pang of jealousy pierced him. It made him want to rush over to the mandrake and take Merewyn back. But not before he killed Blaise for making her look at him like that.

How dumb was that? Yet there was no denying what he felt. He wanted her to smile at him.

Trying to distract himself from his thoughts, he caught up to them in just a few strides. 'How far do you think the valley runs?' he asked Blaise.

'I honestly have no idea. Like I said, dragons can't fly overhead and to my knowledge they never have been able to. Anyone who was ever sent in here never returned.' He looked around at the black trees and thorned brambles. 'My guess is they all died here.'

Varian shook his head. 'I don't believe that. Some of the people Morgen has banished were too mean to die that easily. Of course, that means that they're probably still in here and are extremely pissed off.'

'Joy, oh joy,' Blaise said sarcastically. 'I can't wait to see them.'

'I wouldn't worry overmuch. I'm banking that we make it through.'

'That's because *he's* too mean to die.'

Blaise laughed at Merewyn's unexpected words. Honestly, Varian was a bit amused by them as well. 'You know, for a woman who can't walk, you're terribly lippy. I'd be nicer to us if I were you.'

'No, you wouldn't.'

In spite of himself, Varian smiled. That was probably true, too. Niceties had never come easily to him.

Insults, sarcasm, and snide remarks were his *raison d'être*.

After all, it wasn't wise to be nice to anyone. All being nice did was allow others an opportunity to shove a knife in your back, which would only make you feel worse in the end. Better to treat everyone with disdain and contempt. That way when their betrayal came, you at least understood why and weren't caught off guard by it. There was none of this sitting around wondering how someone could stab you when all you'd done was be kind and considerate to them. Try to help them.

He knew why people betrayed him. He was an asshole through and through, and he expected it from everyone else. So it never came as a surprise when people betrayed or attacked him. That's what people did. And the only thing friendship accomplished was it allowed them an opening and means to take him down.

Even now part of him couldn't help but wonder how Blaise and Merewyn would use this temporary weakness against him. When they'd strike for vengeance.

Varian ducked under a branch, then pulled it back for them. As he did so, the hair on the back of his neck rose.

Someone was watching them . . .

Blaise cleared his throat, letting him know that the mandrake felt it, too. Merewyn caught his gaze with a look that corroborated her intuition.

So they all felt it.

There was no telling who or what could be in this valley. Had it only been meant as a prison for Morgen, or had the ones who designed it populated it with other destructive things as a means of torture for her as well?

102

Not to mention that confined magick had an unholy knack for running amok. It could have twisted and morphed into just about anything after all these centuries. Morgen had damned a lot of Adoni and other fey creatures here. Every time one of them had used its powers trying to escape, it could have fed into the nether realms and allowed them either to create something new or allowed something from one of those realms to escape and come here.

Which meant that anything could be watching them now and planning their deaths.

With one hand on his sword, he kept his attention rapt for any movement in the dismal forest that surrounded them. Any sound or smell that might give away their watcher and give them even the tiniest advantage.

Varian froze in place as he heard a light, rasping sound. Before he could react, three of the trees beside them burst into flames, including the one in his hand. Releasing the branch, he cursed in pain. Blaise dove to the ground with Merewyn at the same time Varian unsheathed his sword. Even though his palm still burned from the fire, he turned around in a circle, scanning the forest for the source of the flame.

There was nothing.

Absolutely nothing.

More trees erupted.

'I think they're fyrebaums.'

Varian looked down at Blaise, who was leaning up on his elbows as he studied one of the black trees that was burning. 'What?'

'The trees.' Blaise indicated them. 'They're fyrebaums. Remember? Emrys gave one to Arthur for Michaelmas – not long after you'd been left at Camelot.'

It took Varian a minute to pluck that out of his memory. He hadn't thought of, or seen, that tree in centuries. Morgen had chopped it down the instant she'd taken over Camelot. But now that Blaise mentioned it, he did recall the gift. It'd only been a sapling that Emrys had brought back from the shores of Annwn – a netherworld where many of the older gods had taken refuge from the world of man.

Like the trees around him, it'd had sharply defined black bark and brittle black-and-silver leaves. Emrys had said the trees had been created to be a source of light in the darkness. That they were symbolic of benevolent strength, dignity, and rebirth, which was why he'd given one to Arthur. Emrys had believed their fire was cleansing for the soul, and that any person who'd been exposed to it would be able to repent their past and find a new future.

Varian didn't know about that, but he'd been captivated by the tree as a child. He'd stared at it for hours, trying to understand the source of the orange flame. Not even Merlin had been able to adequately explain it to him.

As Varian started away from the tree, he felt something cold brush against his neck. It was a whispered touch. Gentle and quiet. Like a fey woman's ...

'Why are you here?' The question was spoken in a delicate tone, but the source of it remained invisible.

Even so, Varian knew instantly who was speaking to him. There was only one creature with a touch like that. 'We come seeking refuge, Mother Sylph.'

The trees belched more fire that danced and entwined ten feet above them. Varian looked up as the flames formed into the image of a young, beautiful woman. Every part of her from her flowing gown, to her facial features, to her limbs were made by the flames' spirals. She stared down at them with a blank expression as her flame hair danced around her body.

Her visage turned to anger.

'Refuge? Since when does a son of the Adoni seek anything but violence and turmoil?' She turned her burning gaze toward Blaise. She cocked her head curiously. 'You're a son of Emrys Penmerlin?'

'I am.'

Her anger seemed to mount as the flames moved even faster. Their temperature increased to a point that Varian was beginning to sweat from it. 'Why are you in my valley, mandrake, when your kind doesn't venture here?'

'I'm friend to the Adoni warrior.'

Varian had to stop himself from showing his surprise at Blaise's declaration. Though they'd known each other for centuries, they'd never been friends.

Her lips curled. 'While your devotion to him is admirable, Emrys is no friend to the Conifer Sylphs of this valley. Kill them!'

'Oh bloody good choice, Blaise,' Varian snarled, as all the trees around them burst into flames. No wonder he profaned friendship.

Look at what it got him.

The trees began shooting balls of fire at them. Varian ducked the blasts.

Blaise cursed as he struggled desperately to keep either himself or Merewyn from being struck. 'I take it back. I'm fatherless. I swear it!'

'I concur. He's a total bastard.' When they didn't slow their attack, Varian snarled at him. 'You had to be honest, didn't you? See why you should never answer a question until you know why someone's asking it?' He deflected balls with his sword, trying to cover Blaise's retreat.

'Well it's not like she liked you either.'

A vine from one tree shot out, tripping Blaise. He and Merewyn rolled to the ground. Varian stood between them and the trees, which shot blast after blast at him. He deflected them, but even so the heat from the fire was scorching.

'Go, Blaise,' he said. 'Get Merewyn out of here.'

Blaise nodded before he crawled to Merewyn under the barrage.

'Hold!'

The blasts stopped as the three of them froze into place.

Again the woman appeared in the fire to stare at them maliciously. 'What is it you do?'

'I'm crawling,' Blaise answered.

'Not you.' Her tone was irritable as she turned her gaze toward Varian. 'Why are you protecting the woman?'

Yeah right, like he was going to answer that and get screwed again? How stupid did she think he was? 'Why do you want to know?'

She shot a blast at him, but he deftly ducked it. Or so he thought. Instead of flying off, the fireball curled back and knocked him off his feet. He tried to rise, only to have another blast pin him to the ground and hold him there on his back. The fire burned on his armor but didn't scorch or burn him. It merely held him in place.

'Why do they protect you?' she asked Merewyn.

'Because they gave me their word that they would do so, my lady. We're fleeing from Morgen and her army.'

'An Adoni's promise is worthless,' the Sylph queen spat at Merewyn.

Merewyn shook her head. 'Varian's isn't, as you have seen for yourself. He has protected me, as he

106

promised, even when it would have been best for him to abandon me.'

The fire petered out on his chest. Then another bit of it curled around him and lifted him to his feet. It did the same for Merewyn and Blaise. The only difference was that in the case of Merewyn, the fire coated her entire body yet didn't burn or singe her.

The Sylph lowered herself from the top of the trees, down to the ground so that she could approach them. She passed a look first to Blaise, then pinned her fiery gaze on Varian. 'You men owe your lives to a woman. I want you to remember that.'

'All men owe their lives to a woman,' Blaise said sincerely. 'It's only through our mothers that we're born.'

The Sylph nodded in approval. 'And it's a wise man who realizes that.' She jerked her chin toward the path that led deeper into the valley. 'Go in peace and remember to avoid still water.'

Before Varian could question her about that, she vanished. The fire around Merewyn went out completely. To his surprise, she remained on her feet.

Retrieving his sword and sheathing it, he went to her side. 'Can you walk?'

Merewyn took a breath as she felt some of her queasiness subside. 'My legs are still shaky, but they seem able to hold me now. I think she repaired my body.'

It was what Varian did next that shocked her even more than when he'd carried her. He held his arm out for her. Without thinking, she tucked her hand into the crook of his elbow. He placed his strong, callused hand over hers. That gesture sent a wave of heat over her. No one had ever treated her with such regard. No one.

'Are you ready, Blaise?' he asked over his shoulder.

'I think so.'

Helping her walk, Varian again renewed their journey down the small path.

How very strange to her. She'd never walked like this with any man except for her father. There was something unsettling and at the same time invigorating about the sensation of having his subdued power beside her. There was really no reason for him to help her. Aye, he'd given her his word, but so few people followed through with their promises that she found his honor refreshing and precious.

An unfamiliar tenderness swept through her. It made her want to hug him close for being like this, but she knew better than to even try. Varian wasn't the kind of man to be so emotional around. Even though he was an Adoni, he was extremely standoffish, which was another reason she was surprised he allowed her to touch him.

She glanced back to see Blaise trailing after them. He looked as tired as she felt, and his face was still swollen from their rough landing. Unable to believe what these two men had been through for her, she stopped.

Varian faced her with an arch stare. 'Is something wrong?'

She shook her head as gratitude choked her. 'Thank you, Varian.' She rose up on her tiptoes to kiss him on his grizzled cheek. Then she turned and did the same for Blaise. 'And thank you, too. I owe you both every-thing.'

'I wouldn't say that,' Varian said, as if her gratitude made him uncomfortable. 'We're not out of the woods yet. Literally.'

Blaise snorted at his bad pun before he started singing, 'Ain't no valley low enough . . .'

Varian let out an anguished cry as he covered his ears. 'Stop! Not that song. It'll be going through my head for the rest of the day, and, no offense, I'd rather be chained to the wall and tortured by Morgen.'

When Blaise broke into another chorus of it, Varian shot his hand out. He grimaced as he realized it was futile. 'I really resent the loss of my magick.'

Merewyn laughed at his childlike pout. 'I'm sure Blaise doesn't.'

'I'm sure he doesn't, too,' Blaise said with a wicked smile. 'Kind of damned glad he can't blast me.'

'I could still skewer you though. Especially now that you're worthless to me.'

Blaise threw his hand up to his heart. 'Oh the pain of those words, you wound me, V.'

Varian scoffed. 'I haven't yet, but the day's still young.'

Merewyn shook her head at their good-natured play.

As Varian started on his way, Merewyn returned to his side and placed her hand again on his arm. He didn't protest as he led the way through the forest.

There was such an odd camaraderie between them. It'd been countless centuries since she last felt this kind of friendship. Since she'd seen people tease each other without malice or cruelty.

It was absolutely endearing.

They walked on for several hours without speaking while passing more of the black trees, some of which would erupt into flames without warning and for no apparent reason. But the eeriest part about the valley was that there were no animal sounds. It was so quiet that it was oppressive against her ears.

The path turned sharply to the right. She and Varian had only taken three steps when Blaise called out. 'Wait. There's water here.'

Varian released her arm to investigate it. It was a small pond with black water that didn't ripple even though there was a fair breeze stirring around them.

'It's still. We'd best leave it alone.'

Blaise looked doubtful. 'I don't know ... do you really trust a woman who lives in a tree ... one who tried to kill us? Maybe she was lying so that we'd die of thirst.'

'Maybe.' Varian picked up a stone from the side of the path and tossed it into the water. It exploded with a sound so loud that Merewyn had to bite back a shriek.

The rock rained down on them in a fine ash.

Varian gave him a smug look. 'Or maybe she told us the truth, huh?'

Blaise brushed the ash from his hair and clothes. 'Note to self, listen to women who live in trees, even if they do try to kill me.'

Merewyn stared at the water, which still hadn't rippled even the slightest bit. The rock had never broken the surface. As soon as it'd touched the black water, it had violently disintegrated. 'What do you think caused it to do that?'

Varian shrugged. 'Most likely it was someone's idea of a sick joke.'

She agreed completely. 'That probably explains the lack of animals here.'

'Yeah,' Varian said, his voice heavy with sarcasm. 'Dipping your head down for a drink is one quick way to ruin Bambi's day.'

Blaise frowned as he looked at them. 'So what are *we* going to do for water?'

'Hope to find water that moves,' Merewyn said.

That didn't placate the mandrake. 'And if we don't?'

It was Varian who answered. 'We probably will die,

but that's not something I want to think about right now, Mary Sunshine. Shall we continue on our way?'

Blaise mocked him before he sobered and gave a heavy sigh. 'How did I get myself into this? Oh wait, I didn't. Merewyn dragged me into it. I was minding my own business when she popped into my room and asked me for a favor.'

She pretended to be miffed at his teasing. 'You could have said no.'

'And well I should have.'

Her mirth died as she heard something in the woods. 'Sh . . . what's that sound?'

They grew quiet to listen. It was a faint, almost indiscernible bell-like sound.

Varian pulled his sword out again as he cocked his head to listen for a moment. But it was Blaise who caught the direction and headed for it.

Merewyn held the hem of her gown up as she followed after him, with Varian only one step behind.

Blaise drew up so short that she actually walked into him. Frowning, she opened her mouth to ask why he'd stopped, then slammed it shut as she saw the obvious answer.

Hanging in the trees were the remains of several knights. It was the spur of one who was swinging against a tree that accounted for the small metallic sound.

Bile rose in Merewyn's throat as she stumbled away from the ghastly sight. She'd never seen anything more revolting or disturbing. Varian caught her in his arms as she shuddered in horror.

'Cut them down,' Varian said in a thick voice.

Blaise hesitated. 'I think we should leave them until we figure out what put them there, lest we join them.'

Releasing her, Varian stepped forward with a look of

grim anger on his handsome face. 'You don't disrespect the dead. Cut them down or you *will* join them.'

Blaise exchanged a confused look with her before he moved to help Varian cut down the bodies. She held her hand to her nose in an effort to quell her queasiness. Some of the bodies were nothing more than bones, while others were still decomposing. She didn't understand how Varian and Blaise could go near them without vomiting.

'Who were they?' she asked, trying not to look at the bodies for fear of being sick.

'There's no telling,' Blaise said in a tone that told her he was having to fight his own nausea. 'I don't recognize the arms on any of them.'

Varian didn't speak at all as he freed the men, then piled their bodies reverently for a pyre. There were sixteen of them in all.

'Do you think any of them were grail knights?' Merewyn asked.

Blaise caught one of the bodies that Varian cut down, then took him to the others. 'I think some of the older ones might have been the original group who quested for it. But the newer ones ... There's no telling. Maybe they're Morgen's lovers.'

'Whoever they were, they were damned unfortunate,' Varian said.

Merewyn agreed. Poor men to be killed, then left to hang like this.

Blaise stood back as Varian added the last body to the pile. 'You know we can't bury them, V.'

'I know,' he said, his voice heavy with emotion. Varian went to one of the fyrebaums and broke a branch off.

She walked over to Blaise and together they stared at Varian, who appeared sad and tormented by the company of knights he'd freed from the oak trees. 'Is he all right?' she asked Blaise in a low tone.

'I don't know. I've never seen him like this before. Something about it disturbs him a lot more than it should. I mean, it's gross, no doubt, and I feel sorry for the poor men. But there's more to his mood than that.'

It took several minutes before one of the trees burst into flames. Varian held the branch until it caught fire, then he returned to the bodies so that he could burn them. The flames caught against the surcoat of the knight on top, then spread quickly to consume the others. It was a funeral ceremony very similar to the ones her Saxon brethren had practiced.

Merewyn watched as Varian whispered a small Adoni prayer for their souls. It was so strange having lived with the Adoni to see one so compassionate. Had she not witnessed it, she would never have believed it.

There was a heart inside Varian duFey. He wasn't the cold-blooded killer that the stories spoke of. This was a man who felt deeply for others. Unlike his mother, he thought of more than his own selfish needs, and it made her want to hold him until his sadness passed.

'I hate to rush you,' Blaise said quietly. 'But we should probably go before the fire draws unwanted attention to our location.'

Varian nodded before he tossed the branch onto the pyre, then turned to leave.

Merewyn hastened her steps to catch up to him, but she didn't try to touch him. His stance was too rigid for that. He obviously wanted to be alone. 'You look troubled, Varian.'

A muscle worked in his whiskered jaw. 'Needless death always troubles me.'

His feelings didn't make sense to her. They were at odds with his occupation. 'But you're an assassin for Merlin.'

'And those I kill are traitors who sacrifice innocent people to Morgen's vanity and machinations. What I do, I do for the good of all. Trust me, the men I've killed were no loss to humanity. Not even the mothers who whelped them would mourn their passing.' His gaze was harsh as he met her quizzical stare. 'But that doesn't mean I like what I do.'

His tone touched her and made her ache for him. 'I overheard you asking the bartender in Glastonbury about the grail knight the MODs killed.'

He nodded. 'That's why I was in Camelot. I wanted to know what he'd told them during his torture.'

She cringed as she remembered the poor man they had brought to Morgen in chains. Like Varian, he'd stood strong before them. At least at first. By the end of his torture, they had reduced him to a crying babe before they mercifully had ended his life. 'He told them nothing.'

'That's what the MODs told me, too.'

The color faded from Blaise's cheeks. 'There was a grail knight killed?'

Varian looked back at him. 'Did you not know?'

'No. Who was it?'

'Tarynce of Essex. Merlin sent me to Glastonbury Abbey to return him to Avalon and find out who betrayed him to Morgen.' He narrowed his gaze on Blaise. 'How is it he was killed in Camelot, and you didn't know it?'

'The same way you were captured and tortured without my knowledge. Since I took off with Kerrigan, I'm not exactly on the list of people they trust.'

Merewyn grimaced as she thought of the brutal way

114

Blaise had been treated since his return. None of Morgen's court could stand him before he left. Since he'd returned, they were openly hostile and crude. 'Why did you come back?'

'Merlin needed a spy.'

Varian snorted. 'No offense, haven't you been a bit inadequate since you never seem to know what's going on?'

Blaise's lavender eyes snapped with heated fury. 'Shut up, Varian. Trust me, no one's more upset by Tarynce's death than I am.'

'So you say.'

'What's that supposed to mean?'

Varian paused to confront him on the trail. He turned around and faced the mandrake. 'How do I know you're not the one who betrayed him?'

By the look on his face, she half expected Blaise to shove or hit him. 'You're not serious with that bull-shit.'

Still, Varian didn't back down. There was so much tension between them that it was tangible and frighten-ing. If they started fighting, there would be nothing she could do to stop them.

'Maybe I am.'

Seeking to diffuse their mutual anger, she spoke up quickly. 'Blaise didn't do it.'

Varian gave her an exasperated stare. 'How do you know?'

'I know,' she said emphatically.

'And I'm just supposed to accept your word on it?'

She looked at Blaise. 'Tell him what you are.'

He was petulant. 'Why should I?'

And that just irritated her to the core of her being. Men! They were ever prideful, never wanting to back down from an argument. 'You would withhold that from him when you know it would allow him to trust you?'

'Why not? If he doesn't trust me without it, why should I tell him?'

Varian scowled at them. 'Tell me what?'

'Tell him, Blaise,' she insisted.

Varian glared at the mandrake, who remained sullenly silent. 'Whatever.'

She growled at the mandrake. 'Blaise!'

He let out a tired sigh before he relented. 'I'm a grail knight, Varian.'

Varian came to a dead stop as those words went through him. Blaise was a grail knight? That didn't make any sense. 'What did you say?'

'You heard him,' Merewyn said. 'It was how I knew he'd help me to free you.'

Blaise turned on her then. 'My question is, how did you know what I was? You touched me right on my mark when you asked for my help.'

Her cheeks flushed becomingly before she answered. 'I saw you bathing one day in the stream by the castle. I thought the mark was curious, but put it out of my mind until I saw them bring in Tarynce. They ripped his armor from his shoulder to show the mark to Morgen. It was then I knew what it meant.'

He appeared baffled by her actions. 'Why didn't you tell Morgen about me when you knew she would reward you greatly for that knowledge?'

'I told you. I don't betray my friends.'

'But I've never been that friendly to you.'

It was true, he hadn't. 'No, but you were never cruel to me either. That's the closest thing I've had to a friend since Narishka took me from my home.'

Varian shook his head at her words. How pathetic the two of them were that it took so little to touch them. That she would willingly hide Blaise's identity

116

because he'd merely treated her cordially.

It was a foolish thing he would do.

'How did Morgen learn about the mark in the first place?' Varian asked her.

'There was a knight who came to her one evening and explained the mark. I didn't understand that it was the same as Blaise's mark until I saw it for myself. That knight was the one who told her about Tarynce and where she could find him. He said that Tarynce could lead her to the location of the grail.'

Varian's heart sped up at her words. 'Who was this knight?'

'I don't know. I'd never seen him before. He wasn't one of the circle members who serve Morgen. Rather he was from the outside.'

'Could you describe him?'

'He was a bit short, with a belly pooch. He had brown hair and eyes and the look of malice on his face. I didn't hear his name, but I'd know him if I saw him again.'

'Are you sure?' Varian asked.

Her eyes were fierce with anger. 'Absolutely. He spat on me as he passed and shoved me out of his way. He called me a pathetic hoarish hag. I never forget men such as he.'

Those words angered him. There was no excuse in anyone treating her that way. As if she were nothing, and he hoped that that one act of cruelty had marked the man so well in her mind that it would prove to be the act to bring him down. It would only be fitting.

Varian met Blaise's bemused stare. 'Whatever happens, we have to get her back to Merlin so that Merewyn can identify our traitor.'

Blaise nodded. 'And then we can both beat him for his cruelty.'

Varian couldn't agree more. 'Definitely.' And with

that, they needed to be under way again. He turned to lead them.

Merewyn followed a step behind him with Blaise by her side. 'Can I ask you a question, Blaise?'

'Sure.'

'Why haven't you asked me about my newfound beauty?'

'Because you were always beautiful to me.'

Merewyn paused as her emotions choked her. 'You lie. Everyone knows that mandrakes and Adoni are only attracted to physical beauty.'

'I'm blind, Merewyn. I could never see your appearance to judge it.'

Still, she didn't believe him. He had to be lying to her. 'Only as a man, and even then you're only partially blind.' She'd known this for years since, in spite of his claim of blindness, he always seemed to know where everyone and everything stood in relation to him. 'As a dragon you have perfect sight.'

'And in both incarnations I don't judge beauty by the outside but rather by the heart. As I said, you were always beautiful to me.'

She felt a tear slide down her cheek as she felt more haggish now than she'd ever felt before. She had sold out Varian for vanity. Her only saving grace was that she'd at least tried to correct her mistake.

'Thank you, Blaise.'

She felt a strange tickle on her neck. Glancing up, she caught an angry look on Varian's face as he looked at them over his shoulder. 'Is something wrong?'

He didn't respond as he quickened his steps.

She couldn't understand what about their exchange could possibly have angered him. But they continued on in silence for almost an hour before Blaise called out to them.

'Yo, Varian, we need to stop for a few.'

'Why?'

He indicated the woods with his thumb. 'I have private business to take care of.'

Merewyn blushed at his words, but now that he mentioned it ... 'As do I.'

Varian let out a sound of aggravation. 'Fine.'

Merewyn headed to the right while Blaise went to the left. She searched the woods for a comfortable and private spot before she quickly took care of her needs. She'd barely finished and stood up when she heard the sound of running feet. Her heartbeat quickened as she looked about for the source of it.

Hastening her stride, she headed toward Varian. But before she could reach him, something grabbed her from behind.

Chapter Nine

'Varian!'

Varian jerked around at the sound of Merewyn screaming his name. His heart racing, he headed at a dead run for the area where she'd vanished. He jumped over fallen logs as thorns batted against his armor, tearing at his exposed hands and face. He didn't care. All that mattered was saving her.

But he couldn't find her anywhere. She'd vanished into thin air. It was as if the forest had swallowed her whole. And the gods knew that in this place, that might be a very real possibility.

'Merewyn!' he called, looking everywhere for some telltale sign of her.

There was no answer. No glimpse. It looked as if she'd never existed.

How could she be gone?

He heard someone coming at his back. Unsheathing his sword, he spun about, ready to confront his attacker, only to find Blaise there.

The mandrake froze instantly, holding up his hands in surrender. 'Whoa! Friend. Don't skewer the dragon. It would really ruin my day.'

'Help! Please! Varian!'

Varian held his breath as he heard Merewyn again. It sounded far away and uneven. As if she were being jostled.

They both ran in the direction of her call, but again all they could find was the black forest and foliage that surrounded them. It concealed everything. He had no idea if they were even headed in the right direction. No idea if she was still moving, or if someone or something had hidden her in the underbrush.

He could be right beside her and not even know it. That thought angered him.

Varian had all but given up hope of finding her when they finally broke into a small clearing. There on the other side was Merewyn over the shoulder of a tall man who was sprinting away with her.

Varian narrowed his eyes as rage filled him. Skidding to a stop before they vanished again, he launched his sword with all his strength at the man. It whistled through the air and went straight to his target, pinning the man's sleeve to the tree he was passing.

The man dropped Merewyn as he struggled to free himself from the tree. She immediately scrambled away from him and headed toward them.

He and Blaise wasted no time crossing the field, especially since Varian fully intended to kill the bastard when he got close enough.

But before they could reclaim Merewyn or she could reach them, another man, identical to the first, scooped her up from behind and tossed her over his shoulder.

'Derrick!' the first man shouted. 'Help me get free.'

Before Derrick could help his twin, Varian dove at him and captured him about his waist. The three of them went tumbling. He landed on top of Derrick as Merewyn quickly scooted away from them, toward

Blaise. Blaise put her at his back to block her from the reach of the other two while Varian punched Derrick.

'She's ours,' Derrick said from between clenched teeth as he tried to escape Varian's hold. 'We've been waiting for centuries for Morgen to send a woman through the portal. There's no way we're not taking her. Now get off me!' He kicked Varian away.

Varian caught his balance, then started for him, only to have Merewyn shove Blaise aside and kick the man in the crotch for all she was worth. Derrick let out a scream of feral pain so loud it would have made a seven-year-old girl proud before he cupped himself and fell straight to his knees in front of them. But even that wasn't enough. Still writhing, he fell to his side, then his back.

Varian stiffened in empathy as he fought the need to cup himself out of habit.

'I belong to no man,' she said angrily to Derrick. 'I am not your wench to be tossed over your shoulder and carted off. How dare you grab me like that.'

She turned on Varian, who backed up, wary of her foot while she was so angry. 'I was only trying to help.'

The fury in her eyes cut him to the marrow of his bones. 'Then you shouldn't have thrown a sword at me. Have you no sense at all? I could have been killed.'

'Not really,' he tried to assure her. 'I do that a lot and have only killed one innocent bystander who fool-ishly stepped out in front of the blade while it was in flight.'

'Is that supposed to comfort me?'

'A little.' There was no reprieve in her expression, which actually made Varian squirm even though he didn't know why. 'Maybe?'

The man who was pinned to the tree finally ripped himself free to confront them. By his face it was obvious that he intended to grab her again.

Merewyn braced herself.

Varian straightened up immediately, grabbed the sword from the tree, and turned the blade toward him. 'Don't even think it.'

Tall with dark blond hair and blue eyes, the man had sharp patrician features that were flawless. Though he was fairly well built, his demeanor didn't strike Varian as that of a soldier or knight. In fact, he, like his brother, was dressed in a navy blue jerkin and hose with no obvious weapon of any kind. He was too soft and held himself as a man who wasn't proficient at arms or fighting. More likely, he was an aristocrat of some sort.

'Oh come on,' the man begged. 'Have a pity on us. Have you any idea how hard, and let me seriously emphasize the *hard* part, it is to go three hundred years without a woman?'

Not really. He'd gone a few months, but never centuries. Honestly, it was too horrifying to contemplate, but that wasn't his problem. The fact that they'd intended to rape Merewyn was. 'You're not helping your cause any.'

'Wait,' Merewyn said slowly as she narrowed her eyes on the blond man and his brother. 'I do remember you at Camelot, but weren't there three of you?'

The man nodded. 'There still are.'

Varian stiffened as he looked about for the other. 'And where's the third one hiding?'

He pointed to the shrub next to where his brother was still squirming on the ground where a small ferret was eyeing them cautiously. 'That's Erik there.'

Varian actually gaped at the sight of the ferret, who

appeared a bit peeved by the attention. But even more disturbing than the fact one of the brothers had become a ferret was the ghastliness of their names. 'Derrick, Erik, and . . .'

'Merrick,' the man said proudly. 'We're identical triplets. Or at least we were until Erik became a ferret. Luckily Derrick and I weren't so cursed.'

'Hence Morgen's fascination with them,' Merewyn explained. 'They were all her lovers at one time. She used to parade them around at her banquets, and they doted on her constantly. It's how I remember them. She's had many lovers who were twins, but they are the only threesome I've ever known about.'

'Aye,' Merrick said caustically. 'At least we were her lovers until Erik got drunk one night. After he failed to please her, she insulted his manhood, and he called her a frigid bitch incapable of human emotion, never mind an orgasm.'

Varian sucked his breath in sharply between his teeth. That was an insult Morgen would never take lying down . . . obviously given the fact she'd turned the man into a ferret.

The ferret chattered angrily at his brother. It even shook one small fist as it railed.

'Oh don't start again, Erik. That's exactly the way it happened. Why do you think she turned you into a ferret, you moron?'

He chattered even more and jumped up and down in the brush, but Merrick dismissed him with a wave of his hand. 'My brother's in denial. He thinks that Morgen will one day miss us and return to set us free.'

'He's an idiot,' Derrick said as he slowly returned to his feet. His face was still pale as he limped toward them. He let out a long breath as if he were trying to stave off the pain. He clenched his teeth as he eyed

Merewyn with malice. 'Figures the only woman to touch my cock in over three hundred years damn near rammed it up my throat.'

'Serves you right,' Merewyn said defiantly. 'Your mother should have taught you better. You don't just grab a woman and haul her off.'

Merrick snorted. 'You do when you're desperate.'

Varian exchanged an amused look with Blaise. 'Better desperate than dead, which is what you'd have been had we not caught you.'

Still, Derrick showed no remorse for his actions. 'Not from where we're standing or, in my case, limping. At least death would cure my blue balls.'

'And his stupidity,' Merrick added.

Varian shook his head at them and their brotherly barbs.

Derrick's gaze sharpened as he looked at the three of them. 'So what did you do to Morgen to make her dump the three of you here?'

Varian rubbed his jaw as bitter amusement welled inside him. 'We didn't. We're running *from* her.'

Derrick and Merrick laughed until they realized that Varian was serious.

'You're not joking?' Merrick asked.

'No. Not in the least. This seemed like the lesser evil. At least it did until we met the three of you.'

'Excuse me?' Derrick said irritably. 'I don't think you should be insulting the only ones who are in a position to help you get acclimated to your new home.'

A wry smile curved Blaise's lips. 'I should think better we insult you than kick your private parts.'

Varian had to bite back a laugh at Blaise's dry sarcasm.

'That's not amusing,' Derrick snapped at him.

Merewyn looked at Varian. 'Can you stop them?'

'I'm not in this fight. I completely absolve myself from their conflict.'

'I should have left you chained to the wall,' she said under her breath. Then louder, she addressed the triplets. 'Do you know where we can find food and shelter?'

'We do,' Merrick said.

Derrick stiffened at his brother's words. 'But why should we share it? What's in it for us?'

Varian didn't hesitate with his answer. 'A serious butt-whipping if you don't.'

The ferret chattered angrily.

'That's right,' Derrick snapped. 'You don't scare us.'

Varian arched a brow at Blaise. 'They're not really this stupid, are they?'

'One of them *is* a ferret.'

'Good point.'

Merewyn cleared her throat. 'Could you please stop for a moment.' She turned toward the triplets. 'What exactly do you have in mind as trade?'

Blaise laughed out loud. 'Merewyn, think. They want us to trade *you* for food.'

Merewyn gasped as she saw the look on their faces that confirmed it. 'Forget it, I'd rather starve.'

Derrick's entire demeanor changed as he sidled over to her. 'Don't be that way, love. We're actually very skilled at what we do.'

Jealous anger poured through Varian as he saw red over the man's actions. 'So am I.' He angled the tip of his sword at Derrick. 'Touch her, and I'll skewer you.'

The ferret started chattering again.

Merrick sighed heavily. 'Oh very well. He says that we should be kind to you before you make good that threat.'

'That's not exactly what he said,' Blaise said.

The two brothers gaped at him.

'What?' Derrick asked.

'He said the best way to get under Merewyn's skirt is by kindness.'

Varian arched a brow. 'Didn't know you spoke ferret.'

'Ah, you know us rodents, we stick together.'

'I thought dragons were reptilian,' Varian said, grinning at Blaise's offbeat humor.

'Rodent, reptile, we're all slimy creatures who are hated by others.'

'I don't hate you,' Merewyn said unexpectedly, and again Varian felt a misplaced prickle of jealousy. What was it with him?

'We do,' the triplets said quickly.

Blaise curled his lip at them. 'Ah, your mother was a hamster.'

Varian shook his head at Blaise. 'I think the Python reference is lost on them. I doubt they have many theaters here in hell.'

'Damn pity that. I'd shoot myself if I had to live without Monty.'

'Well you know, it's lost on me as well,' Merewyn said. 'I know nothing of this Monty person you keep speaking of.'

Blaise placed his hand over his heart as if her words wounded him. 'When we get to Avalon, my lady, it's something you *have* to see.'

'Avalon?' Merrick said with a strange note in his voice. 'You're trying to get to Avalon?'

Varian nodded. 'That's the plan.'

The triplets burst out laughing. Even the ferret was rolling on the ground, its paws holding its belly.

'What?' Varian snapped.

127

Derrick was the first to sober enough to explain. 'No one leaves the valley. Ever. You can forget ever trying to reach Avalon from here. Or anyplace else for that matter.'

'I refuse to believe that.'

'You can refuse all you want, but it doesn't change the fact that Merlin will never let you go.'

That one name gave Varian pause. 'What do you mean *Merlin* won't allow it?'

Derrick cleared his throat. 'Merlin controls everything here. Well, everything but the sylphs. Nimue controls them, and they're usually at war with him.'

Blaise frowned. 'I thought you said there were no women here.'

'There aren't. Sylphs have no interest in men, and Nimue hates all of Morgen's ex-lovers. If anyone tries to be nice to her or seduce her, Merlin hangs them in the trees for everyone to see. He might not be able to handle Nimue, but he'll be damned before he lets anyone else near her.'

'Emrys Penmerlin?' Varian asked slowly.

'Is there any other?'

Actually there had been many others. But this particular one had served Arthur, and he'd gone missing not long before Arthur had died. 'I thought he was encased in ice.'

'He was,' Merrick said. 'Now he's not. He got out sometime ago.'

'How?'

They shrugged. 'He didn't exactly say, and he's not the sort of person to confide in others. He'd much rather gut you and leave you for the elements to decay. He's terribly morbid that way.'

Varian was having trouble with this bit of news. He couldn't believe that he'd found Emrys. All this time,

128

they'd assumed he was either at Stonehenge or somewhere under Avalon. No one had ever guessed the valley. 'But he is here? Alive?'

'Yes. Very.'

'He'll help us,' Blaise said in a decisive tone.

Varian was still skeptical. 'How do you know?'

'I'm his son. I know the man.'

Merrick took a step back as Derrick eyed Blaise warily. 'You don't look like him.'

'He adopted me when I was barely more than a hatchling, and he raised me. I know him like the back of my claw. Now take us to him.'

The brothers still looked hesitant. It was as if they knew a secret they didn't want to let the others in on.

Merrick moved to stand beside his brother. He wrapped his arm around his shoulders so that he could whisper in his ear without their overhearing it.

Derrick stared intently at them while he listened.

Blaise ground his teeth at the actions. 'You know, V, one well-placed skewer would nail them both in that position.'

'Don't tempt me.'

Merewyn was a little more rational. 'Perhaps we should whisper amongst ourselves and make them wonder what we speak of?'

Blaise wagged his eyebrows at her before he pulled her into his arms. 'Works well for me. Put your arms around my neck, and I'll breathe in your ear.'

Varian put the blade of his sword between them. 'You can whisper from there.'

Blaise appeared appalled. 'What are you? An old maid?'

'I promised her my protection.'

The mandrake shook his head. 'You're gay, aren't you?' Varian raised the blade to rest against Blaise's

Adam's apple. He carefully pressed it close. Not so much that it drew blood, but enough to let him know that he wasn't amused. 'Or not.'

Varian used the blade to push him away from Merewyn. His gaze met hers, and he felt the heat of his desire for her all the way through his body. At the moment, he wished he were gay. Then she wouldn't tempt him so. 'Or not. Definitely *or not*.'

Merewyn felt a strange flutter at Varian's protection of her, and she wasn't sure why. Maybe it was the novelty of it. As a crone, no man had ever cared what befell her.

Now she was standing in a circle of handsome men, none of whom was belittling her or insulting her. It was such a strange moment. Even though Merrick and Derrick had offended her with their actions, there was a tiny, tiny part of her flattered by their failed abduction.

But there was a bigger part of her highly offended that if she were in her haggish form, they'd have run in the opposite direction.

The brothers broke apart finally. Merrick moved forward to address them. 'Very well. We shall take you to Merlin.'

'Why do I have a feeling this isn't a good thing?' Blaise said under his breath.

She didn't know, but she concurred. There was something very strange about these men. She didn't trust them at all.

'Follow us.' Merrick headed deeper into the woods.

Merewyn and her companions hesitated before they followed.

'How far is it?' she asked, as they caught up to him.

Derrick stopped to pick up Erik from the ground and place him on his shoulder. The ferret wrapped itself around his neck and eyed them coldly. 'It's a day and half from here. We'll get as far as the bridge by day's end, then camp on this side of it. On the morrow, we'll cross over to the valley proper. Then it's only a small way to Merlin's.'

That didn't make sense to her. Why pause there? 'Why don't we cross the bridge tonight?'

The brothers laughed even though she didn't find anything funny about her question. 'No one crosses the bridge at dusk.'

'Why?' Blaise asked. 'Is Tim the Enchanter going to get us, or is it the killer bunny we have to fear?'

Varian frowned at him. 'Whoever let you see that movie?'

'It wasn't the movie that hooked me. It was the *Spamalot* play.' Blaise winked at him. 'I'm surprised you don't love it. Both your father and your brother come off as morons. And in the play, Lancelot's gay.'

'I should have been so fortunate.' Then louder Varian said to him, 'Stop your taunting, you English kanigit.'

Merewyn shook her head. 'I think I definitely need to see this play.'

'Trust me,' Blaise said, 'you'll love it.'

'It does sound amusing.'

Varian didn't speak while Blaise told Merewyn all about the *Spamalot* play and *Holy Grail* movie while they walked through the forest. But what enchanted him most was the sound of her laughter. It was so gentle and pleasant.

And when Blaise began teaching her the songs, and he heard the beauty of her voice, he was absolutely beguiled by it. Sara Ramirez had nothing on Merewyn. The cadence of her tone actually sent a shiver down his spine. One that went straight to his groin and made

131

him heavy and aching for her. He didn't know why, but he'd always loved the sound of a woman singing.

And by the awkward way the brothers were now walking, he could tell they were equally drawn to the sound of her voice.

But the most amazing part was her capacity to learn each song. Blaise only had to sing it once, and she had it committed to memory.

When she began to sing 'Find Your Grail,' he actually got a lump in his throat.

'Good God, I've become maudlin,' he said under his breath. What was wrong with him?

'Come on, Varian,' Blaise said with his usual cheerful mien. 'Why don't you join us? I know you know the words.'

Yeah, right. He didn't really think for one minute that public humiliation suited him, did he? 'I don't sing in public. Private either, for that matter.'

'Oh come on, Varian,' Merewyn said with a smile. 'Join us for a bit of merriment.'

He so didn't understand this woman. 'How can you be happy? We're stuck in a—'

'Dark and very expensive forest?'

'Cease the *Spamalot* quotes, Blaise.' He softened his tone as he addressed Merewyn again. 'As I was saying, we're stuck in a hellhole with exploding water and trees. We don't know if we'll ever get out of this, and the two of you are back there singing show tunes. How can you do that?'

She shrugged. 'That's because I'm so thrilled to be away from your mother for even one day that to me it is worth celebrating. And what better way than to sing?'

'Always look on the bright side of life—'

'Blaise!' Varian snapped.

'I can't help myself. I'm addicted.'

He growled at the incorrigible mandrake. 'I can't believe Kerrigan never cut your head off for irritating him.'

'I'm too entertaining to die.'

'Don't wager me on that. I'd dearly like to put you out of my misery.'

'We'll join you for singing, my lady,' Merrick said, interrupting them. 'Won't we, Derrick?'

Even Erik chattered in agreement.

Varian groaned as the whole company of them started singing 'I'm Not Dead Yet.' If only he were dead, then he'd be spared. While Merewyn's voice was lovely, Blaise's was passable, but the other two . . .

They wouldn't know a key if someone put it in their hands. It was absolute torture to be subjected to the lot of them.

'Isn't there something fierce in this forest that your singing could lure out of hiding?'

The triplet beside him paused in his singing. 'Well, there are a few things now that you mention it.'

Varian stopped dead in his tracks to look at Merrick, or maybe it was Derrick. He couldn't really tell them apart. 'Then why are you singing?'

'The lady wanted to, and we thought it would be a way to woo her to our bed.'

Merewyn swallowed as she looked about nervously. 'Is there really something that could attack us?'

'Of course,' the one with the ferret around his neck said. 'We're in the Forest of Woe. It's aptly named.'

Merewyn became even more nervous.

Wanting to console her, he reached out to touch her soft hand, which only served to remind him of how good that hand had felt on his face as she caressed him.

133

'Don't worry,' one of the triplets assured her. 'We won't let anything happen to you, dearest Merewyn. We're too desperate to seduce you to let you die.'

She scoffed at him. 'Am I supposed to be flattered by that?'

'Of course you are. We were legendary in our time.'

Varian scoffed. 'Legends in their own minds, he means.'

'You're just jealous Morgen never chose you.'

'Please. I wouldn't touch that . . .' Varian paused as he realized what an imbecilic argument they were having. Was there even a point to it? 'Why am I having this discussion with you?'

'Because you know we're right.'

Varian looked at Merewyn. 'You can't argue with lunatics. Why do I even try?'

She shrugged. 'I have no idea. Perhaps you like banging your head against the wall?'

He shook his head as she flounced off in front of him.

Two seconds later, she vanished.

Chapter Ten

'Merewyn!' Varian sprinted after her, only to have Merrick stop him. She'd fallen into a small hole of some kind, but Merrick wouldn't let Varian pull her out. Every time he tried to get around him, Merrick forced him back.

'You can't reach for her.'

He shoved at Merrick, who somehow managed to stay in his path. 'The hell I can't. Get out of my way.'

'No!' He put his hands on Varian's arms as he insisted Varian calm down. 'Listen to me. She's fallen into a pit of despair. Getting her out isn't as easy as you think it is.'

Those words caught him off guard. Was the man serious? '*A pit of what?*'

'Pit of despair.' Merrick released him and gestured toward the hole. 'Just listen to her for a second.'

He did as Merrick said, then felt his jaw slacken at her mindless tirade.

'Oh, good grief, look at me. I'm worthless. It's hopeless. Life is rotten. My life in particular is rotten. It's awful. Horrid. Miserable. Why should I even bother? I should just lie here in this hole and die. Aye, that's what I'll do. I'll just lie down and die. No one even cares. They'd all be happy if I were gone ...'

It was Merewyn's voice, but the tone was incredibly pathetic and filled with doom. 'I don't understand why all of this is happening to me. What did I do to deserve this life? Why oh why ... oh why? Is it too much to ask that my life have one minute of easiness? Of joy? Of mediocre relief? No. First I'm tortured by an evil bitch and her minions. Then I try to make myself pretty so that others will at least look at me without cringing and what happens? I get stuck with a lunatic good guy/bad guy who is so boring I can't stand it and a mandrake who is just plain odd. Neither of them has a brain. Neither of them gives two spits for me. Now we're being led along by three freaks of nature, and the smartest one of them is the ferret! Oh how did this happen? How?'

Varian was stunned by her tirade.

'Ah, close your mouth,' Derrick snapped at Varian as he adjusted Erik on his shoulders. 'She doesn't mean any of it. It's just the pit talking.'

Blaise duplicated Varian's frown as they looked down into the hole where Merewyn was sitting in the middle of it, on the ground, wringing her hands and rocking back and forth as if oblivious to the fact she was trapped.

Varian glanced to Merrick. 'What do you mean "the pit talking"?'

Moving to the edge of the path, Derrick reached up to cut a stout vine away from a nearby ash tree where it was wrapped. Varian ended up having to help him cut it with his sword.

'There's some kind of gas that collects in the bottom of the pits. Anyone who inhales it becomes weepy and depressed.'

'But unfortunately not suicidal,' Merrick interrupted

as he helped them loosen the vine from the tree. 'Those infected just carry on until everyone around them wants to cut their own wrists or cut out their tongue for the babbling.'

Derrick nodded. 'You start spouting off all kinds of things. It'll wear off after a few hours once we get her out of there.'

A few hours? Oh that just sounded wrong to him.

'Why did this happen to me?' Merewyn moaned from her pit. 'Why, Lord, why? Can't I have one day free of strife? One day just for me? No. It's my lot in life to suffer. Suffering is all I'll ever have ... And pain. Lots and lots of pain. Why did you give me this life? Why did you put me in the company of such boring people? Why couldn't I be with friends? Someone who loves me? Someone who wouldn't leave me here all alone? I don't want to be with a mutant knight and a half-wit dragon.'

'I don't know,' Blaise said drolly. 'I'm thinking we ought to leave her in there. I'm getting a little tired of being bashed. You know if anyone has a right to complain, it should be me. I was just minding my own business when *she* dragged me into all this.'

'Really,' Merrick insisted, 'she doesn't mean anything she says right now.'

'She better not.'

Varian lowered the vine into the pit and dangled the end of it right in front of her. 'Merewyn!' he said sternly. 'Wrap this around yourself, and we'll pull you up.'

'Why bother?' she asked forlornly. 'You might as well leave me here. Trapped. Alone. Suffering. It's no use anyway. Everything is awful. Life is meaningless and pointless. We're all meant to suffer without end. I should just cut my wrists and end it all, rather than have one more minute of undeserved misery.'

Thank the gods she wasn't like this normally. He really would have to kill her if she were. 'Come on, Merewyn,' he said, trying to take the agitation out of his voice. 'Put the vine around your waist and let us help you up.'

Complaining every step of the way, she finally started wrapping it around her waist. 'It's never going to work. You're just going to drop me. I know it. I'm sure I'll break something when I fall, then you'll leave me for dead or worse, you'll leave me with the sex fiends to use as their plaything.'

Merrick gave him a hopeful look. 'Would you?'

Varian snorted. 'I'd kill her first.'

Derrick thought about that for a second. 'You know that wouldn't be so bad as long as her body wasn't cold or stiff.'

That disturbed him on a level he didn't even want to contemplate. 'You're disgusting.'

'Three. Hundred. Years,' Merrick said each word slowly. 'No sex. Think about it.'

Very well, he might have a point with that. Any man would be rather desperate after that amount of time . . .

Unwilling to stay on that course of thought, Varian pulled the vine and hoisted her out of the hole, which sealed up as soon as she was clear of it.

Merewyn lay on the ground in a heap as she bemoaned every minute and misfortune of her life. 'Can you imagine being stuck here? With you? Can you?'

Varian untied the vine from her waist. 'Sorry I'm such a chore.'

'Oh, you've no idea,' she said breathlessly as she sat up to confront him. 'The burden of you men. Why couldn't women be left alone without you and your cockfighting and your cocks . . .'

Varian choked. 'Our what?'

'Your cocks.' Her tone was completely rational and yet he found it hard to believe she knew what she was saying. 'You know, the way you walk like all of you own the world, and we women are nothing but your servants. And me, I am a servant. Ugly and twisted. Why? Why did I make such a bargain? What was I thinking?'

Derrick plugged his ears. 'Can we knock her out until this wears off?'

Blaise laughed as he tossed the vine into the forest. 'I don't know. Now she's becoming entertaining. Let's go revisit the whole cock thing.'

'Let's not, Blaise.' Varian tried to help her to her feet, but she sank back to the ground.

'Why bother getting up? We're just going to die here. All of us. One by one, until we're nothing but dust. Dust under someone else's feet. Dust blowing aimlessly through the woods and into lakes and food. We're nothing. None of us. Just sacks of bones moving from cradle to grave with no purpose except to die after living long, miserable lives of pointless endeavoring to quantify our worthless existence.'

Blaise laughed again at her morbid tirade. 'Good thing this isn't the twentieth century and she doesn't work for the suicide hot line, huh?'

Derrick scoffed. 'Much more of the cradle-to-grave, useless bit, and we might become it ourselves.'

Varian rubbed at the sudden pain in his skull. 'Yeah, Camus has nothing on her.'

Still Blaise appeared amused by her bitter musings. 'Yes, but curiosity is riding me hard. Let me take a tumble in the pit and see what comes out, shall we?'

Varian was still trying to get Merewyn up from the ground, but she was actually fighting him. For a small slip, she was strong when she wanted to be. 'You're not cute enough to tolerate like this, Blaise. You, we *would* kill.'

'That just hurts my feelings.'

'You'll get over it.' Giving up on her walking on her own, Varian picked her up.

'See!' she snapped at him. 'You men are all brutish. You force your strength and will on us as if we matter for naught and then you wonder why we don't *like*' – she spat the word at him – 'you. Really? Is it any wonder? Why would any woman want to subject herself to the male ego? Why?'

She looked down at his body as a sudden heat came into her gaze that made him instantly nervous. 'Sure, you're a handsome beastie with kissable lips when they're not bleeding. You're fair in form with big, bulging—' He actually cringed in fear of the word 'cock' coming out of her mouth again, but luckily she averted her thoughts as her gaze met his.

For the first time the despair left her voice. 'Your eyes are so beautiful.' She ran one finger over his brow, making him instantly hard for her. 'Did you know that?' Then the gloomy tone returned as she dropped her hand from his face. 'Of course you do. You're a worthless man. Just like all the others.'

'Yeah,' Blaise teased. 'You're worthless, Varian. And what on him bulges again, Merewyn?'

Varian glared at the mandrake, who merely continued to laugh at him.

'Everything. His arms, his legs, his—'

'Enough, Merewyn,' Varian said from between clenched teeth.

'Well, you do bulge. I've seen it.'

'We've all seen it,' Merrick said, his voice filled with humor, 'And it's sickening.'

Varian glared at the triplets, especially the ferret, who was laughing and rolling around his brother's neck. 'When she is over this, I'm going to kill all of you.'

Merewyn let out a long-suffering sigh. 'Of course you will. That's what men do. They destroy everything. Everything. Because you're all worthless whoremongers.'

Varian winced at her choice of words.

'Whoremongers?' Blaise repeated with a laugh.

'Yes. You all go out with your giant lances, spearing anything you can find. Nailing your targets against trees and walls, while you gallop from field to field, bragging over your conquests, uncaring of who you've hurt while you quest for more glory.'

'Good gods,' Merrick said, his face horrified. 'Is she speaking of what I think she is?'

'Do you mean warmongers?' Varian asked her.

'No! Whoremongers. All of you.' She looked over at the triplets. 'Especially *them.*'

Laughing uproariously, Blaise took a step back, only to have Merrick grab him and haul him forward again. 'Remember, the pit is right there.'

Blaise sobered as he scanned the ground around him. 'Where?'

'There!' Merrick scooted closer to it to show him. 'You can tell the pits by the small grayish outline around their parameters and the tufts of grass over them.'

Varian didn't see the line of demarcation that seemed to be clear to Merrick.

Blaise looked up at him. 'Am I totally stupid, or do you not see it either?'

'Yes,' Varian said in a dry tone, 'you are totally stupid. Seeing the pit has nothing to do with that.'

Blaise actually picked up and lobbed a clump of dirt at him, which he ducked, while Merewyn cursed the mandrake.

'Do you see the damn hole or not?' Blaise demanded.

Varian tilted his head and squinted at the ground. 'Sort of. How you would see it while walking, beats me. I'm surprised we haven't fallen into one before now.'

'It's all so hopeless,' Merewyn lamented. 'You, me, Blaise, we're all going to die. Die!'

Varian let out a sound of exasperation. 'We're not going to die today unless I really do kill someone, which, to my chagrin, isn't looking likely, so don't worry.'

'How can you say that?' she asked with a note of hysteria in her voice. 'Can't you feel your life just ticking away? Tick. Tick. Tick. Tick ... tick. We're heading toward our deaths. Every second, we're getting closer and closer. The end is coming for us, and we're powerless to stop it.'

Frustrated, he turned toward Derrick and the ferret. 'Is there an antidote for this?'

'No. But you can look on the bright side. You weren't here when we first discovered it. The only saving grace was that Erik was the one who fell in. So we locked him in a cage and left him in the woods until he got over it.'

How he wished they could do that to Merewyn.

Erik chattered at them.

'I don't want to hear it,' his brother snapped. 'You're lucky we didn't turn you into trim the way you carried on.'

'So how do we avoid these things in the future?' Blaise asked, interrupting them.

'Look for the gray tuft.' Merrick tossed a rock onto said tuft, which immediately disintegrated into a pit.

So it was pressure-released. That was nice, and at the same time, scary to know.

'Just out of curiosity, why are those pits here?'

Merrick shrugged. 'Merlin made them one day when Nimue had angered him. She made the exploding water to get back at him for the pits. I think she was hoping to blow his head off, but it failed. He may still be limping from the experience though.'

Derrick nodded. 'Most of the things here are from the two of them warring with each other. There are the lava rocks you don't want to touch ... they're yellow and extremely hot, but the worst part is they make you stink for days on end. Then there's the boiling water that's ice-cold to touch.'

'The stinging lizards and of course,' Merrick said, 'my personal favorite ... the Tourista Shrub.'

Blaise scowled. 'The what?'

Varian curled his lip at the thought of making contact with said shrub. 'Think about it, Blaise. What happens to tourists when they visit a new place? Montezuma's revenge ring a bell?'

The mandrake screwed his face up in distaste. 'That's so sick.'

Merrick laughed. 'That's the idea. Merlin and Nimue were really angry people for the first few hundred years they were trapped here together. Since then, they've mellowed.'

'Somewhat,' Derrick qualified.

'My brother does have a point. Sometimes they still erupt at each other, and the rest of us have to take cover from the ensuing battle it causes.'

'Doomed!' Merewyn threw back her head against his shoulder. 'We're all doomed.'

Varian groaned. 'All right. We're doomed, but before we die horrible deaths after living a horrible life, I think we need to keep moving while we can.'

'Why bother?'

Blaise snorted. 'Would you like me to choke her?'

'No. If there's any choking to be done, I think I've earned the honors.'

Derrick started for the path, while Merewyn continued to drone on and on with her dire predictions. 'I still say we should knock her out until it wears off.'

Varian was beginning to agree with him. 'Any idea how long this will last?'

'Not really. As I said, we put Erik in a cage and left him alone until he was over it.'

It's going to be a long day. 'I think I liked it better when she was singing show tunes.'

'I'm all alone . . .' she began, singing the one lachrymose song in *Spamalot*, but that was at least better than her chattering about doom. The song was actually funny. 'No one to comfort me or guide me . . .'

Varian looked over at Blaise. 'Since I'm not comforting her, can I drop her?'

'I would say yes, but I know you would never do that.'

'What makes you so sure?'

Blaise stepped close enough so that the others wouldn't overhear him. 'I've seen the way you've been taking care of her. You're not the badass you pretend to be. I've always wondered why Merlin tolerated you. Now I know.'

'Don't let my attention to her fool you.'

'Yeah, I know, you can and will kick my ass. I can defend myself against you. But I've noticed you're not real keen on attacking anyone who can't.'

'Shut up, Blaise.'

Grinning, he drifted away.

Varian didn't speak as he carried her while she swung from periods of singing to whining. It bothered him that Blaise had been able to peg him so well. He prided himself on being complex and mysterious. He didn't like for anyone to know anything about him. It kept people away, and it allowed him to have the peace he craved.

He still wasn't sure why he allowed Merewyn into his circle. It wasn't like him to do such a thing. Especially since he knew she'd sold him out for her beauty.

Not really, his inner voice argued. All she'd done was exchange her haggishness for the chore of tending him. It was her own desperate foolishness that had turned her into his mother's pawn. His mother was a master at manipulation. She could even pretend to be kind and sweet when she wanted to.

It was when the kindness ended that you needed to take cover.

'Tell me, Varian,' Merewyn said as she wrapped her arms around his neck and tucked her head under his chin. 'Do you think the world is an ugly place?'

'It can be, I suppose.' There was something so tender about her actions that it touched him in the strangest place.

His heart.

The way she held him was so very trusting, almost childlike. No woman had ever really held him. Sure they'd embraced him during sex, but there had never been a gentle hug. A friendly hug. Never anything like this.

'There is no supposing,' she said in a low tone. 'Why do people have to be so mean? I don't under-

145

stand it. But what's worse is that I know I was one of them, too. The whole reason I made a bargain with your mother was so that I wouldn't have to marry an ugly man.'

She tightened her hold on his neck as her voice trembled and her breath tickled his neck. 'I've lied to myself for centuries saying it was because he didn't respect me or see me, but in the end, I know the truth. He was so much older and scarred with cold, beady eyes and a bald head. All he wanted was a broodmare to mother his heir. I couldn't even get him to converse with me. Every time I tried, he would only answer that it was the will of God that women have no opinion save that that is given to them by father or husband. All women should be meek and silent.'

'You're certainly not silent.'

'Yes, I am. At least normally while in Camelot. I only speak under my breath because to speak to others when you're hideous only invites their scorn. Or the backs of their hands.'

A wave of anger seized him at her words. Like her, he hated that people could be so cruel. 'But you're not ugly anymore.'

'No. I'm beautiful. The ugliness is inside now. So I ask you, which is better? To be ugly inside or out?'

He didn't even have to contemplate that answer. 'You've met my mother. Which do you think I prefer?'

She lifted her head to look at him. 'You say that, but have you ever taken an ugly woman to your bed?'

Varian fell silent as he realized the truth. 'No.'

There was no missing the disappointment in her gaze. 'Then you are as bad as all the others.' She paused and chewed her lip for a moment, lost in thought. 'Or are you? You did save me when I was ugly, didn't you?'

146

'Aye.'

'Why?'

He answered with the truth. 'I can't stand to see anyone abused.'

'Yet you kill people for Merlin. Is that not abuse?'

Unwilling to discuss it or his motivations, he scowled at her. 'How can you be intoxicated and carry on a serious ethical debate?'

'Because ...' Her voice trailed off as her eyes turned glassy.

Varian stopped the instant he realized what was wrong with her. Unfortunately, that came an instant too late as she unloaded her stomach all over him.

He cringed in horror.

'I'm so sorry,' she gasped.

'So am I.'

'No, really, I'm sorry.'

Really, so was he. But he didn't want to embarrass her any further for something she couldn't help. 'Don't worry about it. It's easy enough to fix.' He set her down on her feet before he closed his eyes and used his limited magick to remove the armor from his body. 'But don't do it again,' he teased.

Merewyn nodded. She was absolutely mortified over what she'd done to him. Unfortunately, she wasn't through. Running toward a tree, she felt her body rebelling again.

'Oh man,' Blaise grumbled as he turned his back to her. 'Are you all right?'

'Aye,' she gasped.

'Good. I think I'm going to walk ahead a bit while you ... uh ... take care of your business.'

'Us, too,' the brothers said in unison. They took off so fast that Erik flew from the shoulders of his brother, then ran after them, chattering indignantly.

Alone, Merewyn leaned against the tree and let the poison work its way out of her system. As she bent forward again, she felt someone lift her hair back from her face. To her shock, it was Varian, who didn't try to speak to her while she was sick.

When she was finished, he handed her a small cool cloth. 'Better?'

'I think so.' She wiped her mouth, then held the cloth to the base of her neck to help calm her angry stomach. 'Thank you.'

'Least I could do for you.'

No, it wasn't. He could have easily joined the others and left her to her own means. It meant a lot to her that he'd stayed. 'You didn't have to.'

'I know, but you didn't need to be left alone. You keep getting yourself in trouble.' He winked at her.

In spite of her embarrassment, she smiled. Her heart fluttered at his kindness. Most men would have done what the brothers and Blaise had done – they'd have run and not looked back.

'Is the doom-saying all over now?'

She nodded. 'Thankfully. I'm so sorry for all that I said. I really didn't mean it. I wanted desperately to shut up, yet it kept spewing out of my mouth without cessation.'

To her amazement, he draped an arm over her in an affectionate embrace. 'Have no worries over it.'

'Thank you for being so patient with me.'

'It's not a chore.'

Merewyn was positive now that he was being far too generous and disingenuous as well. 'I think you would have disagreed with that ten minutes ago.'

Even though he didn't look at her, his gaze softened. 'I will give you that argument.'

Then he gave her a smile that completely beguiled

148

her. He didn't smile often, and it was probably a good thing given the effect it had on her body. She was warm all over, and an odd, giddy rush went through her. She'd never seen a more handsome man and, given the fact that she'd lived with the Adoni for centuries, that said something. And it wasn't just his beauty, there was an inner tranquillity to him that seemed to soothe a part of her even though the rest of her was highly excited.

It was such a strange contradiction.

She fell into an awkward silence as they walked. Varian let his arm fall away from her shoulders, which brought a peculiar ache to her chest as his warmth receded from her. She wanted to be closer to him, not farther away.

'Varian?'

He paused to face her. 'Yes?'

Her nerve faltered at the look of him. How could she ask when he might push her away even more?

Ask, Merewyn. But it wasn't that easy. What she wanted was forbidden. It was exotic.

But she wanted to know.

She *had* to know.

'Would you kiss me?'

Varian's breath caught as he heard the very last thing he'd expected her to ask him.

'Please?'

How could any man deny that? Certainly not one who was more sinner than saint. He could already taste those lips. But a part of him was unsure. 'Is that the pit asking?'

'No. It's me.'

His heart racing, he gently pulled her close even though he wanted to crush her against him. This would be her first kiss, and he wanted it to be tender and sweet. Something that would warm her when she thought back on it, not scare her. Everyone's first kiss should be memorable and unrushed.

He dipped his head and hovered his lips just over hers so that he could savor the sensation of her breath on his skin. It was featherlight and sweet. And it fired his blood to a fevered pitch.

How could he resign himself to a simple kiss and nothing else when he wanted so much more than that from her? But he had no choice. His wasn't a life he could ever share with anyone else, and she wasn't the kind of woman a man could play with lightly and walk away from. There was something about her that was completely unforgettable. And he knew the taste of her lips would be with him long after he returned to Avalon.

Merewyn could barely breathe as she watched Varian through hooded eyes, waiting for that first taste of a man's passion. She'd spent centuries wondering what a kiss would taste like.

Feel like.

In all honesty, she'd given up hope of ever having one herself. Now she would know ...

His arms tightened around her an instant before he lowered his lips to hers. Her head reeled at the sensation of being held by him so intimately. He teased her lips with his teeth, nibbling them ever so sweetly before he nudged them apart so that he could explore every inch of her mouth with his.

She inhaled the scent of him as his whiskers scraped softly against her chin. Sinking her hand in his soft hair, she let the silken strands wrap around her fingers while she kissed him back with everything she had. Her breasts tightened as heat flooded her in a demanding rhythm that wanted so much more than this.

She wanted to be touched by him ... to know why Narishka and Morgen were never sated by their lovers, no matter how skilled they were. What was it about sex that was so all-consuming that it caused people to risk their very lives to have it? That they would lie and cheat for one taste of another person?

But if his kiss was any example of what Varian would be like in her bed, then she was beginning to understand. There was magick in his lips. Magick in his touch. It radiated through her body, making her ache for him.

Varian pressed her closer to him as his body burned out of control. The only thought he had was taking her straight to some secluded area to lay her down on the grass so that he could further explore her body, slow and easy. He wanted to find someplace where he could take his time tasting every inch of her. But that would be a tremendous mistake. The last thing he needed was to be involved with anyone. He had too many enemies for that.

Besides, he knew nothing of love or relationships. He was Adoni. A race that was known for its bloody ruthlessness. More than that, his own father had been a faithless bastard who'd ruined the lives of every woman he'd ever cared for. That was Varian's legacy, which was about as worthless as he was.

Merewyn deserved so much better than that. She'd already been screwed over by his mother. The last thing he wanted was to hurt her any more. She'd been through enough.

Wishing he could go back and take away the damage his mother had done to her, he pulled back from their kiss reluctantly. She stood there for several heartbeats with her eyes closed as if she still could feel him kissing her. The sight of her like that set a fire inside him so hot that it was almost overwhelming.

When she opened her eyes, the desire there cut straight through him. 'Thank you,' she breathed. 'I've always wanted to know what that was like and I certainly couldn't ask Merrick or Derrick.'

But she could have asked Blaise. And he was grateful she hadn't.

Shifting himself to relieve the pain in his groin, he still couldn't resist teasing her. 'If you'd like to explore anything beyond that kiss, my lady, let me know. I am ever your servant.' He winked at her.

Her cheeks pinkened as she looked away from him. It was the most adorable thing he'd ever seen.

'There is one thing I should like.'

He held his breath as his groin jerked in greedy expectation. 'Yes?'

She hesitated.

He smiled down at her. 'Come on, Merewyn. No need to be bashful after all the two of us have shared. Near death. Tauntings aplenty and three lunatics in a forest . . . Tell me what it is that you'd like?'

She looked away as if the wrong answer would hurt so much that she couldn't bear to see his face should he deny her. 'Do you think that if we get out of here you could return me to my time? I should like desperately to go home again.'

Varian ached for those heartfelt words even though he didn't really understand the sentiment. He'd never had much of a home to miss. 'What of your father and the way he treated you?'

'I don't want to go back for him. I should like to make amends to the man I betrayed. He wanted to marry me, and I should have made good my betrothal. I was wrong for doing what I did to him.'

Her words amazed him. 'You would suffer a

marriage with him just to apologize?'

'Since the day I ran from my home, I've suffered far worse. It's time I grew up and acted accordingly.' Her gaze met his, and the sincerity of it scorched him. 'Would you please help me do this?'

A part of him screamed out against it, but she was right, and, like Arthur, she was trying to do the right thing for the right reasons. 'I will.'

'Thank you.'

He inclined his head to her and would have kissed her again had a scream not rung out.

Jerking back, he cocked his head to locate it. Not that he needed to bother. Another rang out just behind it.

Chapter Eleven

Varian led the way toward the sound, eager to see what'd happened now. He was expecting the very worst so when he broke through the forest to find a group of harmless greenish gray rocks surrounding Merrick, he was a bit perturbed by the man's screaming.

Eyes wide, Merrick had pressed himself against a tree as if terrified of the inanimate objects.

Varian glanced around to look for Merrick's brothers and Blaise, but they were nowhere to be seen. 'Where are the others?'

'Sh!' he snapped angrily, 'They'll turn on you if you speak too loudly.'

Varian exchanged a frown with Merewyn. 'I think he's lost his mind.'

A wicked gleam lightened her eyes. 'Maybe the rocks ate the others.'

Varian laughed at the absurd idea until two of the rocks turned slowly toward them as if they were sizing them up. He didn't even have time to speak before the rocks flew at him of their own volition.

'Run!' he shouted, ducking out of their way. But they didn't fly straight. Instead, they turned about and came at him like lightning. The first one hit him in the back, and the second struck his leg, knocking him to the ground. He was forced to lie on his stomach to keep them from striking his face. But as soon as he did that, they started pounding him along his back and on top of his head.

Damn! It hurt.

Merewyn squeaked, then ran to try to help him, which only caused the rocks to attack her as well.

'What are these things?' he shouted at Merrick before he summoned his armor back on his body to protect him. It worked only in that it kept the rocks from breaking his skull or bones, but he still couldn't rise under the force of their combined attack.

'Gaulstones,' Merrick said from between clenched teeth as he pressed himself even closer to the tree. Given his fervor and fear, Varian was actually surprised the man wasn't climbing it.

But that didn't change the fact that the rocks were still hammering him. 'Gallstones? They attack from the inside, not out.'

'No,' Blaise said from behind him, 'they're goyle-stones.'

Varian looked to Blaise, who was running toward them from the right. The mandrake rushed toward Merewyn to chase the stones away from her while Varian was still trying to pry them off his back.

'What the hell is a goylestone?' he asked the mandrake.

Instead of answering, Blaise, who had himself wrapped around Merewyn, made a deep, echoing dragon's growl.

The rocks actually shuddered and cried before they scattered by rolling and running into the forest. Varian scowled at the sight of a couple of them that appeared to be waving stubby arms above their heads as they rushed off. They looked strangely like people.

That was the damnedest thing he'd ever seen, and as a sorcerer, he'd seen some rather freakish things in his lifetime. Rolling over, all he could do was gape at their flight.

Crossing the distance between them, Blaise held his hand out to Varian to help him up. 'To answer your question, goylestones are the rocks that grow into gargoyles. It's what makes them. They're not particularly intelligent, which is why they have to be controlled for the most part by others, but they are highly mobile.'

Merewyn didn't appear to be harmed, but Merrick was still clinging to his tree as if afraid they'd come right back.

Removing his helm, Varian rubbed at the back of his head, where a small lump was forming from the rock that had struck him there. 'Yeah, well, at the moment, I think they may have rattled my brains, too.' He winced as he rubbed a particularly tender spot. 'Why have I never seen one of them before?'

'They don't normally come out in the daylight. Like gargoyles, they're nocturnal. Maybe it's something here in the valley that makes them feel safe.'

Merewyn frowned. 'I thought gargoyles couldn't move in daylight at all unless Morgen or another commanded them to.'

'The free ones can move independently during the day, they just don't like to. But the goylestones, since they're not as capable of defending themselves, usually hide from everything and everyone.'

Varian considered that. There were two kinds of gargoyles. Those who were born as such and those who were made. The latter were humans or Adoni who'd been cursed into gargoyle form. They generally weren't a happy bunch, but they were highly intelligent. The former were servants, and Morgen used many of them to fight in her army.

'So why did they run from you?' he asked Blaise.

'When in dragon form, mandrakes eat them, and they fear being our food. They have a high concentrate of pyrite, flint, and coal, which our bodies break down internally and use to make fire.'

There was something he hadn't known before. 'Wow, Blaise,' he said dryly, 'and here I thought you only annoyed me.'

Blaise rolled his eyes at him.

'You eat babies?' Merewyn asked in a startled tone as she joined them.

'Well, they're not really babies, they're rocks.'

She gave him a suspicious, doubting stare. 'You just said they were baby gargoyles.'

'I don't eat the big ones. I eat the small ones.'

'The babies!'

Blaise opened his mouth.

'Save yourself,' Varian said. 'You've lost this match, Blaise. You're a baby gargoyle killer. Face it.'

'But ... they're rocks. I don't eat the ones that move around.'

Varian snorted. 'Sure you don't. That's what all the baby-rock killers say.'

Blaise screwed his face up in disgust.

But before he could say anything, Merewyn spoke up. 'Will they return?' She brushed at the dirt on her dress.

Blaise looked back at the forest where they'd vanished. 'Probably. As I said, they're not real bright.'

Varian recalled the former knights of the Round Table, whom Morgen had cursed when they'd defied

157

her during Arthur's rule. 'Makes me pity Garafyn and the others who were turned into gargoyles.'

Blaise concurred. 'Definitely.'

Merrick was a bit hesitant as he moved away from his tree to join them. 'Where are Derrick and Erik?'

Blaise shrugged. 'I don't know. They were right with me a few minutes ago when we heard you screaming ... so how did you fall behind anyway?'

'I thought I heard Varian and Merewyn in the woods. I went to tell them where we were when all of a sudden I was attacked by the rocks. They were pummeling me so badly that I couldn't move away from the tree.'

Blaise scoffed. 'Yeah, it's a damn shame to get your butt kicked by rocks.'

Merrick was indignant over his laughing tone. 'Stoning's a vicious way to go.'

Varian rubbed the back of his head where his lump was growing significantly. 'Not that I particularly want to defend Merrick, but those little rocks did happen to hurt. Thank the gods for armor.'

Merewyn gave him a sweet, sympathetic pout. 'Poor baby.' She reached up to rub his sore spot, but honestly he'd much rather have her rub something else that was bothering him. The touch of her hand made his entire body break out into chills. Not to mention that the smell of her so close played total havoc with his hormones.

He honestly wanted to curl up beside her and start purring like a cat.

More than that, he had a vicious need to nibble her body until he was drunk on her scent. And there was a thought that made him glad he was wearing his armor again since it kept his erection hidden from the ones around him.

Stepping away from her before he actually did purr, he looked at Merrick. 'What other nasty surprises do we have in store for us?'

'I have no idea. They're pretty much countless here, and they change daily as Merlin and Nimue go at each other.'

Oh, that just made it all so special. Nothing like dangers galore to brighten up the day and make him want to go skipping through the forest, singing a giddy tune or two. 'I just love my life.'

'Better than loving your death,' Blaise said with a crooked grin.

'Yeah ...' Varian wasn't willing to concede that fully. 'Maybe.'

As they started forward, a small, whining sound stopped them dead in their tracks.

Merewyn scanned the area around them until she saw that one of the rocks had returned. As strange as it sounded, the rock seemed to be crying. Since she was closest to it, it rolled over to her and gently nudged at her leg. The action reminded her of a pet dog, wanting attention and affection. It was so tall, it almost reached to her knee, and it appeared to have two small arms growing out of it that it wrapped around her calf.

She looked up at the men, trying to understand what was happening.

'It's sprouting,' Merrick explained. 'Once they reach a certain size, they begin to mutate into gargoyles. No one knows why.'

'It's their molecular structure.'

They all stared at Blaise.

'What? I was raised around Merlins. You learn these things. The goylestones are a by-product of when the original dragons were formed. Legend says they

159

breathed their fire on them, and it altered their structure. The fire birthed them, and over time, they evolved into gargoyles, which my people believe are malformed dragons. It's why they have wings and fangs like us. But because they're born of rock and not flesh, they never fully develop into the higher form of dragon.' He pointed to the one at Merewyn's leg. 'That's called a bantling there, and anytime between tomorrow and two weeks, it'll turn into a gargoyle. In six months, it'll be full-sized.'

Her heart softened as she looked down and stroked the top of its ... well, it wasn't really a head. More like a large lump. 'It's a baby?'

'Essentially. It must have fallen behind while the others ran off, so it's trying to find something to cling to for comfort.'

It didn't make sense, but that touched her. She could understand feeling lost and scared, and wanting something, no, anything, to cling to. 'You poor thing,' she said, bending down so that her face was even with where his might be if it were fully formed. 'Are you scared?'

The rock cried.

Merewyn wrapped her arms around the cold stone to hold it, and it actually stopped crying.

'It's a rock, Merewyn,' Merrick said in an irritated tone.

She shook her head. 'No. It's sentient.' She gave him a sideways glance, 'Unlike some people I could mention.'

Varian laughed out loud while Merrick's face flushed red.

'But it's very stupid,' Merrick said defensively.

Blaise snorted. 'So are a lot of beings that are supposed to be intelligent.'

160

Merrick's features softened as if those words amused him. 'That would be Erik.'

It was Varian's turn to pick on Merrick. 'That would be anyone dumb enough to bed down with Morgen.'

Merrick threw his hands up in surrender. 'Fine, so I'm stupid, too. I'm still not a rock.'

Ignoring them, Merewyn tried to pick up the rock, only to find it too heavy.

'What are you doing?' Merrick asked.

'We can't leave him here. He's scared.'

'He's a rock.'

Varian sighed. 'No. He's a baby gargoyle, and he has a number of enemies who could kill him.'

Merewyn frowned. 'Such as?'

'Anything that uses magick. They can chip him down and use his pieces for various spells.'

She gasped in fear. That thought hadn't even occurred to her. She put the rock behind her skirt instinctively to protect it and kept her hand on his head.

Merrick gave her, then Varian, a peeved glare. 'He's a rock. It's not like he could feel it, and how do you know it's a he anyway?'

'He would feel it,' Blaise said sternly. 'They are living creatures, Merrick.'

Merewyn's stomach shrank at the thought of someone hurting him. She couldn't allow that. 'We can't leave him here.'

'How do you know it's a he?' Merrick asked again.

Merewyn shrugged as she looked behind her to where the rock was clinging to her leg, staring up at her. She could swear she saw his scared little face. 'He seems like a he.'

'It's a he,' Blaise said definitively. 'But he has no name. He won't be able to name himself until his mouth forms, and he can speak clearly.'

Merewyn took one of his arms in her hand. 'Would you like to come with us?'

It made a soft mumbling noise of agreement.

Merrick still wasn't convinced. 'It'll only slow us down. Get us caught.'

Varian stepped forward between Merewyn and Merrick. 'Then it slows us down until we find the rest of its ...' He paused to frown at Blaise. 'What the hell do they call their groups?'

Blaise laughed. 'Kith. Their units are call kiths.'

Merewyn patted the rock's head affectionately. 'Then we shall be your kith until you find the others.'

Merrick shook his head in disgust. 'I can't believe we're dragging a rock behind us. Isn't that called an anchor?'

Varian narrowed his eyes on the man. 'Shut up, Merrick. The lady's happy, and so are we.'

Grateful for Varian's support, she took the rock's hand.

'I'm not happy,' Merrick mumbled under his breath.

'And no one cares,' Varian and Blaise said in unison.

Paying their naysayer no attention, they started back on their path through the woods, with Varian leading the way and Blaise pulling up the rear.

It wasn't long before they found Derrick and Erik, who were walking in circles as if they'd lost their way and couldn't find a direction to go in.

Erik was on the ground at Derrick's feet as he scowled at the rock beside Merewyn. 'What is *that*?'

The ferret approached it cautiously so that he could smell it.

Merrick looked at his brother wryly before he kicked dirt and leaves over Erik, who raised a tiny fist and chattered angrily at him. 'Merewyn and Varian had a baby while you two bastards left me behind to die.'

'Really?' Derrick said sarcastically, 'Impressive timing, but what an ugly child.'

Varian gestured toward the rock. 'Sic 'im, Rocky. Make him pay for that insult.'

To Merewyn's surprise, the goylestone actually rolled over to Derrick and jumped on his foot. Cursing, Derrick pulled back and kicked him, which only hurt his foot more, while the rock put his hands on his hips and gave a rather smug pose.

Blaise laughed. 'Proves your earlier point about intelligence, huh?'

Merewyn and Varian joined his laughter. The brothers, on the other hand, appeared less than amused.

Varian crossed his arms over his chest as he smiled devilishly at them. 'You have a ferret and we have a rock. It's fair.'

'Besides,' Merewyn couldn't resist adding, 'our rock is smarter.'

'Definitely. He didn't sleep with Morgen.'

As if he approved of their support, Rocky rolled back toward them and wrapped his arms around Merewyn's leg.

Blaise shook his head at her actions. 'You know, it takes a special woman to love a rock.'

Varian agreed. 'True enough.' He started forward. 'Shall we continue on our way, good people?'

Blaise held his arm out to indicate their path. 'After you, of course.'

Merrick picked Erik up and placed him on his shoulders so that the ferret could wrap around his brother's neck.

Varian and Derrick took the lead. Merrick followed them, then Merewyn and Rocky, with Blaise once more at their rear.

Even with the brothers grumbling, they walked on

through the day in fairly easy comradery, with their rock and ferret. It was about an hour to dusk when they reached the bridge. Varian left Blaise and Rocky with Merewyn while he and the others went in search of food.

Blaise gathered wood, then used his magick to make a small fire for cooking and warmth. Something that caused Rocky to run screaming to Merewyn for protection.

'Don't worry, I won't let him hurt you.'

'Besides, I can't eat you unless I'm in dragon form anyway, and right now that's impossible for me to do.'

Still, he trembled in her arms as if terrified. Merewyn comforted him as best she could, but she hated for him to be so scared. 'I didn't know gargoyles were ever this afraid.'

'They're not once they're old enough to fly and they weigh more. He's still young enough to be splintered.'

That made sense to her even while Rocky wailed in panic. She tried her best to soothe him, but he seemed inconsolable. So she decided to try to distract his attention from Blaise. 'So what shall we call you? I'm not really happy with Rocky, are you?'

Calming down a degree, he made a noise of disapproval.

'Hmmm ...' Merewyn sat down on the ground in front of him. She held his arms as she looked him up and down, trying to think of a suitable name for her new friend. 'How about Peter?'

He whined loudly in protest.

'Very well, no Peter.'

'How about Beauroche?' Blaise asked.

He stopped making noises and appeared to stare at her.

'It means handsome rock,' Blaise explained.

Rocky actually purred in approval.

He was definitely a male rock. Laughing, Merewyn shook his hand. 'Nice to meet you, Beauroche. Would you mind if I called you Beau for short?'

Beau nuzzled against her in an affectionate hug.

To her surprise, Blaise came over to them and held his hand out in friendship. 'Welcome to our motley crew, Beau.'

Beau eeked and rolled to Merewyn's side, where he stared up at Blaise. After a few seconds, he peeked around her shoulder, then hesitantly held his hand out to Blaise, who shook it gently.

Merewyn was curious about his actions. 'How is it he can see?'

Blaise shrugged as he moved to tend their fire. 'Not sure really. It's one of those strange things in nature. Rocks, trees, even the soil can see. They don't always have the ability to understand what they're viewing, but they can see it. It's why you have to be careful. A powerful sorcerer can use that ability to spy.'

'Really?' She didn't know why she found that so shocking. It actually made sense now that she thought about it. 'Is that how Narishka is able to learn so many things about others?'

He put a few more pieces of wood on the fire. Embers shot up and rained down harmlessly on the ground. 'Probably. But it's not an easy thing to do, and it takes its toll on the one who does it.'

He dusted his hands off on his brown leather breeches. 'I remember when Varian was a young boy. There was a pupil of my father's, an older adolescent, who had him do it. Because he was so young, it ruptured part of Varian's brain and caused him to have a seizure. It damned near killed him.'

Her heart clenched in sympathetic pain as she tried

to imagine the fear and pain Varian must have felt. 'Are you serious?'

He nodded. 'When Varian's father learned what had caused his illness, he beat Varian for it and almost killed him again.'

That was so harsh that she couldn't even fathom it. 'Why would he do such a thing?'

Blaise shrugged. 'Even though he was born from a Merlin's bloodline, Lancelot hated anything to do with magick, especially the darker part of it. Some say that's why he never really quested for the grail. He never wanted it found because of the magick it holds.'

'Is that why he hated Varian? Because he was part Adoni?'

Blaise's lavender eyes were sad as if he felt for his friend. 'Lancelot hated him for numerous reasons. There weren't many at Arthur's Camelot who would suffer Varian's presence without insult or injury.'

That didn't make sense to her. Why would Varian stay where he wasn't wanted? 'Then why hasn't he joined his mother's side?'

Blaise pinned her with a gaze that was filled with aged wisdom. 'Would it be any better there? Honestly?'

No, and Varian was a smart man to realize that. Most wouldn't see it that way, and they would use it as an opportunity to strike back at the ones who'd hurt them. It said a lot for Varian that he hadn't succumbed to that need for vengeance.

'I don't understand why the Lords of Avalon can't see him for what he is.'

'What is he, Merewyn?'

'He's a champion.'

'A champion who tries to tempt the Lords of Avalon from the path of light and when they fall, he kills them for it.'

She frowned at him and his harsh words. 'You make him sound ruthless.'

Blaise came to sit before her. 'Don't get me wrong. I respect Varian for who he is and what he does, but never mistake him. He is ruthless, my lady. To the core of his being. He was born of the darkest of his mother's powers, and he has a direct line to them even now.'

'I don't understand. Why did Lancelot sleep with Narishka when he hated dark magick?'

'He didn't.'

That confused her even more. 'Then how was Varian conceived?'

Blaise let out a long breath as he reached to pluck a blade of grass from the ground beside him. He twirled it idly between his long, graceful fingers as he appeared to gather his thoughts so that he could explain this to her.

'I guess I should go back to the beginning. From the moment she first heard of Lancelot, Elaine of Corbenic was in love with him. So much so that she was willing to do anything to have him. *Anything*. Even make a deal with an Adoni.'

Now she was beginning to understand. Elaine had been as foolish as she had. 'She summoned Varian's mother.'

He nodded darkly as the flames highlighted the sharp angles of his handsome face. It made the lavender of his eyes practically glow.

'Narishka agreed to help her, and her price was simple. Elaine would spend one night with Lancelot and conceive his children. Two sons. One for Elaine to use to tie him to her and one for Narishka, who didn't want the pain of childbirth, but who wanted a son born of a Merlin's bloodline. To make sure that the child

167

would be a blending of her Adoni blood and a Merlin's, Narishka implanted one of her own ovaries inside Elaine.'

That didn't make sense to Merewyn. There wasn't even a tiny hint of motherly instinct inside the Adoni. 'Why did she want a child so badly?'

'Narishka believed that a child born of Lancelot's genes and hers would have powers even greater than Morgen's and her son Mordred's.'

'Does he?'

Blaise gave a very subtle nod. 'There are some who speculate that Varian's are even greater than any of the Merlins'. But Varian refuses to prove or disprove that theory. He believes his powers are his, and what they are or aren't is no one's business but his own.'

And again she was impressed. Most people, male or female, would be more than happy to show the world the exact extent of their abilities. Especially those who'd been so tormented.

But that being said, she found it odd that Blaise knew so much about someone who preferred to keep to himself and not interact with others. 'You seem to know a lot about Varian.'

Blaise looked down at the blade of grass in his hands as he continued to wind it about his index finger. 'Yes and no. I was there at Camelot, and I remember well the angry boy he was, not that it wasn't well justified. Both his father and his stepmother scorned him. Even though Elaine had carried and birthed him, she held Varian up to everyone as worthless. I think it was a toss-up as to who hated him more, Elaine or Lancelot.'

'It still doesn't make sense that his father hated him so for something he had no control over.'

Blaise met her gaze and held it. 'You have to understand what happened the night Varian was conceived.

Elaine didn't appear to Lancelot as Elaine, like she'd planned. Narishka had disguised her so that she was Guinevere. Lancelot had been drugged during supper and wasn't in his full senses. He tried to do what was right and push her away, but she refused to leave him. For that matter, she practically raped him. It wasn't until after they'd had sex and Lancelot had passed out that Elaine saw her reflection and realized she was Guinevere – when she'd made her bargain, she'd told Narishka she wanted to be irresistible to him. She forgot to stipulate how, and so Narishka gave her the one form that Lancelot wouldn't be able to deny – Guinevere's. In the morning when he awoke and Elaine was again in her own body, Lancelot was sickened by the sight of her and the deal she'd made.'

Merewyn understood. It was bad enough that he'd been duped, he'd also been found out with irrefutable proof. 'Elaine knew his secret.' He'd been in love with his queen.

Blaise nodded grimly. 'And she threatened to expose it to Arthur unless Lancelot married her.'

Merewyn winced in sympathetic pain at how betrayed Lancelot must have felt. 'That poor man.'

'You've no idea. Lancelot was born from the grail merlin and had spent his entire life wanting to follow in his mother's footsteps, trying to prove himself worthy of her. With that one action, his chances of being pure enough to achieve the status of grail merlin was taken from him. He'd been corrupted by the Adoni, by his love for a woman he could never have, and by Elaine, who'd blackmailed him over that love. He was never the same again.'

Closing her eyes, Merewyn hated to see anyone so hurt over something that should bring happiness. Love shouldn't hurt. But what was so bad was that he'd turned on the one person he shouldn't have – his own son. 'Did he hate Galahad, too?'

She saw the pain clearly in Blaise's eyes. 'No. Even though Galahad's mother had deceived him, her Merlin's bloodline was pure, and so was Galahad's. The sad thing is, Lancelot would have loved Varian, too, had Narishka not come to claim him an hour after his birth. When Lancelot tried to drive her away, she told him of the bargain Elaine had made and that Varian was her son, not Elaine's. Lancelot was so angry, he tried to kill Varian before Narishka could take him.'

Tears pricked the back of her eyes as her heart ached for Varian. How awful to be so hated over something he'd had no part in. 'How do you know all this?'

'I was there when Narishka came for him. Because Galahad and Varian were born from a Merlin's bloodline, my father, being the Arthur's Penmerlin, was there for their births. Back in those days, the birth of any Merlin was watched closely, and each Merlin was carefully raised to protect their purity.'

As opposed to now. After the fall of Camelot and Arthur, the Merlins and the magical objects they governed had been sent out into the world to hide them from Morgen so that she couldn't use them to spread her evil to the other side of the veil and subjugate mankind. It was why Morgen and Narishka both had spies trying to locate the Merlins and their objects.

'Varian's purity wasn't protected.'

He shook his head. 'Even though Merlin tried to stop it, he couldn't. By the laws of magick and the Adoni, Varian was Narishka's son, and she was fully entitled to him. So Varian was taken to live with his mother's people in their nether realm. And it was there that he learned the darkest arts imaginable . . .' Blaise paused to give her a sad smile. 'Then again, you've seen enough of Narishka's work to be able to imagine them quite well.'

Yes, she had. Narishka's cruelty was second only to Morgen's, and even then it was a thin margin Morgen led by.

'But he was returned to his father. Why?'

Blaise leaned back on his arms. 'Varian was born of light and dark. Those two parts of him are at war with each other, and they won't let him walk purely on either side. He's too dark to be true to the light and too pure to walk solely in darkness. It's his hell to be caught between the two forever.'

Still, that didn't make sense to her. 'Why can't he just choose one side or the other?'

'He has too much conscience for evil and too much id for sainthood. It's what makes him unpredictable. In any given situation he could be good or evil. It just depends on which part of him wins the internal battle. That's why none of the Lords of Avalon trust him. And it's why Varian doesn't even trust himself. When we went to war against Morgen at Camlann, Varian stayed home.'

She was stunned by that news. The battle of Camlann was the one where both Arthur and Morgen's son Mordred had been fatally wounded. That battle had been the one that destroyed the knights of the Round Table. After their defeat, they had fled to Avalon to regroup while Morgen had marched her army to Camelot and seized Arthur's throne.

The two groups had been battling ever since. Morgen trying to keep her throne and the Lords of Avalon who were trying to rid her of it forever.

She couldn't imagine a man like Varian not even taking part in such an important event. 'Why didn't he fight?'

171

'You have to remember, Varian was just seventeen when the battle came and he'd only been knighted a few weeks before it. He was still mastering his powers and torn greatly between his father and mother. Since he despised his father, he was afraid he'd see Lancelot on the battlefield and turn against Arthur, and he loved Arthur too much for that. Arthur was the closest thing to a father Varian had ever had and the last thing he wanted was to take a chance that his mother or someone else would turn him to Morgen's side. So he stayed in Glastonbury while we rode out.'

'And Arthur was killed.'

He nodded, his eyes dark with his own pain. It was obvious Blaise had loved Arthur, too, and Merewyn wished she'd met the man who'd inspired such love and loyalty from these men. He must have been great indeed. 'Varian has never forgiven himself for not being there to fight by Arthur's side.'

'But he won't fight for evil. You saw how they beat him in the dungeon, and still he refused to serve them.'

'And yet he would have allowed your throat to be cut before he joined them. A purely good man would never sacrifice an innocent life for any reason. Varian would. As I said, he's not firmly planted on either side.'

Perhaps that was true. Perhaps it wasn't. But she refused to believe that Varian would ever be purely evil.

'Not all of you hate him, Blaise. You don't.'

'Only because I understand him.'

'And his brother—'

'Hates him bitterly.'

She was surprised by that. Even though Varian had refused to speak of Galahad, she would have assumed his brother, who was reported to be so noble and pure, would be able to love Varian in spite of everything. 'Why would he hate him?'

'He blames Varian for Elaine's suicide.'

She frowned at him. 'Why?'

'Elaine was brutal to Varian after Narishka returned him to Camelot. She couldn't stand to see him because he reminded both her and Lancelot of Narishka's treachery. Elaine was embittered by the fact that her husband loved someone else. She'd tried everything to win Lancelot's love, but it was hopeless. Even though he never touched Guinevere, he loved her more than his life. Since Elaine couldn't hurt Lancelot without ruining herself and Galahad, or attack Narishka, she turned her hatred to Varian.' He flinched as if something had struck him.

'What?'

Blaise wiped his hand over his face. 'I was thinking of one summer day when Elaine had caught Varian boasting to other boys that he would grow to be the noblest knight in all the land. One who would fight for Arthur and drive back the evil in the kingdom. He was wearing Lancelot's grail medallion. Enraged by the sight of it and by his words, Elaine tore it off him and washed his mouth out for lying. But not even that soothed her. She sheared the hair from his head with a dagger that left him bleeding, then threw him out into the sty with the pigs and told him to stay there until his father returned that night.'

His words nauseated her. How could any woman do something like that to a child? 'What did Lancelot do?'

'He had Varian whipped for daring to touch his medallion. When it was over, he cut Varian from the post and kicked him over. He'd heated the medallion, and while Varian lay sobbing on the ground, begging

173

for his father's mercy, Lancelot branded the medallion's symbol into Varian's shoulder. 'That's as close to the grail as you will ever come, worm,' he'd said to him. 'Let it serve as a reminder to you of what happens when the unworthy touch it. Maybe its goodness will burn the evil out of you.' Then he cooled the medallion down and gave it to Galahad.'

A single tear fled down her cheek as her throat closed from the agony of such a thing happening to anyone. Clearing her throat, she wiped the tear hastily away. 'Didn't anyone stop it?'

'The only one who had the authority to do that was Arthur, and he wasn't there at the time.'

'No one else would stand up for him? My God, he was only a child.'

He shook his head sadly. 'After that, Varian never spoke of being noble or a knight again.'

'Yet he's a knight now.'

'Only because Arthur went against his entire court to make it so. Lancelot was so angry over it that neither he nor Galahad even attended. Instead of the ceremony and celebration that men enjoy when they're knighted, Varian was actually booed by the knights of the Round Table when he took his vows. The entire Brotherhood of the Table turned their backs to him when he stood up to receive his sword. Disgusted with all of them, Varian never took the sword from Arthur's hand. He took his dagger from his waist, cut the mantle from his shoulders, and walked out with his head held high.'

'Why would they do such a thing?'

'Because they all expected him to turn on them. *All* of them. Even Arthur, I think.'

'But that doesn't explain why Galahad blames him for his mother's death.'

Blaise drew a ragged breath before he continued. 'Picture this. Varian was twelve, tall for his age and extremely thin. Arthur had chosen him to be one of the royal squires, and he was at a crowded banquet, serving wine to the guests. When he drew near Elaine, she began her usual condemnations of him that had the people around her laughing. As he withdrew, he accidentally spilled a bit on Elaine's dress sleeve. Incensed, she started berating him on how worthless he was. Varian had suffered her tongue in silence for years, but that night, as people laughed at the insults she dealt him, something inside him snapped. He turned on her with the fired eyes of an Adoni and snarled at her, 'They may laugh at me openly, Elaine, but you they mock behind your back. Why not, for once, speak the truth of why you hate me so? We all know it. You hate me because I'm nothing but a reminder of the fact that my father doesn't love you. He never has, and he never will. You had to trick him to marry you because he loves someone else.'

'Arthur shouted at him to be silent, but Varian refused. Too many years of their cruelty had built up inside him. He scanned everyone there, and curled his lip. 'All of you have made deals with the Adoni, and you hate me because I know who you are and what deals you've made. I may be a bastard whose conception was bartered so that a whore could have one night's pleasure and a knight-merlin to call husband, but at least my sins are on the table for all to see. I don't hide them from the person sitting next to me who thinks he's my friend while I secretly plot his destruction. So laugh at me if you will. Insult me if you want. But in the end, it doesn't change the fact that I know all of you. *All* of you and the meanness that you hide from everyone, even yourselves.'

175

'And then he looked at Elaine. 'You could never be the woman my father loves. She's kind where you're cruel. She's beautiful where you're ugly. You're not even fit to lick her hem. I'm his own flesh and bone, and he hates me. What makes you think for one minute that he'll ever forgive you for the lie you told? And every time he sees me, he hates you even more. Admit it, you're nothing but a selfish whore who is a laughingstock to everyone.' Then he set his wine decanter down and walked from the hall with nothing but silence following in his wake.'

Merewyn was aghast at what he'd done. She understood it, but at the same time, it must have horrified Elaine and everyone who witnessed it. 'What did she do?'

'She sat there mortified with her gaze on the floor. No one knew what to do or say until Emrys Penmerlin came forward. He told everyone to ignore Varian. He was only an angry child who would be lashed later for his insolence ... and he was. But Elaine knew how true Varian's words were and later that night, she poisoned herself in her chambers.'

Merewyn covered her mouth as horror filled her. It was tragic what'd been done to them all and for what? So that Narishka could have a child she didn't even want?

'And Varian? What did he do?'

'He didn't speak for two years after that. Not a single word to anyone. He blamed himself solely for Elaine's death. There hadn't been any love between him and Galahad before her suicide. After it ...' He shook his head as if the truth of their relationship was so brutal he couldn't even speak of it.

'So he's been alone all his life.'

Blaise nodded.

Merewyn looked away as grief and anger for Varian washed through her. How awful to have been so hated. She still couldn't understand why none of them could embrace a boy who had most likely been scared.

And now his mother had turned on him again. An unreasoning fury consumed her. How dare Narishka do that to him! She wished for one moment that she had the powers of an Adoni. That she could go and make Narishka pay for what she'd done.

But she was just a woman. One who had no powers. No strength. Nothing to fight with.

'Why so glum?'

She looked up at Varian's voice to see him and the brothers approaching the fire. He was carrying a small string of three hares. His armor was gone again, and he was dressed in black leather breeches and a thin leather jerkin.

'We were just discussing the uselessness of life,' Blaise said, pushing himself up from the ground.

Varian dropped the hares by the fire. 'No wonder. That's enough to depress even the manic.'

Merewyn rose more slowly as Merrick and Derrick eyed her.

'It'll be good to have a woman's cooking again.'

She arched a brow at that. 'I can't cook.'

Merrick scoffed. 'Of course you can. All women are good cooks.'

'No, we're not. I was a princess in Mercia and have been a servant to Narishka ever since. I've never cooked anything in my life.'

Varian pulled out a small dagger. 'I can make do.'

Blaise snorted as he held his hand out for the weapon. 'And I happen to be a great cook, so before you burn it or poison me with undercooked meat, let me do it.'

Varian handed over the dagger. 'No arguments from me.'

Derrick screwed his face up. 'This better be worth eating, mandrake.'

'Can you do better?'

'No,' Merrick said at the same time Erik chattered, 'He can't cook for shit. None of us can.'

Erik rolled over onto his back and feigned a violent, choking death.

Merrick gestured at the ferret. 'Exactly.'

'Oh shut up both of you,' Derrick snarled.

Blaise cut the hares free from the string. 'Make yourselves useful while I skin these and go get more firewood.'

Grumbling, they obliged.

Varian knelt beside her and handed her a small bladder. 'We found a stream with freshwater ... moving water, obviously.'

She offered him a smile as she took the bladder. 'Thank you.'

As she took a drink, she watched Varian pass a gentle hand over Beau. 'How's Rocky doing?'

'Merewyn renamed him. He's now called Beau.'

'Beau, huh? Well, it's a pleasure to meet you, Beau.' He leaned against Varian's shoulder.

Touched by his kindness when, in all honesty, he shouldn't know anything at all about it, she handed him the bladder.

Varian didn't speak as he tilted his head and took a drink. The light shadowed his face, making him look tired. But even so, he was still breathtaking. His black hair was shaggy, and he still had several days' growth of beard on his face.

'You should rest while Blaise cooks.'

'Rest is for the weak. I'm fine.'

She gave him a peeved glare. 'You won't do any of us any good if you're too weak to continue, or if you get ill from lack of rest. Take a moment, Varian, and lay your head down.'

Varian was perplexed by the strange note in Merewyn's voice.

'She's right, V. It'll be a while before these are ready. Take a nap before you collapse, and I leave your hoary hide for the Sylphs.'

'Just don't leave me for the kobold.'

Blaise frowned at him. 'The what?'

Merewyn laughed. 'We were attacked before you came back to get us.'

'Ah. Okay.' Blaise returned to skinning the hares.

Then she gave him a motherly glare. 'Lie down, Varian. I know you haven't been able to sleep comfortably in days.'

It was true. He was exhausted, and now that he was seated, it was hard to keep his eyes open. Conceding that they might be right, he pulled the sword from his hip and stretched out on the ground. He held the sword under his body so that he could get to it quickly and closed his eyes.

Merewyn shook her head at the sight of him clutching the sword as if ready for someone to try and kill him. Leaning forward on one arm, she brushed her hand through his tousled hair. His eyes opened immediately.

'Relax, Varian. I mean you no harm.'

But his expression told her that he didn't really believe it. And she couldn't blame him for that suspicion. Everyone else had meant him harm. Why should she be different?

You would have sold him out for beauty ...

Guilt ate at her. Things were different now. She knew better than to hurt him.

179

'Sleep,' she admonished, closing his eye with her finger.

He let out a deep breath before he relaxed, and she returned to stroking his hair. He was such a beautiful man. His long body was stretched out, but even so she could feel the power of him. The strength.

And as she stared down at him, she made a silent promise. *I will never cause you harm, Varian duFey. You've been through enough.*

Yet even as she whispered that vow in her mind, she wondered if she'd be able to keep it. They still had a long way to go, and Narishka and Morgen were out there, plotting their destruction. If she knew anything about those two bitches, it was that they didn't lose easily. They would be coming for them.

And neither one would stop until they had killed everyone in Merewyn's group.

Chapter Twelve

Varian's dreams drifted through fragmented images of Merewyn like a broken kaleidoscope as he felt a warm comfort the likes of which he'd never known before. It was as if he were wrapped in a heated blanket on a cold winter's night. He could hear her soft voice, whispering gently to him while her tender fingers caressed his skin in what felt like a loving touch.

It was so wonderful until a brittle voice intruded. *'Varian? Where are you ...?'*

He jerked at the sound of his mother's lilting accent whispering through his head as it tore away the succor of his dream.

'Varian? Answer me! You know you can't hide from us. We will find you. You're only making it worse on yourself by running ...'

His gut instinct was to tell her to shove her threats, but then that was exactly what she wanted – it would be the worst kind of stupidity. The minute he said anything to her mentally, she'd be able to find him.

His comfort ruined, he opened his eyes to find Merewyn asleep by his side. She was turned into him with her hand resting softly against his whiskered cheek while her head was tucked under his chin. Beau lay on the other side of her and made a noise that sounded oddly like a quiet snore.

Not wanting to disturb them, he pulled back slowly. But the instant he did, Merewyn awoke with a panicked gasp. She jerked so sharply that her head slammed into his chin, causing him to bite his lip.

Varian cursed as he tasted blood.

'Oh no,' she whispered, looking up at him. 'I'm so sorry, Varian. I didn't realize it was you waking me.'

He wiped at the blood on his lip as the cut throbbed. Most likely not. Knowing his mother and her ilk, he was sure Merewyn was usually awakened harshly, with insults and blows. No wonder she was jumpy. He should have thought of that before he moved. 'It's all right. I didn't mean to disturb you.'

Her brow furrowed by worry, she reached up and turned his head so that she could see where he'd bitten his lip. 'Please forgive me?'

How could he not? No one had ever been so concerned over hurting him before. 'It's nothing. Really.'

'Yes, it is. There's nothing worse than waking to pain.'

God, how he wanted to kiss her. The scent of her skin, the look on her face . . . it tore through him. And he probably would have yielded to that urge had someone not sneezed.

Rolling over, he realized that the others were all bedded down, too. And by the looks of them, they'd been asleep for quite some time. It was completely dark, with the moon high in the sky while the campfire burned low.

It had to be after midnight . . .

'How long have I slept?'

'Hours. I wouldn't let them wake you once supper

was ready, but we saved you some of the meat.'

He doubted there was really a 'we' in there. Merewyn must have put the food aside for him.

She started to sit up, but before she could, he pulled her back into his arms. Her lips hovered just over his as he cupped her face in his hands and stared at the delicate beauty of her features. And before he could think better of it, he gave her the hot kiss he was dying to. He didn't know why, but he had to have a taste of that sweet mouth.

Merewyn closed her eyes and savored the sensation of his tongue sweeping against hers. His whiskers burned her skin as his callused hands scraped against her cheeks. And when he pulled back, she was paralyzed by the tenderness in those deep green eyes. Unable to cope with the heat it ignited in her body, she averted her gaze slightly and noticed a small scar that darted from his hairline to just below his left ear.

Frowning, she reached out to touch it, only to realize that it went farther back into his hair. It must have been a vicious wound when he'd received it.

He pulled her hand away and by the severe flash of pain on his face, she realized it must be one of the scars made the day Elaine had shaved his head because he'd wanted to be a noble knight.

Her heart aching for him, she closed her hand around his and brought it to her lips to press a gentle kiss on his scarred knuckles that also told the story of the countless battles this man had fought. Even the most hardened of warriors needed some succor once in a while. No one should live their life alone, surrounded by enemies.

Varian felt his breath catch as her tongue swept against his flesh. His entire body felt on edge as it begged for a real taste of this woman. His groin was heavy and throbbing, and when she parted her lips, all he could think of was taking her under him and riding her for the rest of the night.

Had they been alone, he probably would have. But he couldn't take her out here with no privacy. She wasn't an Adoni, who would gladly screw him in the open and beg for the others to join them. She'd been a princess.

And she was a lady still. One who deserved only the best things. Her life had been every bit as harsh as his. He would never intentionally add to her bad memories or pain.

Releasing her, he closed his eyes and wished for a tub of ice to bathe in. It would be the only way to chill the fire that raged inside him. Every part of his body was alert, begging for her touch. Even his nipples were sensitive as the leather of his jerkin rubbed against them. But it wasn't the leather he wanted to feel there. It was her touch ...

Her tongue ...

Damn, it'd been too long since he'd last had a woman. And at the end of the day, he was Adoni, too. His mother's people possessed the libido of raging nymphomaniacs. They were ever on the make for any kind of sexual stimulation. And he'd always been as randy as the rest of them. He'd just had a few more scruples about whom he took and where.

But the longer he was around Merewyn with his body aching for her, the more those scruples were coming into question.

'Are you all right, Varian?'

He opened his eyes to find her frowning down at him. 'Not really.'

'Is there anything I can do to help you?'

He dropped his gaze to her gown where her laces

had loosened enough so that he could see just a hint of the skin between her breasts. *Let me lick those* . . .

'No,' he said aloud, trying to banish that thought. 'I just need . . .' *You to strip naked and let me make love to you until dawn.*

'You need?'

'Nothing. I'm fine.'

She cocked her head and frowned down at him. 'Are you blushing?'

Before he could answer, her gaze dropped down to where his desire was more than evident. Her mouth formed a small o at the sight of his erection. Now it was *her* face that was blushing profusely.

Varian ground his teeth as he tried to think of something, anything that would quell his body.

Still she didn't avert her gaze. She stared at him curiously, which only made his desire more acute as he wondered what it would feel like to have her touching him with her soft caress. Or better yet, her lips . . .

'Does it hurt when it does that?'

Damn her curiosity, which wasn't helping him at all. All it did was make him wonder if she'd be so bold with both of them naked. 'If I don't put it to use, yes.'

Merewyn knew she should look away, but she couldn't. She'd seen more than her fair share of erect men, both clothed and unclothed as they'd serviced Narishka, Morgen, and others in Camelot. But no man had ever been hard for her. She'd never inspired desire. They'd only looked at her with scorn and anger. But Varian didn't look at her like that. He hadn't even scorned her when she'd been hideous.

She felt strangely powerful that she could affect a man like Varian this way. That he wanted her, at least physically.

More than that, she wondered what it would feel

like to sleep with him. To have him thrusting deep inside her. She knew from the others just how pleasurable it could be. During celebrations and orgies, the cries of orgasms filled the halls of the castle.

But she'd never had one herself.

Now her body begged for a taste of his as her mind ached to know what it would be like to be completely pleasured. Deep in the center of her being was a hungry throb that didn't want to be denied. It wanted Varian. It craved him.

Turn away, Merewyn.

She couldn't. She'd been more than willing to give her virginity to gain her freedom. And now that she had it, it only seemed right that she should ease some of this suffering she caused him.

Before Merewyn could stop herself, she reached out to touch him.

Varian's breath caught in his throat as he realized where her hand was headed . . . straight for his swollen cock. It jerked in expectation, but just when she would have touched him, he grabbed her wrist and pulled her hand away even though what he really wanted to do was guide it into his breeches and have her stroke him until he found peace again.

She gave him a startled look. 'I would like to know how . . .' Her voice faded out as if she were too embarrassed to finish.

It was all he wanted, too. To have her hand caress him. To feel her soft palm cupping him. But he couldn't. Taking her would be an award-winning act of stupidity and he knew it.

He couldn't trust her, and he damned sure didn't trust himself. He liked living his life free of entanglements and emotions. It was the only way he knew how to get through the endless days. And he was too set in his ways to change them now.

'Sorry, love. I don't sleep with women I know. Ever.'

She stiffened so badly that he actually felt it all the way to her wrist. 'Excuse me?' She snatched her hand from his grasp.

'It's too complicated. Acquaintances have expectations.'

'So you'd rather be intimate with strangers?'

He nodded. 'They don't mind when you get up and leave afterward, and they don't expect anything more than an orgasm or two.'

She screwed her face up in distaste. 'You *are* Adoni.'

He couldn't have been more insulted had she slapped him, but he'd be gutted before he let her know that. Besides, she only spoke the truth. He was his mother's son. 'I am.'

She pulled back with her eyes snapping her fury at him. 'Then you deserve to suffer.'

'That's what they tell me.'

Merewyn felt her stomach tighten at the pain she heard in his voice, and she instantly regretted her harsh tone and words. 'Varian—'

'It's all right,' he said, getting up and moving away from her. 'I know what I am, and I'm happy with it.'

His tone said otherwise. 'Varian, please. I didn't mean what I said.'

'Of course you didn't,' he said snidely. 'No one ever does. People always speak without thought. But it's amazing how much damage thoughtless words can wreak, isn't it?'

And then she knew ... he wasn't speaking about this. He was talking about his final words to Elaine. 'You didn't cause her death.'

He turned to face her. The flames were highlighted

in his eyes as his long hair obscured most of his features from her. 'What?'

She'd been too bold with him, and what's more, she'd betrayed a confidence Blaise had given her. She shouldn't have said anything, but since she'd come this far, she might as well finish it. 'Elaine. Blaise told me what happened the night she died. It wasn't your fault.'

He glared in Blaise's direction where the mandrake slept in peace. 'Well hot Jim Dandy Brown, wasn't that nice of the old mandrake to run his mouth? What else did he tell you?'

She was taken aback by his hostility. She started to lie, but then stopped herself. He'd been through enough in his life. She wasn't about to lie to him on top of that. 'He told me about your past. How Lancelot and Elaine treated you. The day you were knighted ...'

Torment flashed in his eyes before he hid it as effectively as the veil that concealed their world from that of man. 'I see. And now you pity me.'

'No.' She started toward him, only to have him move away again.

She forced herself to stand by the fire even though all she wanted was to touch his rigid body.

When he spoke, his words were flat and empty. 'I don't need your sympathy, Merewyn. I don't need anyone's. You don't have to worry. There are no scars inside me that need to be healed. There's no little boy wanting comfort. I'm at peace with my past.'

Was he? In spite of his words, she didn't believe it. 'Then why do you only sleep with strangers? What are you afraid of, Varian?'

'That they won't shut up so that he can sleep,' Derrick snarled sleepily from the ground.

Varian slung his hand out as if he would send a

sorcerer's blast at Derrick, but when nothing happened, he cursed. His eyes full of anger, he closed the distance between them, and whispered coldly in her ear, 'I fear nothing.'

She met his gaze boldly because she knew those words for the lie they were. 'Then you *are* scared, and you *are* scarred.'

'How do you figure?'

His breath fell against her face as his power reached out to her. He could kill her, he could, and yet she wasn't afraid of him.

What's more, she refused to back down. Varian needed someone to show him the lie he lived. 'If you weren't, then you would have fear. Only a man who feels nothing, who has nothing, can hold no fear of anything. If you weren't scarred by your past and afraid of reliving it, you would be afraid of losing what you've gained. But you've gained nothing in all these centuries. You hold on to nothing because you're afraid that by opening yourself up to someone, they will hurt you. You are scared, and you are scarred.'

He curled his lip in distaste. 'Bah, what do you know?'

Her throat tight, she answered honestly. 'I know what it feels like to be mocked and insulted. And I know what it's like to be afraid of letting someone close enough to hurt me even more. The words of strangers burn badly enough, but it's the words of those we trust that sting the deepest. That's why I'm sorry for what I said to you. I of all people know better than to speak in anger.'

Varian froze at her words and at the fact that she could see so clearly into his soul. She looked so naive, and yet she held as much wisdom as a Merlin.

She crossed the distance between them and laid her

hand on his cheek. Part of him wanted to knock her away, and the other part just wanted to feel that gentle touch on him for all eternity.

'I would be your friend, Varian. If you'd let me.'

He clenched his teeth in anger before he stepped back, out of her reach. 'Friends are only enemies who are able to come at your back. No offense, I'd rather keep my enemies in front of me so that I can watch them.'

Her gaze turned sad, but there was no pity there as she lowered her hand to her side. 'When you're ready to trust—'

'I won't be. Ever. You've already told me that you would bleed for nothing.'

She gave him a wry smile. 'And you think of yourself as nothing.'

Her words confused him as did her tone of voice. 'So what are you saying? That you would bleed for me?'

'Yes.'

Varian laughed at the idea and at the sincerity she showed him. He was used to actors who could lie with the utmost conviction. He could even do it himself. 'Just because you play in my hair and bring me food doesn't mean you'd suffer to do so.'

Still, she held earnestness in her gaze. 'I don't speak lightly, Varian. I know very well what true suffering is and what I'm offering you. You *are* a noble knight and you are worth such sacrifice.'

Those words burned him. He hated the very thought of being in the same league as his father . . . his brother. 'And you are delusional. It's never worth bleeding for someone who will only turn on you in the end. My only allegiance is to myself.'

'Then why did you let your mother beat you instead of joining their cause?'

'Because it pisses her off and may the gods forbid that I ever do *anything* to please that bitch.'

She shook her head. 'I don't believe you would have suffered that much just to make her angry. You are noble, Varian, I know it.'

'There is nothing noble in me. There never was.'

'Then why am I here? You've carried me when an ignoble man would have fled so that he could save himself. You've tended me when others have left me to my own defenses. If that's not noble, tell me what is?'

Merrick snarled from the other side of the fire. 'Letting the rest of us get some friggin' sleep!'

Varian glared at the man, then let all of his emotions pour out of him until he felt nothing but the deep emptiness that made up his life. This discussion was over. He had no interest in revisiting it. He was what he was, and she was a fool to put any faith in him. 'You should sleep, too.'

'What of you?'

He moved toward the fire. 'I was getting food.'

'And after you've eaten?'

Varian looked away from her, unable to face the invitation that was there. She was his for the taking, and he wasn't sure how long he could deny the part of himself that only wanted to claim her. 'Go back to bed, Merewyn.'

Merewyn let out a tired breath. That was the last thing she wanted, but she could tell by the sound of his voice that he was no longer hearing her. He'd already withdrawn back into himself. There was nothing more she could do or say to sway him.

Lying back down, she watched as he walked over to where she'd left the meat, wrapped in cloth that Blaise had provided. Varian sat down beside the fire and ate silently in the darkness. She watched as the dancing light cast shadows over his long, muscular body. The way his jaw flexed as he ate and the way he avoided looking in her direction as if afraid of what he might find. He was troubled, but whether by their conversation or their predicament, she couldn't be sure.

All she wanted to do was soothe him. If only he'd allow it. But Varian wasn't that kind of man. She wasn't sure if he'd tolerate anyone to comfort him. Ever.

When he was finished eating, he glanced over at her. She didn't know why, but she immediately closed her eyes and feigned sleep. He wrapped the leftover hare in the cloth again. Brushing his hands against his breeches, he got up a moment later and left the cloth by the fire before he vanished into the forest.

Thinking he'd gone to relieve himself, she waited for his return.

Only he didn't come back.

Merewyn sat up after a while and looked about. But Varian was nowhere to be seen. Scared something might have happened to him, she got up and went to the edge of the forest where he'd vanished. She gazed into the darkness, but there was no sign of him.

'Varian?' she whispered loudly.

No answer.

Merewyn chewed her lip in indecision. Should she wake the others to search? She looked back to where they slept so peacefully and remembered how they'd growled at them to be silent. They wanted and needed their rest.

Maybe she should search on her own . . .

She returned to the fire to retrieve the dagger Blaise had left there for cooking. It wasn't a particularly large weapon, but at least it was something.

Her heart pounding in trepidation, she headed off in the direction Varian had gone.

You're going to get lost ...

Ignoring her inner voice, she pressed onward. If she didn't see him shortly, she'd head straight back and wake the others to help search for him. As long as she kept in a straight line, she was fine.

She hoped.

But after a few minutes, she realized it was futile. There was no sign of him. No sound anywhere. The forest was so quiet all she could hear was the pounding of her heart and her sharp, quick breaths.

Deciding this was total folly, she was ready to head back for the others when she finally heard something ...

She tilted her head to listen as it was repeated. It sounded like splashing water. But nothing else could be heard. No humming, no voices. No whispering of the wind. Nothing.

She took three more steps forward. The forest was thicker here. The vines overgrown. She had to use the dagger to cut through them, but once she'd cleared the way, she froze where she stood.

The light of the full moon fell down on a narrow river where the moon's shadow rippled and brightened the whole area. Varian's clothes and sword lay just before her on the bank while he stood waist deep in the water, bathing. Merewyn couldn't breathe as she saw him there, sleek and wet. The water ran in rivulets over muscles that were well carved and-defined. She drank in the sight of his beautiful naked body like a parched desert beggar who'd stumbled onto a well.

There had never been a better-looking man created, and it was all she could do not to close the distance between them and touch him to make sure he was real.

At least until her gaze fell to the sight of the scar on his shoulder of the grail with a dragon rising out of it. She'd seen that mark before on the shoulder of the knight they'd killed and on Blaise. It was the mark of a grail knight, and it was from Lancelot's cruelty to his son.

Her stomach shrank. How could any man have done such a thing?

Poor Varian. And it wasn't his only scar. His body was riddled with them. One particularly nasty scar even bisected his left nipple. Accustomed to the Adoni who seldom fought with weapons, she wasn't used to seeing a form so perfect with so much damage. His was a body that told of countless battles and fights. Of pain and war. Not that she hadn't known that already, but to see it like this . . .

It broke her heart.

While she watched, he ducked himself beneath the water and stayed there for several seconds. She waited for him to break the surface, but he didn't. Just when she was sure he was drowning, he finally stood up, this time with his back to her.

He slung his black hair over his broad shoulders and she watched as it slapped against his bare flesh – as it struck another mark on his back.

And in that instant, her world shattered.

On his left shoulder blade was the last thing she'd expected to see.

Varian duFey, evil incarnate. The man who was hated by both the good and the bad. The son of Morgen's right hand was . . .

A grail knight.

Chapter Thirteen

Merewyn stumbled back into the forest, away from Varian and the lush sight he'd made in the moonlight. Fear and apprehension filled her as the foliage swallowed all traces of her.

He was a grail knight . . .

She could still hear Morgen and Narishka scheming to find the six knights so that they could locate the grail. What would Narishka say if she knew one of the men she sought was her own son? How ironic. Narishka had tried to breed a tool for evil, and instead he was firmly entrenched on the side of good.

Or was he?

'Varian was born of light and dark. Those two parts of him are at war with each other, and they won't let him walk purely on either side. He's too dark to be true to the light and too pure to walk solely in darkness. It's his hell to be caught between the two forever.'

And still he'd been chosen to protect the grail. How odd that his father had been judged unworthy while Varian hadn't.

No wonder Varian didn't sleep with women he knew. He most likely went to time periods where they knew nothing of Arthur and his Merlins. A place where women wouldn't understand the significance of that mark.

But she knew. She understood.

She could destroy him with a handful of words. If he ever discovered what she'd learned this night, she was sure he'd kill her. She couldn't even blame him for it. This was a secret to be taken to his grave.

Terrified of what he'd do to her if he caught her, she rushed back to the camp and lay down where she'd been. Her heart continued to pound in a frantic beat as images of him torturing her filled her mind.

I can't let him know, I can't let him know ... The words chased each other around in her head. Closing her eyes, she tried her best to relax, but that was impossible. Varian was his mother's son, and she knew well what Narishka would do in his place.

If she were lucky, he'd just kill her quickly.

Varian waded out of the water to the bank where he'd left his clothes. The air was so still it felt unnatural against his naked skin. Hot. Heavy. But at least he was clean now. He'd never been able to stand dirt on his body.

He wrung his hair out and used his bit of powers to manifest a towel. After drying his face, he slung it over his right shoulder as he stared at the bracelet with malice. There had to be some way to get it off so that he could use the full strength of his magick again. It pissed him off not to have access to the very thing he'd spent his life building.

Putting that thought out of his mind since there was nothing he could do, he quickly toweled himself off and dressed. But as he did so, he caught the flash of something on the forest floor. It glinted eerily in the moonlight. Curious, he buckled his sword to his hips, then went to investigate.

The silver flash turned out to be a small dagger hidden in the weeds.

Varian picked it up and frowned as he recognized the dagger Blaise had loaned him for hunting. The same dagger he'd returned to Blaise so that the mandrake could cook.

How had it come to be here?

Closing his eyes, he was grateful he had enough powers left to feel for its last user's essence. But it wasn't a man he saw holding it.

It was Merewyn.

A chill went down his spine as he saw her dropping it and scooting back into the woods. Had she come to spy on him while he bathed? He didn't know why, but that thought sent a wave of heat straight to his groin. It amused him to think that she'd have hidden here to watch him.

Had it turned her on?

That thought only excited him more until he realized what she could have seen ... his mark.

She was one of the few women who would know what it was and what it signified. He curled his fingers around the hilt of the dagger as anger swept through him. Was his mark what had sent her scurrying off?

And before he could stop it, his memories surged straight to the past.

After the battle of Camlann, and once the surviving knights of the Round Table had withdrawn to the shores of Avalon, Aquila Penmerlin had gathered together the thirteen magical objects Emrys Penmerlin had assembled to help Arthur rule over Britain.

Even though he'd refused to fight, Varian had come at her summoning and borne the insults and hostility of the survivors. Like them, he'd stood in the hall of the

Penmerlin's castle and listened to Aquila's wisdom.

'We have lost Camelot. We have lost Arthur. Morgen is at our borders and will come here to attack us at dawn and claim Arthur's treasure. We cannot allow this. Should Morgen possess Arthur's gifts, there will be no stopping her. Her evil will pour out over the land until she has destroyed everything. No one, human or otherwise, will be safe from her.'

'We have enough Merlins to hold her,' Galahad had boasted. 'She won't take Avalon.'

Varian had scoffed at his brother. 'And they kicked your asses at Camlann, Merlins and all. With Arthur and his sons at your helm. What makes you think she can't defeat you here?'

The words were out before he realized he should have stayed silent.

'Adoni traitor!' Ademar had drawn his sword and headed for him. 'I say we should start by sacrificing the cowards who refused to fight with us.'

Merlin had placed herself between them. 'Varian did what he felt was necessary to help us. You will not harm him on this soil or any other.'

Ademar had reluctantly withdrawn, but his eyes had promised a quiet murder should he ever happen upon Varian's back.

At the time, Varian had had no idea why Aquila had wanted him there. Why she'd summoned him.

All he knew was that he'd found himself among his enemies yet again.

Merlin had pushed Ademar back before she'd addressed the others. 'I want the Merlins to take their objects out into the world of man to hide them far away from Morgen and her army. Do whatever it takes to preserve them from evil. Protect yourselves, but guard your charges as if the fate of the world hinges on them, because it does.'

Percival had stepped forward then. 'I'll hide the grail at once.'

'No,' she said quickly. 'As powerful as the other twelve are, that one object alone overrules them all. It's too much of a burden for one man to carry. We will have six chosen ones who will hold a piece of the puzzle that will allow Arthur's son to find it when the time is right.'

Percival had frowned at her. 'But who will hide it?'

'I will.'

All eyes had turned to Guinevere as she pushed her way through the angry and perplexed crowd. Tall and proud, she'd been one of the most beautiful women ever to live. Her long, curly black hair had been pulled back in a braid, with small tendrils of it escaping to frame her lovely face. Her blue eyes had been honest and sweet, her mouth a perfect Cupid's bow.

Gawain and Agravain, who'd carried the lie of her infidelity to Arthur, looked away, shamefaced. With the full grace and dignity of her position as Arthur's queen and consort, she'd turned to address the gathered knights.

'My most noble husband is dead. My youngest son slain by his side. My eldest asleep to await the day when Morgen raises Mordred to fight again.' She turned a sympathetic eye toward her accusers. 'Tongues have borne the lies and mischief of others, and now Lancelot is in the hands of Morgen. There is no hope for him as I'm sure he will tell her nothing. Save him if you can so that mayhap he will forgive those of you who turned against him. As for myself, I loved Arthur with all my heart, and I know better than anyone the love he gave this land. I will not see his work and death go for naught. I will take the grail and carry it to a place where no one will find it. Ever. Once I'm sure it's safe, I'll do what my husband and children have done. I will send clues back to Merlin so that Draig may one day find it. Then I will give my life for the security of our people. Morgen's treachery and evil will not win.'

The crowd began shouting in protest until Merlin held her hand up to silence them. 'It's been decided that this is how it will be. There's no other way to protect that which cannot fall into Morgen's hands. It must be done. And when midnight strikes tonight, everyone is to be here in Avalon. I, and the Merlins who remain, are going to raise a shield to limit the reach of Morgen and her people. Avalon and Camelot are going to be removed from the realm of man and will from this day forward be hidden behind a veil so that none of them will even know we exist. So long as a Penmerlin reigns here at Avalon, the veil will remain, and the world of man will be protected from Morgen and her army. We will hold the line here for eternity or until the day Morgen draws her last breath.'

Cries for and against Merlin's plan had rung out.

Unable to stand any more of their fighting, Varian had left the hall and passed the black serge that marked the walls, reminding them all that the king and his sons had fallen. The Camelot of old was gone. Arthur would never be here again to lead them. Tomorrow was completely uncertain, except for one thing. They would have a long, hard battle against Morgen and her evil. No one here would ever be safe again.

Varian had felt ill with his sadness.

As he reached the door to the bailey, he'd been shoved hard from behind. Angry, he'd turned to find Bors standing there. The knight still had blood on his armor as he glared his hatred at Varian.

'Are you not going to save your father?'

'No.'

Bors had shoved him again. 'Coward! Bastard! How could you care so little as to leave him to Morgen?'

Varian said nothing because he knew the one thing Bors didn't. He was too young to fight his mother. His powers too green. If he were to go to Camelot for his father, he wouldn't return. At least not to fight with this army.

Even now, he could hear his mother calling to him, promising him his heart's delight to serve her. The Adoni were dark in their ways, but when it came to his mother . . .

She knew what brewed inside him, and she knew how to twist it to make him join her. If she gained control of his burgeoning powers, there would be no one to stand against him. No one except Arthur's son Draig, who was locked in stasis. If Varian fell under his mother's spell, he would use the years of buried hatred and knowledge he had for Arthur's knights to destroy them all.

As he remained silent, more knights joined Bors. Together, they moved to attack him.

'Enough!' Varian had roared, sending toward them a sorcerer's blast that rolled out from him in a wave that knocked them off their feet. He felt a silent wind whip around him, as it blew dust all over the others. There was fear in their eyes as they realized the exact extent of his immature powers.

It was why he wouldn't be here tonight when Merlin worked her magick. He would go where he couldn't hurt anyone. Where he wouldn't have to choose sides or be used as a pawn. Where he'd be a danger to no one.

He'd spend the night in Glastonbury ... with Dafyn and the others, and in the morning, he'd wander off and never be a part of this world again.

If only Varian had known then that it was his destiny to be a Merlin. By his going to Glastonbury, it had drawn the dark powers Merlin had tapped into toward that town and caused it to be sucked into the veil along with Camelot and Avalon.

It was his fault alone that Dafyn and the others were cursed, and it was a burden he'd carried ever since. He had destroyed the lives of every person there. But for him, they would have been as ignorant to the veil as everyone else on earth.

His heart heavy, Varian tried to banish the memories. But they refused to go. And this time they settled on the last time he'd seen Guinevere. It'd been at Fey Hollow. That nether time between night and dawn when the doorway to the Adoni world was open and thin.

Guinevere had sent word to him to meet her there at that time. The sky had just been lightening with the dawn when he'd seen her climbing the hill to join him. Pink and orange had laced the dark clouds above as the wind whipped her long, unbound hair around her shoulders. She'd been dressed all in white, her eyes tinged by dark circles that told of her long, hard journey and sacrifice.

Her face stern, she'd stopped just before him. 'Your father is dead.'

'I know.' He'd felt Lancelot's passing earlier that night.

Guinevere's eyes had betrayed her own grief as she patted his arm affectionately. 'He was a noble soul who wasn't always good, Varian. None of us are. But he wasn't as bad as you believe him to be either.'

Unwilling to hear her at that time, he'd snapped at his queen. 'Why am I here?'

'Because I trust you with the most sacred of all secrets.' Guinevere had held out a small, tan scroll toward him. 'I did as I promised. I've hidden the grail where it can't be found, and here are the clues for my Draig. Clues that will only make sense to my son.'

He'd frowned at her. 'Why give it to me?'

'Because Narishka would never think I'd be foolish enough to hand this over to one of her bloodline. But I know you, Varian, born of the fey. You won't betray Arthur any more than your father did.'

She'd stumbled then, and would have fallen had he not caught her against him.

'Your majesty?'

'It's the poison,' she'd whispered in a shaking voice. 'I was hoping it wouldn't spread so quickly.' She placed his hand around the scroll. 'See this to Merlin. All our fates are in your hands now.' She started shivering uncontrollably.

Varian had removed his own cloak and wrapped it around her.

'Take me home, Varian,' she'd whispered. 'Let me die beside Arthur's tomb.'

He'd nodded quietly before he did what she asked. Using his powers, he'd taken her straight to Arthur's final resting place under the castle at Avalon. Her face had lit up the moment she'd seen his gilded image on his sarcophagus.

Two heartbeats later, she'd died in Varian's arms.

Varian had held her there for the longest time as grief overwhelmed him. He'd wanted to cry at the loss, but the tears never came. Only a thick sadness that seeped through his body and permeated every part of his soul.

He'd wanted to change the way things had turned out, but of all men he knew that he couldn't.

After a time, he'd laid his queen down beside her beloved husband and looked at the parchment he held. All he had to do was open it and he would know the most valuable secret in all the world. He could claim the grail and use its powers for himself.

He could make everyone who'd ever insulted or abused him pay . . .

And by doing so, he would disgrace the lives of the only two people who'd ever meant anything to him. It would invalidate the sacrifices Arthur and Guinevere had made.

So he'd tucked the parchment into his pouch and taken Guinevere's body to her favorite place. The hill in Cornwall where she'd played as a girl.

When he was a boy serving in Arthur's house, she'd told him of this place and of the happiness she'd shared there with her sisters. If she couldn't be buried beside Arthur because of the cruelty of others, then he could think of no better place for her to rest.

He didn't use his magick to dig her grave. He'd done it by the sweat of his brow to honor a decent and kind woman who had given everything she had to save her people. It wasn't until he'd finished burying her that he happened to look up at the oak tree that shaded her grave. There in the bark was an old jagged carving that had been distorted by the years.

Forever Guinvere's Arthur.

Those words had burned in his mind as he'd traced the runic letters while pain washed through him. He would never in his lifetime know the love the two of them shared. He would never even begin to comprehend it.

His heart broken, he'd returned to Avalon then and

handed over the scroll, unread. Merlin had stared at him in wonder. Like him, she was new to her role and uncertain.

But there in the first hours of the day, she'd proclaimed him to be the first of the grail knights who would carry one of the sacred clues.

Varian had tried to argue. 'I can't do this, Merlin. I'm not—'

'You are of the bloodline. You might be born of Narishka, but you are also Lancelot's son. I can think of no better protector than one with your strength and power.'

'I didn't even fight with Arthur.'

'But you didn't fight against him either. Half of anyone's strength is knowing one's limitations and weaknesses. You chose not to put yourself in a situation where you would be tempted to evil.'

He'd shaken his head. 'I should have been strong enough to fight.'

'And you will be one day soon, Varian. That is why I've chosen you.'

Varian had bound himself to her then. To be her tool. To be the one who would carry out her orders without question and to use his connection to his mother to find the traitors who would betray Merlin and the others.

He'd spent centuries wondering if he'd chosen correctly that day. He knew full well what would happen should his mother or Morgen ever learn of the symbol he bore in secret.

Now his mother's servant most likely knew the truth of him. Merewyn had already told him that she would bleed for nothing. That she would sacrifice anything for her freedom.

She would sell him out without a single thought.

205

Kill her.

It would be the safest course of action. It would save both him and the others.

Gripping the dagger in a tight fist, Varian made his way slowly back to camp.

Chapter Fourteen

Merewyn was doing her best to feign sleep when she felt Varian standing over her. Even with her eyes closed, she could feel his sharp, penetrating stare like a tangible touch. The scent of leather and man filled her senses, overwhelming her with the power of his presence.

What was he going to do?

Would he kill her?

Her heartbeat sped up as her panic rose. Refusing to be a coward and allow him to strike while she lay there, she opened her eyes and looked up at him. If he intended to kill her, then she wanted to see the death-blow coming. The darkness cast his entire face in shadows so that she had no clue to his mood or thoughts. He stood over her like a giant dark malevolent specter. The only thing she could see clearly was the dagger he held in a tight fist at his side.

He held it like a man bent on slaughter . . .

Her mouth dry, she licked her lips, waiting for him to lunge at her with the weapon.

When he moved, she would have screamed but for the fact that fear lodged itself in her throat and kept her soundless.

And before she could move, he pulled the cloak from his shoulders and laid it out over her. The weight and warmth of the black leather banished the chills on her body as he laid himself down by her side. His spicy scent clung to the material, making her heart pound even more.

He placed the dagger and his sword on the ground beside him, with his hand resting on the sword's hilt.

Did he know she'd seen him while he'd bathed? If he did, he gave no clue.

'Good night, Merewyn.'

Still unsure if he intended to strike her or not, she whispered her reply. 'Good night.'

To her complete shock, he closed his eyes. Bemused by his actions, she crept closer to see if he were merely toying with her before he struck. It was something his mother would have done. Narishka loved to lull her victims into a feeling of comfort before she viciously cut them down. The evil Adoni lived to see the look of shock on her victims' faces before they died at her feet. Merewyn had no intention of giving Varian that satisfaction if such a thing was his intent.

She snuggled a bit closer.

Opening his eyes, he pinned her with a suspicious glare.

'It's cold,' she said truthfully. 'I was thinking we should share your cloak so as not to give you a chill. After all, your hair is soaking wet.'

Varian frowned at her words. Truthfully, he had enough magick to summon another cloak. But before he could tell her that, she scooted over to him and covered their bodies with the heavy leather.

Then she did the strangest thing of all.

She laid her head on his shoulder and settled down to sleep.

He couldn't move as he felt her there, like a lover, by his side, with her hand resting gently at his ribs. The scent of heather was strong from her hair, and her soft breath tickled the skin of his neck. He'd never lain with a woman like this. Never trusted anyone enough to sleep beside him.

And she knew his secret . . .

If he were smart, he'd shove her away from him and rid himself of her threat, but he couldn't bring himself to do that. Trust was an alien concept in his life. Yet what choice did he have at present? They were tied together until the end of this journey. Not to mention that there was no one for her to tell his secret to here except for Blaise, who also shared his cursed status . . .

With no one else around for her to tell about his mark, he should be safe for the time being.

Even so, he slid the dagger beneath his thigh so that she couldn't reach it without his knowledge. Then he moved his hand to his sword.

Just in case.

After a few minutes, he felt her relax against him as she fell asleep. He didn't move; hell, he barely breathed for several seconds as he waited for her to open her eyes and betray him.

She didn't. She merely slept as if all were right in the world.

Could it be she truly intended no malice toward him?

She shifted in her sleep, raising one leg to rest over his thighs as her arm spread out over his chest, and in that instant he realized that her malice on him was far more insidious.

She was going to kill him with lust.

Desire speared him sharply at her actions. The weight of her body, combined with the peaceful look

209

on her beautiful face, was unbearable.

Now how the hell was he supposed to sleep like this?

Unable to take it, he rolled to his side, away from her.

She snuggled up against his spine, spooning her body to his. Yeah, good move. Now all he could feel were her breasts against his back and her thighs against his buttocks. Even worse, her breath was falling against the nape of his neck, sending heat straight to his groin.

Unable to stand it, he pressed his hand to his cock in an effort to alleviate some of the pain. He considered taking matters into his own hand, but then decided against it. He wasn't some callow youth who needed to masturbate in bed. He was a man full grown, and the last thing he wanted was to have Blaise and the others wake up and know what he'd done. Not to mention he didn't feel like taking another bath in the freezing river.

No, he could control himself.

He raised his leg to get more comfortable. At least that had been his plan, but when her hand fell down to touch the skin that was bared by his jerkin riding up, he learned what true torture was. All he could think of was having that small, delicate hand cupping the part of him that was desperate for her.

Grinding his teeth, he could already feel himself sliding slowly between her fingers. Feel her cupping his sac as he feasted on her breasts . . .

Stop it!

He had to put it out of his mind. He was acting like one of the sex-starved triplets. If he didn't get control soon, he'd toss her over his shoulder and run off with her himself.

Then again, given how long the triplets had gone

210

without sex, he honestly felt sorry for them. If they were in as much pain as he was at present, it was a wonder they hadn't killed themselves.

'*Varian?*'

He cringed at the sound of his mother's voice in his head and knew he wouldn't be able to sleep the rest of the night. Asleep, he was weak against her, and she might be able to manipulate his subconscious into telling her what they had planned or where they were.

Resigned to the fact that his life was seriously sucking at the moment, he rolled again to his back. Merewyn's hand dipped to just below his waistband to touch the tender spot on his lower abdomen. Sucking his breath in between his teeth, he was grateful she was asleep. Little did she know that if she were awake and touched him there, he'd have no resistance to her.

Not that he had much as it was.

Especially now that she knew about his mark. The fact that she might see it while they were having sex was no longer a deterrent. In fact, he held a delectable image right now of her nibbling said mark . . .

He clenched his teeth at the thought.

Merlin had been a fool to choose him as a grail knight. He might yet prove his father right by switching his allegiance to the Adoni. Morgen would reward him well for such a thing, and he knew it.

So long as he bore that mark, he'd be able to control and channel the power of the grail. He could unleash a magick so raw that no one would be able to stand in her way or his. It was why he didn't want to know the names of the other knights and why he hadn't looked at the clues that could lead him to where Guinevere had hidden it. He didn't want the temptation of betraying them. He was already afraid of what he might do one day should Bors and the others anger him past his control.

And yet as he lay here with Merewyn snuggled against him, he couldn't imagine ever betraying people like her. They were the ones who would suffer most if he turned. They had no power to negotiate. Nothing Morgen could make use of. They would simply be fodder or pawns for her to abuse and kill for no other reason than she was having a bad hair day.

He felt his eyelids getting heavy. Blinking them open, he reminded himself that he couldn't go to sleep. He couldn't afford to give his mother anything she could use against them.

Merewyn came awake slowly to find herself incredibly warm. She smelled the scent of leather and pleasant musk . . . Varian. It was so comforting that it was all she could do not to burrow her nose against his neck and just inhale him. As it was, she felt the heat of his body, the strength of him pressed against her. But what startled her was the fact that her hand rested against his naked skin. She could feel the short, crisp hairs that ran from his navel down to a thicker pelt where her fingers rested.

Slitting her eyes open, she realized he was still asleep, facing her while her left leg was buried between both of his. Her head was cushioned against his shoulder, and his cloak still covered them both. Her heart pounded at their intimate position. Every inch of her was pressed up against him, with her face literally buried against his neck.

There was no way to pull away without waking him. Bracing herself, she moved back as slowly as possible.

Just as she thought, he woke up immediately. She froze the instant those green eyes met hers.

'Sorry to wake you,' she whispered.

He blinked as if he didn't understand her. And before

212

she could think to remove her leg from his, she felt him harden against her thigh. Heat scalded her face.

But he didn't seem to feel any embarrassment. Instead, he closed his eyes and nuzzled her gently before he withdrew from her. Merewyn was baffled by that. For a man who didn't want to sleep with her, he was strangely tender.

He stretched languidly. 'I can't believe I slept.' There was an odd note in his voice that she didn't understand, but it sounded like he thought sleeping was a mistake.

She tried her best not to notice the way his jerkin pulled against his body, emphasizing the taut muscles that flexed as he moved. It was a most tempting sight he made lying there, and it made her wonder what it would be like to lick that inviting skin the way Narishka did her lovers.

What would he taste like?

Trying to distract herself, she cleared her throat and went back to the topic at hand. 'You were tired.'

Before he could respond, she heard the others stirring awake.

Merewyn got up immediately, before any of them saw the way she and Varian were cuddled, and straightened her gown. She frowned as she looked down at the hem. Had the dress stretched out of shape? It appeared to be longer than it'd been before.

It was as if she'd shrunk during the night . . .

At that thought, a wave of icy trepidation went through her as she turned toward Varian, who was standing beside her.

'Do I . . .?' The words caught on her tongue as fear seized her completely. Please, please don't let her be right in this.

'Do you what?'

'Am I . . .' She had to force the word out of her paranoid throat. 'Normal?'

He frowned at her as if she'd lost her mind. 'Should you not be?'

Merewyn placed her hands over her face, trying to see if Narishka had turned her back into the ogress. To her relief, her skin was still smooth. There were no scars, no bulbous lips. Her face seemed to be as it was.

She gave a nervous laugh. 'I must be imagining things. Sorry.'

He picked his cloak up from the ground and fastened it back around his neck by a silver dragon clip. 'No need to apologize.'

Still she had a bad feeling, as if something about her was different. As if Narishka was somehow here with them. Her mistress's presence hung in the air like a bitter-smelling pall and it made the hair on the back of her neck rise. She continually looked about, half-expecting to find Narishka or one of her minions hiding to spy on them.

The group was mostly silent as they packed up camp, then ate a bit of meat to break their fast.

Beau seemed to be a tad taller, and his arms were a bit more formed as he clung to Merewyn's side while she ate in silence. The strangest thing was that he seemed to be smacking his lips . . . only he didn't have lips yet.

Once they were ready to resume their trek, Derrick audibly gulped. 'I guess it's time to cross the bridge.'

Erik chittered nervously before he ran up Merrick's arm and hid his small head under his brother's collar.

Blaise rolled his eyes. 'What is the deal with the damn bridge?' He exchanged a bemused look with Varian. 'I mean really, how scary can it be?'

'You'll see,' Merrick said, leading them north once more.

'We'll see,' Varian mocked in a feigned spooky tone.

Merewyn shoved playfully at him for picking on the triplets that way.

But that playfulness died a short time later when they approached the old wooden bridge that stretched over a fiery pit – one made of burning dragon scales that shimmered like iridescent jewels below them. Every so often one of the scales would launch itself into the air, then burst into flames. The bursting was bad enough, but the real danger in dragon scales came from the fact that they were razor-sharp and could carve through flesh and bone like a hot knife through butter.

Even so, Varian and Blaise didn't seem to notice the pit at all. It was the bridge that made them pale drastically.

'What?' she asked the men, worried that they knew something she didn't.

They didn't respond to her.

'How is this here?' Varian asked Derrick, his voice low and filled with awe. It was obvious the bridge held some major significance to him that she was unaware of.

Derrick shrugged. 'We don't know. It was here when we arrived and has been here ever since.'

Merewyn scowled at Varan's dire tone. 'What is it?'

'Slaughter Bridge.'

It still meant nothing to her. 'Should I know that?'

Blaise let out a deep breath before he answered. 'It's where Arthur and Mordred fought their last battle.'

Merrick nodded. 'Arthur's blood marks it still. And we have to cross it to get to Merlin's. There's no other way into the valley proper.'

Looking back at the old wooden-and-stone bridge that arced gracefully over the river of fire, Merewyn swallowed as a chill went down her spine. She could only imagine what must be going through Blaise's and Varian's minds as they stood before the very thing that had brought all of them to this point.

On that bridge the course of history had played itself out. The destiny of the world of man and fey had collided and left a permanent rift between them that would most likely never be repaired.

In one day, everything had changed. A king had died, one prince had been killed, and two more had been laid to rest in stasis until they were summoned again to refight this battle. Three cities had been pulled out of time, and Varian and Blaise had been left to try and keep their enemies from ruining the world she'd been born to. They were unknown guardians fighting a thankless, bloody war that had left scars on both of them.

Feeling for their sacrifice, she reached to take Varian's hand in hers.

Varian paused at the foreign sensation of someone's hand holding his. It was the first time in his life that anyone had done that. As a child, his mother and father had grabbed him by the upper arm, hair, or collar of his tunic to drag him about.

And when she laced her fingers in his, something inside him melted.

He offered her a hesitant smile as they followed after the others who were already on the bridge he didn't want to cross. This was a sad reminder of a day he'd just as soon forget. The only man who'd ever meant anything to him had drawn his last breath here.

It was all he could do not to turn and run, but Varian was anything except a coward. Taking a deep breath, he forced himself to approach it.

As he stepped foot on the old wood, his conscience

burned. He could feel Arthur here. He could hear his voice whispering to him. And all too easily, he could see him fighting against his nephew. See the two of them locked in heated battle like two rams who struggled to reign supreme. Even now the sound of sword against armor and shield rang in his ears. The smell of blood infiltrated his head.

It made his heart ache to think of Arthur falling to Mordred. He should have been here that day . . .

A sudden wind stirred, whipping his hair around his face and blinding him. Merewyn let go of his hand to pull her own hair out of her eyes as her face paled. She held it at her neck with both of her hands as she passed a nervous look to him.

Out of nowhere a mist surrounded them. It blocked the light until they were swathed in absolute darkness. There was no sight of the fire below. No sound or smell. It was as if all their sensations were blocked by something evil.

'Who goes there?' a demonic voice roiled out from the mist.

Before he could even part his lips, the two brothers cried out, 'Derrick, Erik, and Merrick. Servants of Merlin.'

There was a brief pause before the voice responded. 'Then you may pass.'

The three of them ran across the bridge to the safety of the other side.

Varian frowned, wondering why they were so afraid when it didn't appear to be that menacing.

The mist curled around Blaise and seemed to swallow him whole. 'And who are you?'

'Blaise, son of Emrys Penmerlin.'

It pulled back until the light highlighted Blaise's form. His long, white-blond hair whipped around his shoulders before it settled quietly into place. 'Be welcome to our domain, son of Merlin.'

Blaise started forward, then paused to look back at Merewyn.

Again the mist thickened around Merewyn as if it were caressing her. 'And who are you, lady?'

She shifted as if it were making her uncomfortable. 'Merewyn of Mercia ... I know nothing of Merlin other than the legends people tell of him, but I am friend to Blaise and the others. And I travel with the bantling named Beau. He can't speak yet, but he's harmless to all.'

'Then you, too, may pass.'

She smiled at Varian before she reached to take his hand again.

Varian started forward with her, only to find his way blocked by some unseen energy. That same *thing* forced their hands apart and pushed Merewyn away even though she visibly fought it.

'Varian!' Merewyn shouted as she and Beau were driven across the bridge.

He inclined his head to her while he waited for the demon to question him.

'And who might you be?' it demanded.

'Varian duFey. Knight of Arthur.' The hot wind blasted him so hard that he wasn't sure how he kept his feet. It smelled of sulfur and fire that was so pungent, it was all he could do not to choke on the stench.

'Traitor!'

Varian tensed as he finally placed the voice who accused him. 'Sagremor?'

The mist cleared to show him the image of a knight who'd died centuries before. Sagremor had been another knight of the Round Table and had died here on this bridge, fighting Mordred before Arthur reached him.

He'd been the first to turn his back when Varian had moved forward to be knighted. But not before the man had spat on the ground before Varian's feet.

Now Sagremor condemned him again. His dull gray armor cast no reflection or light in the darkness. But his eyes blazed red through the slit in his helm. 'How dare you call yourself a knight of Arthur when you wouldn't even defend him!'

Varian curled his lip. 'You know nothing of my loyalties.'

'No, but I know of your cowardice.' Sagremor drew his sword.

'Varian!' Merewyn shouted. 'No! You leave him be!'

To Varian's shock, she actually picked up a rock to throw at Sagremor's back, but it glanced off the armor harmlessly.

Sagremor threw his hand out and shot a blast that knocked her back. Rage suffused every molecule of Varian's body as he drew his sword and charged forward.

'Don't you dare harm her!'

Sagremor turned and brought his sword down hard against Varian's. The force of the strike reverberated through his body as Varian summoned his own black armor into place. If this was to be a fight to his death, then he intended to make it count.

Merewyn pounded her fist against the invisible wall that kept her from the fight. 'Blaise!' She turned to look at him over her shoulder. 'Do something.'

'Like what?'

'Stop them.'

He moved forward to strike against the wall, too.

219

'I'm no more effective than you are.'

Beau then took up her cause, slamming himself uselessly against the wall. But nothing he did made any sort of wave in the field.

Growling in frustration, she splayed her hands against the wall and watched as Varian ducked below one swing and rose to kick Sagremor back. He swung at Sagremor's head only to have the knight raise his sword sideways to block the strike. Sagremor knocked Varian's blade aside, then sliced up from under Varian's arm. Varian twisted away, feinting to the right to slice at the man's leg. Sagremor lifted his foot and kneed Varian hard in the chest, then brought his sword down to slice his back. Varian raised his sword just in time to block the stroke.

He shoved Sagremor back. The knight struck the side of the wall.

'Sagremor!' The disembodied male voice was fierce with anger.

He looked up at the gray sky above them. 'My liege?'

'Release the fey and let him pass.'

'But—'

'There are no buts in this. Do as I say.'

Varian stood back and cast a suspicious look toward Blaise, whose face was ashen.

She knew instinctively to whom the voice must belong. 'Merlin?'

Blaise gave a subtle nod.

Sagremor's eyes glowed a vicious red before he vanished into vapor.

Varian didn't move at first. Instead, he listened for the sound of Sagremor attacking him from behind. After a minute, he finally trusted enough to start his hesitant journey toward Merewyn and Blaise, both of

220

whom were still standing behind the wall.

It didn't recede at his approach. He met Merewyn's sad amber eyes. Wanting to comfort her, he splayed one hand over hers, but still he couldn't feel the warmth of her touch. He held his sword in his right hand as he glanced up toward the dismal sky.

'Merlin?' he called. 'I can't leave the bridge.'

The words had barely left his lips before he felt a rush of air that was followed by the sensation of Merewyn's hand on his. She curled her fingers around his as if afraid something would rip him away from her again.

That sensation gave him more comfort than he ever wanted to admit to feeling. He would have kissed her hand had the others not been watching them so intently. As it was, he walked forward with her by his side.

Beau cooed and hugged his leg as he waddled beside them. What a strange sight they must make.

And as he neared the end of the bridge, the gray lifted from the landscape. It flowed over until everything was lush and green. For the first time since they crossed over, he could hear the sounds of insects and birds.

Merewyn paused, gaping at the breathtaking beauty around them. 'What happened?'

'There's always green here,' Derrick said. 'Merlin keeps the outside dismal so that Morgen won't know that he's free of his prison.'

Varian was baffled by that. 'Why does he stay here?'

Derrick shrugged.

He looked to Blaise for an explanation.

But he was no more helpful than Derrick. 'I never understood his motivation for anything.'

'I'm just glad he's here,' Merewyn said softly.

'Given his powers, he should easily be able to get us into Avalon, right?'

Varian let out a nervous laugh. 'Here's where I have to remind you that nothing has been easy up until now. I find it hard to believe that that's going to change.'

Her gaze bored into his. 'Have faith, Varian.'

He shook his head at her. How could she have faith in anything? Especially given the centuries she'd spent with his mother. But as he looked at her, he found an alien part of himself wanting to believe in her faith. To believe in her.

Unwilling to think about that, he glanced to the triplets. 'How far to Merlin?'

'Not much farther. A few hours.'

'Merlin?' he called, but only the cry of birds breaking into flight answered him.

'He won't speak if you call him,' Merrick said irritably. 'He doesn't like being questioned. We'll have to make our way to him if you want an audience.'

Varian cursed. Unfortunately, that was too much like the man he remembered. 'He was always an unreasonable bastard.'

'Hey now, that's my father you speak of.'

As if that mattered? 'And?'

Blaise shrugged. 'I just felt the need to point that out.'

Varian let out a tired breath before the triplets began to lead the way again. They didn't speak much as they traveled. Rather, the triplets seemed to be keeping their eyes peeled for something, which made both him and Blaise keep their eyes peeled for whatever was unsettling them.

'Should we be concerned?' Merewyn finally asked the unspoken question.

Merrick snorted. 'Always. Haven't you learned that yet?'

Blaise cast a wry grin at Varian. 'Sounds like someone else took a tumble into the pit of despair.'

Varian laughed. 'Yes, but at least we have sunshine now.'

'True, very true.'

Merewyn listened to the men bantering as she and Beau trailed behind them. For hours they walked, and as time passed, she felt more and more strange. She couldn't place the sensation really. It was as if her stomach were troubled and at the same time there wasn't anything really wrong with her.

It wasn't until she brushed her hand through her hair and came away with a handful of it, that she let out a cry of dismay.

The men froze and turned to face her.

She stared at the dark curls that were wrapped around her fingers as horror filled her. 'I'm turning back into a hag, aren't I?'

Merrick and Derrick turned away. Blaise's eyes were filled with pity, but even he didn't dare speak of it.

Varian only gave a subtle nod.

Utter despair filled her as tears gathered in her eyes. But she didn't let them fall. She was stronger than that. Really she was.

What was beauty anyway?

Freedom ...

She stifled that voice as Beau gently stroked her leg. It'd been too much to hope that Narishka would spare her. She should have known the woman's cruelty would drive her to this.

'Please, Beau,' she said, her voice breaking from her tears. 'I want to be alone.'

He made a sad noise before he waddled to Blaise,

who took his rocky limb into his hand. The mandrake's violet eyes betrayed his pity.

The triplets, Beau, and Blaise withdrew, while Varian approached her solemnly. He cupped her cheek in a gentle hand as those green eyes burned her with friendship.

'Don't think about it, Merewyn.'

And that succeeded in bringing her tears out. They streamed down her face as his kindness burned through her. She didn't deserve it. 'I don't want to be a hag again.' She placed her hand over his and held it close to her cheek. 'Please, Varian. Show your mercy. Kill me.'

His grip tightened under her hand as his eyes snapped furiously. 'Don't you *dare* say that to me. You can't give my mother that victory.'

'What victory? She destroyed me long ago.'

'No, she didn't. You've survived her cruelty.'

'To what purpose? What good is my freedom when no one will look at me?'

'I'm looking at you, Merewyn. *I* see you.'

She swallowed at his sincerity. At the kindness of his touch. She gripped his hand tightly in hers before she lowered it from her face and held it between her hands. Her heart heavy, she stared at the strength of the tanned flesh. At the scars that marred his knuckles. His hands were large and capable. Manly.

Never again would she have the chance she had now. 'I know how you feel about this, Varian, but I would ask a favor of you.'

'I will not kill you.'

'Then make love to me.'

Varian froze at her unexpected words. 'What?'

'Before I'm completely ugly again. Before she steals any more of my soul. Make love to me, and I won't end my life. Give me a reason to fight her.'

'And you think that will do it?'

'Please, Varian. I want to know, just once, what it's like to be held by someone. Show me what kindness and intimacy are so that I can hold on to them and fight for them.'

He was aghast at her words, and at the same time, how could he deny her? She was right. As a crone, no one would touch her. His mother had seen to that.

'I will ask nothing more of you. I promise. You can walk away from me as you do the others.'

He somehow doubted it would be that easy for him. Whether he wanted to admit it or not, there was some part of him that seemed integral to her.

Wanting to comfort her, he lifted her hands to his lips and kissed the palm of each one. Already they were losing their beauty. They weren't gnarled yet, but they weren't as long and graceful as they'd been this morning.

He glanced to where the others had vanished. There was no sign of them at all.

His heart heavy, he looked back at Merewyn. 'You don't deserve to be taken out here like an Adoni whore.'

She licked her lips before she led his hand to her breast. 'I dare not wait. She could turn me foul again at any moment, and I don't want you to see me like that. I want to have this as a woman who is beautiful in your eyes.'

'You were always—'

'Don't!' she snapped angrily. 'Don't you dare tell me I was beautiful to you when I know it for a lie. I don't want you to take me with pity in your heart. I want to know that you desire me.'

He could feel her nipple harden through the thin

225

fabric of her gown. That one tiny puckering was enough to send heat straight to his groin.

He wanted her. There was no denying it.

And if that wasn't enough, she lowered her hand until she cupped him gently in her hand. His cock stiffened even more, and it drove away every argument he had. All he could think of was the sweetness of her lips.

Merewyn wasn't expecting the ferocity of his kiss as he pulled her into his arms and held her tight. She could feel his heart racing against hers as his tongue teased hers. Closing her eyes, she inhaled the warm scent of him. This was the moment she'd waited for all her life.

Eager for it, she lifted his jerkin so that she could run her hands over his lean, corded muscles. His skin was soft and ridged by scars. Unable to stand it, she pulled away from his lips to push the jerkin up so that she could see the perfection of his body.

Varian lifted it over his head before he tossed it to the ground. Merewyn hesitated as she saw the burn of Lancelot's mark on his shoulder. She reached a tentative hand toward it as she tried to imagine the pain he'd felt as a child. Every piece of the grail emblem was there, right down to the Latin words that read: *Esse Quam Videri*. To be rather than to seem.

He was what he seemed. There was no falseness to this man. Wanting to comfort him, she leaned forward until she was able to press her lips to the mark.

Varian shivered at the sensation of her lips on his flesh. No woman had ever touched that scar before. Normally when he took a lover, he used his magick to conceal the imperfections of his body. The scars, the welts. Most of all the grail symbols. But he couldn't do that with Merewyn. He was naked before her in a way he'd never been bare before.

And it was why he understood how important this was to her. There was nothing worse than to see pity on a lover's face. Or repugnance.

He hissed as she pressed her tongue to the mark before she kissed it, then moved down to his scarred nipple. His entire body thrummed with heat as she gently laved it. He wanted inside her so badly that it was all he could do to stand there and not pull her to the ground.

But this wasn't about cooling the fire in his blood. This was about giving her a memory that would soothe her pain. One that would make her life a bit more tolerable.

He would be her first and most likely last lover. It was a sobering thought. And for her he wanted this to be a perfect memory.

Merewyn groaned at the taste of his salty skin, at the sensation of his flesh underneath her hands. He was the most beautiful man she'd ever seen.

And when he pulled away, she looked up, afraid he'd changed his mind. Instead he scooped her up in his arms and carried her off into the woods, in the opposite direction from where the others had gone. She frowned up at him.

'I want this to be just between you and me. Unlike my mother's people, I don't perform for an audience.'

She smiled at his kindness as he found a small, sheltered spot in the forest. Setting her on her feet, he removed his cloak from her shoulders before he spread it out on the ground.

This really is happening . . .

She was about to journey down a path from which there would be no escape. But this was what she wanted. One moment with a man so that she could know the sensation that drove Morgen and her court. She wanted to understand the beauty of sharing herself with someone else.

Holding that thought close, she unlaced her gown and let it fall to the ground.

Varian felt his breath leave him as Merewyn bared herself to his hungry gaze. Even though she was a bit thin for his tastes, she was still the most beautiful sight he'd ever beheld as she kicked her shoes off.

And when she reached for the lacings on his breeches, he couldn't hear anything except the pounding of his own heart. She loosened the waistband enough so that she could dip her hand down and touch him. His head spun from the sensation. Holding her hand against his cock, he slowly rocked himself against her palm, delighting in the feel of her gentle touch.

Merewyn licked her lips at the velvety hardness of him. Her face heating, she looked up at him while he stared down at her. The look of pleasure on his face made her giddy.

But she wanted more than this. She wanted to know how he tasted. How he felt ...

Varian frowned as she lowered her gaze to his waist before she pushed his breeches down. He was going to take his boots off, but before he could, she sank down to her knees in front of him.

Surely she wasn't going to ...

He held his breath in sweet expectation as she slowly fingered him from hilt to tip. Her brows were drawn together in curiosity as she examined his body much like a scientist might. At least until she moved her finger to the tip of his cock, where he was already leaking.

She brushed her fingertip over him before she led

her fingers to her mouth.

The sight of her tasting him like that was almost enough to make him come. She locked gazes with him before she lowered her hand and leaned forward.

Varian felt his breath rush out of him as she slowly took him into her mouth, inch by sweet inch, while her tongue swirled around him. He buried his hand in her hair, but took care not to hurt her while she carefully licked and tortured him with pleasure.

He had to brace himself not to thrust against her while she took her time tasting him. But it was sheer agony. Needing to taste her as well, he pulled back.

Merewyn frowned at his actions. 'Did I do something wrong?'

'No.' He literally tore his boots and breeches off before he lay down on the cloak and pulled her on top of him. He kissed her deeply as his hands explored her body. Merewyn moaned against his lips as he gently sank his hand down her cleft. He pulled back with a tender smile. Rolling her onto her side, he slowly kissed his way from her lips to her breast.

She cried out as he slowly tongued her swollen nipple, drawing it back and forth in a rhythm that made her entire body twitch. Moisture exploded as she felt a small pleasurable shudder run through her. A low laugh rumbled in his chest while he dipped his hand back to explore her carefully.

He sank his finger deep inside her as he continued to lave her breast. Cupping his head against her, she spread her legs wide for him.

She'd never felt anything more incredible than the combined stroking of his fingers and tongue. At least not until something foreign ruptured inside her. It rushed over her body with waves of intense pleasure. Her entire body shuddered as she screamed out from it.

And still he played with her, wringing even more pleasure from her. When her body began to settle down, he rose up to smile down at her. 'That, my lady, was your first orgasm.'

'First?'

He continued to swirl his fingers in and out of her in a magical rhythm that was already building more heat inside her. 'Yes. I promise you, you'll have a lot more of those before I'm through with you.'

And with that oath, he began kissing his way back down her body. He turned himself so that she would have access to him before he spread her legs and took her into his mouth.

Merewyn sucked her breath in sharply as she arched her back, drawing his tongue even deeper into her. She bucked ever so slightly as he hit a sensitive spot. Wanting to give him every bit as much as he gave her, she reached up to stroke his cock.

He faltered for a moment before he returned to her full force.

Varian closed his eyes as he tasted her. She was still sticky from her orgasm, but he'd never sampled anything better. She'd never come for another man. He could feel and taste her maidenhead. No man had ever known this part of her.

Only he.

And as she closed her lips around his cock again, he wanted to cry out in pleasure. There was something incredible about being with her.

For the first time in his life, he wasn't with a stranger. He was with a woman who knew his brutal past. One who didn't see a passing stranger. They were more than that.

And now they were lovers . . .

Merewyn moaned at the salty taste of Varian as she

230

took him in as deep into her mouth as she could. She ran her hand over his back, then down to his hips to the crisp hairs on his legs. She wanted to devour him. To keep him like this for the rest of her life.

But that was a stupid thought. A man like Varian would never be content with any one woman. He had too much Adoni in him for that.

Still, she was glad that he was her first. She couldn't imagine anyone being more gentle or patient.

Grateful that he'd given this, she felt her body on the verge of climax. She pulled her mouth away from him an instant before she came again.

Varian refused to pull away as he felt her spasming against him. He wanted to spend the rest of his life making her feel like this. Wanting to feel her nails biting into his skin as she gave the most delectable hiss.

When she started back toward his cock, he stopped her. 'You do that right now, and you'll still be a virgin.'

'I don't understand.'

He gave one long, luscious lick to her that caused her to shudder. 'If I come, love, it'll take me a little bit to rise *fully* back to the occasion.'

A becoming blush stained her cheeks.

Smiling at her, he cupped her face in his hands before he pulled her lips to his for a kiss. He savored the sweet softness of that mouth, the sensation of her tongue exploring his as he rolled over onto his back.

Merewyn was enjoying their kiss immensely as Varian started to guide her hips. She felt the tip of him hard and stern against her core.

She pulled back to stare down at him.

'This is your last chance to escape,' he breathed raggedly.

'Show me.'

His gaze held her captive as he slowly slid her onto his cock. Merewyn sucked her breath in sharply between her teeth at the foreign sensation of his body invading her. To her chagrin, it burned as he broke through her maidenhead.

He paused as if he sensed her pain. 'Deep breaths.'

She did as he suggested and luckily it helped while he continued to enter her. Once he was buried to his hilt, he held her there motionless.

Merewyn couldn't breathe as she felt him deep inside her. It was so strange to have him there. He cupped her breasts tenderly in his hands before he kissed her gently on the lips.

'This is for you, Merewyn. Move when you're ready.'

Bracing herself for more pain, she lifted herself up ever so slightly. The burn was still there, but it wasn't nearly as bad as before. And when he dipped his head to suckle her breast, it all but vanished.

Encouraged by that, she started to move even faster.

Varian held himself completely still as he let her find her rhythm. She was hesitant at first, but over the course of the next few minutes, she began to rock herself against him with more force. Amazed by her passion, he watched her through hooded eyes. She was incredible.

When she appeared to be adjusted to him, he lifted his hips, driving himself even deeper into her. He growled at the ferocity of the pleasure that ripped through him.

Holding her hips in his hands, he continued to lift himself as she lowered herself on him. His breathing ragged, he felt something foreign seep through him. All his life, he'd thought that having the same woman over and over again would grow boring.

But she was so eager and curious that he wondered if a man could ever be bored by her.

It was rare to find a woman, never mind a virgin, with an appetite so strong. If he didn't know better, he might think her part Adoni.

Lacing his hand with hers, he felt his pleasure mounting. But he held it back until he couldn't stand it anymore.

Merewyn felt Varian's grip tighten on her hand an instant before he cried out. She watched the ecstasy on his face while he shuddered beneath her. He arched his back, driving himself deep inside her before he froze.

She could feel his explosion. His breathing ragged, he relaxed under her as his body slowly withdrew from her. She moved to his side and expected it to end there.

It didn't. Varian gathered her into his arms and kissed her gently on the cheek before he parted her lips and sampled her mouth again.

'Are you all right?' he asked, wringing a spike of pleasure from his concern.

'I am.'

'And was it what you thought?'

'No,' she said, snuggling against his side as she felt him stiffen against her. 'It was better.'

Varian felt a strange sensation tighten his throat at her words. He didn't know why they touched him, but they did. Deeply. He buried his hand in her soft hair before he kissed her forehead. They needed to get up from here and go after the others before they came back to search for them.

But he didn't want to move. He just wanted to stay with her like this, for eternity.

If only he could.

'Varian?'

'Yes?'

'Is there someplace you can take me where I won't be mocked for my hagishness?'

Those words brought a severe ache to his chest. 'I gave you my word, Merewyn, that I'd keep you safe.' But even as he spoke, he wondered if he could honestly keep that vow. He couldn't even stop the ones who taunted him. How could he keep them from her?

Yet as they lay entwined on the forest floor, and he felt the warmth of her body against his, he knew that he would find some way to fulfill that promise.

She'd been hurt enough, and today she'd given him a moment of peace the likes of which he'd never known before.

'No one will mock you ever again, my lady.'

'How can you be so certain?'

He wanted to lie to her, but she'd been told enough of those in her life. He wouldn't add himself to her list of betrayers. 'I don't know. But somehow I will keep you from it.'

Merewyn's throat tightened at his vow. But she knew better than to trust in it. His mother was ruthless, and she wouldn't stop until Varian was her slave, and Merewyn was even more hideous than she'd been before.

She'd told him to have faith, but right now even she was finding it hard to hold on to it.

'Merewyn?'

She stiffened at the sound of Blaise's voice.

'Varian?'

Their interlude was over.

'We're coming,' Varian shouted. Somehow he manifested a small cloth and handed it to her. 'Give us a minute.'

She quickly used it to clean herself before Varian helped her to dress. She paused as she looked down to see her hands, which suddenly had a dull, grayish cast to them.

Varian covered them with his. 'Don't think about it.'

How could she not? 'Do you think Merlin can help? Maybe he can counter her spell.'

His eyes were troubled before he shook his head. 'One sorcerer can never undo another one's spell. You can alter it somewhat, but never eliminate it.'

'Alter it how?'

'Make you an ugly duckling or mare.'

'Could he not at least take away some of my deformity?'

'No. If he tried, it'd only make it worse. It could even kill you.'

From where she stood, that wasn't such a bad thing. She would rather be dead than to return to her old life.

Varian pulled his breeches and boots back on. It took them both a second to remember that his jerkin had been left on the trail. As they went to search for it, they found Blaise holding it with a curious look on his brow.

'I thought you were blind,' Varian snapped as he snatched it away from the mandrake.

'You don't cover up that heinous body of yours soon, I will lose what little sight I have.'

Varian grimaced at him before he pulled it on over his head and laced the front.

'Should I ask what you two were doing?'

Varian gave her a sideways glance before he answered. 'Not if you want to continue breathing.'

'Very well then.' Blaise turned toward her and froze. His features turned completely blank.

Merewyn knew that look all too well. It was the same one Blaise had always worn around her in the past. One of careful emptiness to keep from offending her. 'I'm back, aren't I?'

'No,' Varian said quietly. 'It's not as bad right now.'

Not as bad. Was that supposed to comfort her? Unable to bear the thought, she pulled his cloak around her and raised the cowl so that no one would be able to see her now.

I will get my beauty back.

I will.

Varian gave her arm a gentle squeeze. 'Come, Merewyn.'

'You lead,' she said to them. 'I wish to hang back a bit.'

Blaise frowned. 'You sure?'

'Yes. Please.' To her relief, they did as she asked, and with every step she took, she hated herself more and more.

'*Merewyn?*'

She hesitated as she heard Narishka's voice in her head. She glanced to Varian and Blaise, but neither of them seemed aware of it.

'*Are you there, hag?*'

Merewyn ground her teeth in bitter anger. '*Go away.*'

She heard laughter in her head. '*So you are there. Tell me how you like the new look of yourself?*'

'*Leave me alone.*'

'*I could do that. But if I go, you'll be stuck like this forever.*'

In spite of her common sense, which begged her to insult Narishka, she couldn't stop the sudden flutter of hope in her breast.

'*I can return your beauty to you.*'

'*At what price?*'

'*You know the price. Return my son to me.*'

Merewyn's heart thundered in panic as she watched

236

Varian bantering with Blaise.

'*I can't.*'

'*Can't or won't?*'

Before she could answer, she felt a brutal pain lance through her leg. One that almost caused her to fall. Gasping at the effort of staying on her feet, she realized that her hump was back ... as was her bad leg.

But even worse than that, one of her arms started to curl in toward her chest, useless.

'No,' she choked under her breath as she hobbled forward.

Varian turned around at the sound of her voice. A look of abject horror filled his eyes before he blanked his expression. He moved toward her. 'Merewyn ...'

She recoiled from him. 'Don't touch me. Don't look at me.'

He glanced to Blaise, who now stared at her with the same guarded look. It tore her heart asunder to see that. It was worse than the curled lips of others because she had seen them look at her like a person.

Now they pitied her.

'*You can be beautiful again. Say the word, Merewyn, and you will be what you were.*'

She looked up at Varian, who still held himself in check, and in that instant, she made her decision.

Chapter Fifteen

Varian wanted to comfort her so badly that he could honestly taste it, but Merewyn would have none of it. Every time he tried to close the distance between them, she moved away.

Her features contorted by pain, she railed at him. Even so, he knew her anger wasn't for him so much as it was for what his mother had done to her. 'Don't touch me while I know I sicken you.'

'No, Merewyn,' he said, trying to make her understand the truth, 'you don't.' He tried to touch her only to have her wrest herself away from him.

Still, doubt was painted plainly on her distorted features. 'How dumb do you think I am that I can't tell the difference in your eyes when you look at me? I see your pity and your disgust. You can't even hide it.'

Varian wanted to curse at her for her stubborn blind interpretation of feelings he didn't have. Okay fine, so she didn't exactly set his hormones on fire in this condition. He still wanted to hold her. To soothe her. No matter how she looked on the outside, there was no denying that he cared for her. And he'd given his word that he would keep her safe.

'You don't sicken me.' That was the truth.

'Stop lying to me.'

Varian tried to cup her face, but she slapped his hand away. He actually hissed from the pain of it. She was incredibly strong in this form. His hand stinging, he looked at Blaise, hoping he would have a suggestion as to what he should say or do to ease her.

Blaise merely shrugged as Merewyn stomped her way toward the path where the brothers and Beau still waited for them.

Varian sighed as he watched her limping gait. How could he make her understand that he didn't care about her looks? That wasn't what had allowed her into his circle. He honestly wasn't sure what part of her had wormed its way into his heart. All he knew was that her pain hurt him, too. That even in this distorted form, he still saw her as she really was ... an extremely beautiful woman whose looks were incidental to him.

But there was no way she'd ever believe that.

Was there?

Varian quickened his steps so that he could pull her to a stop. Her face bore her torment and pain.

He couldn't leave her like this. 'Tell me something, Merewyn? If I were suddenly to lose my looks, would I sicken you?'

She scowled at him. 'What?'

Varian indicated his body with a wave of his arm. 'The scars I bear all over me. Do they sicken you? Do you find them repugnant? If I were to take a sword stroke to my face that left me with one eye missing and a disfiguring gash, would you never want to look at me again?'

She wiped her bulging lips with the back of her hand to remove the excessive moisture. Then she indicated her face in the same manner he'd indicated his body. 'This is a bit more extreme than that, don't you think?'

'No, I don't,' he said, his voice thick with the weight of his sincerity. 'You are still what you were before this. You are what you are, no matter how you look.'

Merewyn felt the tears in her eyes as they welled up and blurred her vision, but she refused to cry. She wouldn't give Narishka that satisfaction.

She wanted to believe Varian's words. Desperately. Yet how could she? Men loved with their eyes. She knew that. And in this form, there was no hope for her to appeal to him. Ever. 'If I were to make myself naked for you now, would you take me?'

He didn't hesitate with his answer. 'Yes.'

She curled her lip at the lie he spoke. 'But you wouldn't desire me.'

He caught her arm as she started away. Those green eyes actually bit into her as they snapped with fury. 'Listen to me, Merewyn. Listen well. I'm not going to lie to you. This form doesn't exactly inspire me to throw you down on the ground and screw you until we're both blind from it. But you don't repel me in any manner.' He took her hand in his and led it to his cock, where he was starting to bulge once more. 'Even though I just had you, I could take you again.'

He wasn't lying about that. She could feel him harden even more as he held her hand against him. It was inconceivable to her.

'It's *you* who attracts me, Merewyn. Not your body or your looks.'

A tear slid down her cheek as she walked herself into his arms. He encircled her with his strength as she tucked her head beneath his chin while he held her close. She felt so safe here. So wanted. Never once in her life had she ever experienced anything like this.

Anything like him. His warmth invaded her. He was so much more than she'd ever dreamed of.

How could anyone have ever been cruel to a man so kind?

She buried her face against his neck and just inhaled the scent of his skin before she lifted one hand to bury it deep in his dark hair. He looked down at her with a clear, open gaze before he tilted his head down toward hers.

She held her breath, wondering if he'd really be able to meet her kiss ... and just as their lips would have met, she heard someone approaching.

Varian pulled back from her to see who it was.

Frustrated, she looked past him to find Merrick and Derrick frozen before them.

Derrick screwed his face up in disgust as he looked at her. 'Oh. My. God. What is *that*?'

Merrick's face showed his own repugnance. 'Did a kobold eat Merewyn?'

Even Beau was hesitant to approach her.

Her heart shattering, she tore herself away from Varian with a cry of dismay.

'Merewyn!' Varian snapped as he went after her. 'Don't listen to them.'

But how could she not? They only spoke the truth. She was hideous. Hideous! Unable to bear the truth of it, she turned from him and ran back into the woods, where she almost collided with Blaise. The mandrake caught her against his chest to keep her from stumbling. Her tears blinding her, she twisted out of his grip, to continue her mad trek through the trees.

With no destination in mind, she only wanted to escape the pain she felt inside. She wanted to get away from the men who looked at her as if she were too lowly to breathe their air.

241

Varian ran after Merewyn. He was afraid of what she might do in this state. Honestly, he could kill the brothers for their idiocy. How could they have insulted her so? Then again, they weren't exactly rocket scientists.

He could hear Merewyn's sobs as she ran, and they tore through him with resounding pain. To be so deformed, she was amazingly swift. Lowering his head, he quickened his steps until he was able to overtake her. Even though she tried to outmaneuver him, he scooped her up in his arms and turned her to face him.

In that instant he gaped at her face.

She was beautiful again. Perfect.

And that terrified him. 'What happened?'

She stopped struggling against him and looked down at herself, at her hands. Her features aghast, she lifted her hands to cup her face where her skin was once more smooth and supple. 'W-w-what? What's going on?'

Varian's eyes narrowed at his mother's cruelty. 'My mother's playing with you.'

Merewyn sucked her breath in sharply. '*That* bitch! How dare she.'

He blinked at her raw and unexpected language. 'Are you all right?'

She turned on him with blazing eyes. 'What do you think? How dare she toy with me after all she's put me through.' She turned around and scanned the forest as if seeking his mother's presence. 'I hate you, you evil troll. I wish you'd choke and die on your own venom.'

Well, she was certainly creative in this mood. 'You do realize that would only amuse her *if* she could hear you?'

She looked at him with such anger that he actually

242

took a step back. 'Don't you *dare* make light of this.'

'I'm not, believe me.'

Curling her lip at him, she started past him, only to pause as she stared into the forest.

Varian looked to see Blaise there, watching them with a frown. 'Is something wrong?'

'I'm just wondering why Narishka is playing with Merewyn like this.'

That answer was simple enough. 'Because she's sick.'

'Evil,' Merewyn added. 'To the center of her being.'

He certainly couldn't argue that. Narishka might be his mother, but he wasn't blind to her faults.

Blaise let out a long breath. 'Man, V, you definitely didn't come from choice genetic stock, did you?'

'Not really.' He glanced to Merewyn, whose face still bore her fury. 'Don't worry. We'll get her in the end.'

She scoffed. 'No, we won't. You know it as well as I do. She's been around since the beginning of time, spreading her malice and ruining people's lives. What makes you think for one minute that either of us will ever live to see her fall?'

Again, she had a good point. There was only one answer to her question. 'Faith?'

'You're not funny.'

He wasn't trying to be.

His heart heavy, Varian held his hand out to her. 'Come. Let's be on our way.'

Reluctantly, she took his hand in hers and allowed him to lead her back to the brothers and Beau, who were extremely grateful she'd returned to her more attractive form.

None of them spoke as they continued their journey. It was as if a pall clung to them, sealing out any chance for joy or laughter. Varian wanted to cheer Merewyn, but he couldn't think of anything that wouldn't depress her more.

She was right. His mother had survived for untold centuries, and it would take more than their small band to destroy her. Hell, they'd be lucky just to survive this. So how could he ever cheer her?

Unable to find an answer, he walked stoically by her side.

It was high noon before the brothers stopped walking.

Varian braced himself for an attack. But that wasn't what held their attention.

It was the sight of a young, beautiful woman, waiting in a small clearing. Dressed in a shimmering green-and-gold gown that plunged so far down her torso it barely covered her breasts, she was exquisite. Her hair was a deep auburn that fell in waves of curls from a gold diadem that was laced with delicate gold chains that framed her delicate features.

There was something extremely familiar about her, but Varian couldn't place it.

She crossed her arms at their approach and narrowed a pair of deep green, fey eyes at them. 'You made it, I see.'

The sound of her dulcet voice went through him like a lance. *The fey are no worse to betray their own than anyone else, boy. Just wait. One day you'll see ...*

He remembered well that voice saying those words to him when he was just a child. But it was a voice he'd never thought to hear again. 'Nimue?'

Her gaze softened as it reached him. 'Varian. Beloved nephew, how are you?'

Confused as hell. But then what else was new? 'Since when am I ever beloved?'

244

The crooked smile on her face was geared to charm him, but it didn't work. He didn't dare trust her or anyone else.

'Why do you think I had Merlin spare you from Sagremor?'

'Boredom.'

She laughed. 'Hardly. You are my blood, Varian. The last that I have who still breathes. It's good to see you again.'

Even so, he was suspicious. Nimue had originally been the Merlin for Arthur's Excalibur and one of his grandmother's five sisters. Born of the fey, they'd been the six who held dominion over all of the water Sylphs – hence their moniker of du Lac.

Though the sisters had been united against the world, their fights against each other had been legendary. It was a great fault of the Sylphs that they were all possessed of explosive tempers.

Unable to stand the fighting while pregnant, his grandmother had returned to the land of fey, Landvætyria, to have his father and raise Lancelot there. She'd brought Lancelot to Arthur's court on Lancelot's eighteenth birthday, and she had held him close to her breast until the day the knight Balin had vengefully beheaded her. That action had caused her sisters to curse Balin and his brother Balan to die by each other's hands.

Then the sisters had turned their attention to Morgen, the source of Balin's anger, who had systematically eliminated each one of them . . .

Nimue had been the last one standing. It was why she, along with Emrys Penmerlin, had tried to imprison Morgen here.

They had vanished just before Arthur himself had confronted Morgen. There had been countless speculations as to what had happened. But no matter what version one heard, it all came back to the fact that Morgen had turned the tables on them.

Varian narrowed his gaze at his great-aunt who actually looked even younger than he. 'I thought you were trapped in ice underneath Camelot.'

'Apparently not,' she said sarcastically. 'But make no mistake, I was in ice for a time. Thanks to Emrys and his hormones. We were supposed to trap Morgen here instead. Unfortunately, you men are stupid when a woman is naked, and he spilled his thoughtless guts to one of her spies before we could implement our plans. To get back at us, Morgen imprisoned us. Now, I'm trapped *here*' – she gestured to the forest around her – 'with *him* for all eternity.' She sighed irritably. 'Sucks really.'

'That's why they keep trying to kill each other,' Merrick whispered loudly.

Derrick snorted. 'You mean when they're not screwing wildly.'

That got Derrick a sorcerer's blast from Nimue that knocked him off his feet and slammed him to the ground.

Blaise shook his head. 'Word of advice. Don't tease a sorceress when all you can do to defend yourself is bleed on her. It's highly unwise.'

Derrick sneered. 'Shut up.'

Blaise ignored him as he turned back to Nimue. 'Speaking of, where's my father?'

A sly smile spread slowly over her lips as she lifted her smallest fingernail to her mouth so that she could nip it playfully. 'He's hanging about.'

Varian arched a brow at the smug look of satisfaction on her face. 'I have a feeling you mean literally.'

She laughed. 'He deserved it. Trust me.'

Blaise shook his head. 'Any chance we can free him?'

She cut her gaze back to Blaise as she sized him up. 'Want to join him?'

'Not really. But I would like to see him. If it's not too much trouble.'

She dropped her hand and sighed. 'Oh very well.' She snapped her fingers, and an instant later Emrys Penmerlin appeared by her side.

Varian actually gaped at the sight of him. This wasn't the man he'd known in Arthur's court. Instead of the mature Merlin who had counseled his king, this one was a man no older than his mid twenties. He had short, brown hair and gray eyes. Dressed in a dark green jerkin and brown leather breeches, he glared at Nimue before he scanned the rest of them.

When he met Varian's arch stare, he gave him a sarcastic smirk. 'I age backwards, remember? Lovely curse from a demonspawn I met early on.'

'Oh it's not a curse,' Nimue said with a laugh. 'Worked out very well from where I'm standing. It's the only reason why I haven't killed you yet. You're the only man I know who truly gets better with age . . . in more ways than one.'

'Why they screw like bunnies,' Derrick said under his breath. The words had no sooner left his lips than his entire mouth vanished.

Nimue glared at him. 'Some people shouldn't be allowed to speak.'

'Nim,' Merlin said in an irritated tone. 'Fix the poor boy.'

'Why should I? He annoyed me. This way, he can't further offend me.'

Merlin let out a sound of aggravation. 'You know he can't eat like that, and it was your bright idea to send him after Varian in the first place. So repair his face.'

She mocked his words and expression. 'Oh you're such a spoilsport. Won't let me maim the minions, won't let me rearrange your fyrebaums, or do anything else fun. Bitch, bitch, bitch. You should have been born an old woman.'

Growling at her, Merlin crossed the distance that separated him from Blaise. His features softened instantly into an expression of affection before he embraced the mandrake. 'Good to see you, Blaise.'

Blaise nodded as he withdrew. 'You, too. I can't believe you're still alive.'

Merlin cast an evil glare toward Nimue. 'Personally, I think I'm in hell. But it could be worse. At least she has skills, and I do mean *skills*.' He wagged his eyebrows.

Blaise twisted his face up in distaste. Varian concurred that he didn't really want to go there. Like Blaise, he thought of Merlin as a father figure, and the thought of him having any kind of sexual experience made his stomach queasy, especially since it involved his great-aunt.

Nimue passed a peeved glare to Merewyn. 'Men must ever brag over their conquests. Take a hint from me. Kill whatever man you sleep with. At the very least, cut out his bragging tongue so he can't slander you.'

Merlin cocked a brow at her words. 'I thought you treasured my tongue.'

'Enough!' Blaise said, covering his ears. 'You guys are seriously grossing me out.' He grimaced as he looked over at Varian. 'I wish I were deaf instead of blind.'

'You're not the only one.'

Nimue snorted. 'You're part Adoni,' she said to

Varian. 'What are you complaining about?'

'He complains about lots,' Merrick said. 'And by the way, I vote Derrick remains mute.'

'Hmmm.' Nimue snapped her fingers and returned Derrick's mouth.

'You bastard,' he snarled at his brother.

'Oh like you wouldn't have said it had it been me.'

This time, Merlin snapped his fingers, and the two of them and Erik vanished instantly. 'They can be such a pain.'

'So why did you send them after us?' Varian asked.

'They were to bring you here so that you can begin settling in.'

That had been the last thing he expected to hear. 'Excuse me?'

Merlin seemed to miss the open anger in his tone. 'We've already conjured you a place to live. You should each be comfortable here. Especially Merewyn. The men were quite excited to learn that for once a woman has found her way into our domain. They've been praying for centuries that Morgen would become bisexual so that she'd have women lovers to banish here. Now their prayers are answered.'

Yeah, right ... Varian shook his head. 'We're not staying here.'

Merlin was adamant. 'Oh yes, you are.'

Varian gripped the hilt of his sword as he moved to stare Merlin down. 'We will *not* stay here.'

Merlin blasted him hard in the chest. The force of the hit knocked him back, off his feet. Without thinking, Varian tried to strike back, but it was useless. There wasn't enough magick in him to conjure a blast. And to pull a sword against a man like Merlin was suicide.

As Merlin moved to attack again, Blaise put himself

between them. 'I won't let you hurt him.'

Merlin sneered. 'You're not strong enough to stand against me. Move aside.'

'True, Dad. I'm not. But you'll have to go through me to attack him again.'

Merewyn took a step forward. 'Please, sir. No more attacks. You have to understand that Varian has to return to Avalon. He has information that the new Merlin needs to fight Morgen. It's imperative that he go to her.'

'That's no concern of mine.'

Aghast at his lackadaisical attitude, Varian pushed himself to his feet. 'It used to be.'

'Yes, well, a lot of things used to be my concern,' Merlin said, his eyes burning with rage. 'But times and people change. Nim and I have created a haven here for many beings. For centuries we've kept this place away from Morgen and her poisonous minions, and I'll be damned if you and your crew are going to come in here and ruin all we've built.'

Varian was taken aback at his unwarranted anger.

Nimue let out a deep sigh before she spoke. 'Let me explain this a bit better than my nonesteemed counterpart. Morgen kicked our collective asses centuries ago when we were in our prime. Neither Emrys, nor I are what we were then. We still have a great deal of power, but nothing like we had in our youths. Morgen thinks that we're still trapped in ice and are no threat to her. If she ever learns that her spell faltered, she'll march in here and take us down. And in the process, she'll destroy everyone in the valley.'

Blaise frowned. 'I thought she couldn't come here.'

Merlin shrugged. 'A bit of propaganda on our part. The truth is a bit different. While we do everything to keep her out, we can't really stop her should she decide to cross that bridge. We can control the mandrakes and most of the Adoni, but we can't control them all. They can storm us from the opening, and while Sagremor is good at holding the bridge, he is only one apparition. Against Morgen's magick, he's basically worthless.'

Nimue's featured softened. 'So you see, you have no choice except to stay here.'

Varian exchanged a calculating look with Blaise, who held the same determination in his eyes. They wouldn't stay here, but there was no sense in arguing it any further when it was obvious Merlin and Nimue had made up their minds.

'So where are we to stay?' he asked.

Merlin shook his head. 'Don't think that I'm so foolish as to buy into this sudden capitulation. While *your* powers are bound, mine aren't. I catch you slinking out of here after dark toward Avalon, and you will regret it.'

Varian stiffened at the threat. No one told him what to do. No one. 'You don't control me.'

Before he could blink, he found himself locked in a pair of stocks. Cursing, Varian tried to break free as the wooden structure held him bent over in a painful position. It was useless.

Even Blaise tried to blast him out, but it was no more effective than his own struggles.

Merewyn's face flushed with blood before she actually moved to confront the sorcerer. 'Release him. Now!'

Merlin cast a snide smirk toward her. 'You're biting off more than you can chew, woman. Mind your place.'

'And what is that supposed to mean?' Nimue demanded, arms akimbo. 'What place should a woman mind? Huh?'

251

Merlin stuttered as he seemed to search for an answer that wouldn't get him into trouble.

Merewyn tsked at Nimue. ''Tis a pity to be locked in this valley with someone who doesn't respect you, isn't it?'

'You've no idea.'

Merewyn gestured toward him. 'That's why Varian is so special to me. He never disrespects a woman, even though his mother is an insult to us all.'

Nimue glanced toward him. 'You're right. He was always respectful.' And then anger flashed in her eyes as she returned her glare to Merlin. 'How dare you imprison my nephew.' She blasted Merlin so hard that it sent him rolling over. 'You mind *your* place.'

The stock vanished so quickly, Varian went sprawling on the ground.

The two of them starting blasting each other with everything they had. The blasts went everywhere. Shattering trees. Sparking small fires. Blazing near him.

Varian had to agree with the brothers' earlier observation about Merlin and Nimue – these two got into some wicked fights.

Not wanting to gain their attention while they were furious, he pushed himself up quietly, then took Merewyn's hand. He pulled her away from the two battling sorcerers.

Blaise grabbed Beau's arm and withdrew with them every bit as silently.

Never the kind to retreat, Varian made an exception in this case. With any luck, they might actually survive this.

But they'd only taken a few steps when they ran into another invisible wall. He started to back up, but he rammed into another one.

'They've trapped us,' Blaise said under his breath. 'Damn.'

Varian's sentiment exactly.

Nimue blasted Merlin into a statue before she approached them. 'Just because I fight with Emrys doesn't mean I always disagree with him. In this, Emrys and I are united. No one leaves this valley. Ever.'

Varian couldn't believe what he was hearing. 'You would sacrifice innocent people for this?'

'*I* was sacrificed for this. As was Emrys. We tried to warn Arthur and your father, among others, that Morgen was dangerous. No one listened. They all thought we were insane. And when we tried to help them, we were trapped here, and we heard exactly what was rumored and thought of us by the very ones we were trying to save. Forgive me if I don't feel benevolent toward them.'

'But if Morgen gets the grail—'

'How can she? One grail knight is dead, his clue lost to everyone except Aquila Penmerlin. And two more are trapped here, away from Morgen's reach. I'd say the grail is safer now than it's ever been.'

Blaise gaped at her words before he exchanged a frown with Varian, who couldn't believe what he was hearing.

'How do you know there are grail knights here?' Blaise asked.

'My good dragon, Emrys was Penmerlin, and I am a daughter of a lake Sylph and Damé Fortune. Between the two of us, there is nothing we don't know. Right down to the thought you're having at this moment that says you think I'm a liar. The fear that Merewyn has of being ugly again and Varian's rather loud mental insults that he's leveling at my head.' She glanced down at Beau. 'Not to mention that poor rock, who now believes Merewyn is his mother. Poor thing.' She locked gazes with Varian. 'You are all trapped here. Forever. So get used to it.'

And the next thing they knew, they were transported into a small cottage.

Varian rushed to the door only to find it locked with no way to open it. As if he couldn't have guessed that one. Slamming his fist against the door, he turned to face the others.

'Well, children ... any idea on how we get out of this one?'

Blaise glanced down to Beau. 'We use the rock as a battering ram?'

Merewyn gasped before she gathered Beau into her arms and held him protectively. 'Don't you even think that.'

Varian ignored them as he looked around the spartan cottage. There wasn't much room here. But at least there was a fire and a cupboard that appeared to hold plenty of food for them. It was obvious that the sorcerers truly meant to keep them here forever.

And if he didn't get his magick back, they might very well succeed.

Chapter Sixteen

The next week was virtually unbearable as they paced the small space with no relief ... no way out. No matter what they tried, Merlin and Nimue kept them imprisoned in their cottage. Blaise and Varian had tried everything to combine their limited powers to break out.

Nothing worked. It was beginning to look like they really would spend the rest of eternity here.

During their days of frustration, Beau quickly morphed into a short gargoyle complete with a set of small wings. His face was broad and his fangs not as pronounced as others of his kind. Even so, he was a good-looking gargoyle and Merewyn found him extremely adorable.

He still had a bit of trouble speaking, but one thing was certain, he was as attached to Merewyn as she was to him, and the two had formed an unbreakable bond.

As the days dragged by with aching slowness, the only source of light to their prison was the fact that they all got along. At night, they would retire to their individual rooms even though Varian had to fight himself to keep from seeking out Merewyn. He wanted only to hold her ... at least that was the lie he continually told himself, but he knew better than even to try it. For one thing, holding her would only whet his appetite more and, for another, the last thing he needed was to add any more complications to his life.

He had to stay focused. There was still a traitor out there who was seeking grail knights. If their traitor had found Tarynce, then it was only a matter of time before he turned over another innocent man to Morgen. Not to mention, said traitor could do untold damage in other ways.

Varian had to get Merewyn to Avalon so that she could identify their turncoat and he could stop the man dead in his tracks. But that required them breaking Merlin's spell first. While no sorcerer could interfere with another's spell, there was always a loophole that allowed the bespelled to free themselves. It was only a matter of time until they broke through.

On the eighth day of their captivity, Varian woke up feeling extremely ill. So ill, he couldn't even stand. He lay on his cot, his stomach churning as he wondered what he'd eaten the night before to cause such misery. He'd never felt worse. But it wasn't a cold. At least it didn't feel like one to him.

He could hear the others in the main room as Blaise made breakfast. Once it was ready, Merewyn came to get him.

'Varian?'

When he didn't answer right away, she crossed the room to open the window and allow daylight in. He hissed as pain tore through him. The light made his eyes ache as if someone were plunging daggers into them.

Merewyn immediately shut the wooden shutters as Varian recoiled from the light as if he were being burned. Concerned about him, she went to the bed. 'Are you all right, Varian?'

He'd withdrawn completely beneath his blanket. 'I don't feel good.'

Thinking it was a cold, she pulled the blanket back to find him in a fetal position on the bed with his fists balled against his eyes. His entire body was covered with a fine sheet of perspiration. Even his hair was slicked back from his face by his sweating.

When she laid her hand against his brow, it was unbelievably hot. She cupped his whiskered cheek which was even hotter than his brow. Never had she seen such a fever on any person.

When he glanced up at her, she gasped.

There was a grayish cast to his skin, and his eyes were no longer purely green. Strange orangish red streaks marred them. They started at his pupil and cut across the iris straight to the whites of his eyes.

'Oh my God,' she breathed. She turned to call for Blaise over her shoulder.

He came instantly. 'Yeah?'

'Something's wrong with Varian.'

Blaise took one look at him and recoiled in horror. 'Oh man.'

'What?' Varian asked.

'It's magick-poisoning.'

Varian cursed.

'It's what?' Merewyn asked. She'd never heard of such a thing.

'You can't bottle up magick. Anytime you restrict it, it has a nasty way of escaping. I would say from his condition that Varian's is trying to eat its way out of him.'

'Thanks,' Varian said from between clenched teeth.

Shrugging, Blaise somehow managed to appear both sympathetic and uncaring. 'You got a better explanation?'

Varian didn't respond.

Merewyn felt terrible for him. There was no denying that he was in extreme pain. 'What can we do?' she asked Blaise.

'We have to get that bracelet off him.'

'How?'

'I don't know. In case you missed it, we've been trying to figure that one out all week.'

She looked back to Varian, who was shaking uncontrollably as he tried to pull the blanket back over him. But he was trembling so badly that he couldn't quite manage it.

Merewyn immediately covered him. 'Go talk to Merlin and Nimue. Tell them what's happening and see if they can come up with something to help him.'

Blaise nodded before he left them alone.

Merewyn sat on the edge of the bed so that she could rub Varian's back. His skin was so hot that it literally radiated out from beneath the blanket. They had to get his fever down before it caused him damage. But how?

There was no ice in the cottage. Nor anything else that could help.

Getting up, she went to the kitchen for a bowl of tepid water and a cloth. She could hear Blaise in his room, trying to call out for his father and Nimue. They didn't appear to answer him.

As she filled the bowl, Beau flew over to her and perched on the countertop before he tucked his wings in around him. He was only three and a half feet tall, but when he perched as he was doing now, he was much smaller. 'Can I help, my lady?'

She gave Beau a tender smile. 'No, sweeting. We need to free Varian's magick.'

'I wish I could bite through the bracelet for you, my lady. Poxes to his mother for hurting him.'

Merewyn couldn't agree more. She turned the water off.

'Should I try knocking through the field again?'

Her heart warmed at his generosity. Ever since he'd gained his wings, Beau had been doing his best to batter his way through the force field. 'Thank you, but no. I don't want you to chip something off, especially nothing vital.'

He nodded glumly. 'If you need me, call, my lady.'

Thanking him for his kindness, she took the bowl and cloth back to Varian and set it beside the bed before she pulled the blanket back to discover he was completely nude. Heat flooded her cheeks at the sight of him. Every muscle in his body seemed to be rippling, and she couldn't help but remember the way he'd felt in her arms. How those muscles had felt underneath her hands.

How his body had felt deep inside hers ...

But this was no time to think such things. He was ill, and she needed to tend him before that fever caused damage to his brain. She wrung out the cloth and started bathing him while he shivered forcefully.

He tried to push her away. 'I need the blanket.'

'No, Varian. We have to cool your body down.'

'I'm freezing.'

His words wrung her heart. 'I know.' She pushed him back and felt awful as his teeth started chattering. Her gaze fell to the bracelet, and a wave of rage tore through her. Damn his mother for her cruelty.

Varian hissed and growled every time she touched him. Even though the water and cloth were tepid, the instant she placed the cloth to his body, it heated to such an extent it actually steamed. Afraid for him, she tried to pour a bit of water over his chest. It literally boiled and evaporated.

After that, she no longer bothered to wring out the cloth. And still Varian fought against her as he tried to cover himself with the blanket for warmth.

As she trailed the cloth over his chest, his tremors worsened into all-out convulsions. An instant later, the bed lifted two inches from the floor.

Terrified, she pulled back as things in the room started to bang and shift. The bed rattled against the floor. The shutters banged loudly before they were flung open and wrung from their hinges. Her bowl was lifted from the floor and shattered against the wall. The glass windows exploded as she was lifted from the bed. A second later, she was thrown to the floor.

Merewyn covered her head as things flew around her. She tried to call for Beau or Blaise, but they didn't answer. And just as she thought it could get no worse, Varian began to bleed profusely from his mouth and nose. The more things shattered and flew, the more he bled.

She tried to reach him, but some unseen force pinned her to the floor. 'Varian!'

He didn't appear to hear her, any more than Blaise or Beau. A loud, unearthly howl began as a whirlwind swirled through the room. She clutched at the floor as it tried to lift her. Her hair whipped painfully against her skin.

Disembodied laughter filled the room.

Merewyn closed her eyes and tried to cast her thoughts to Varian or Blaise.

She wasn't sure how long the chaos lasted before everything came to a sudden stop. It was as if nothing had ever happened. The windows returned to normal. The bed settled down, and the heaviness that was pressing against her vanished.

The only testament to the ferocity of the attack was the broken pottery.

Scared it would resume, she crawled back to the bed to find Varian unconscious now, his breathing labored. His skin was terrifyingly pale while he continued to bleed from his nose and mouth. 'Blaise!' Merewyn shouted, as she retrieved the cloth to help staunch the blood.

The mandrake opened the door and frowned as he saw her and Varian covered in blood. He crossed the room in two steps 'What's happened?'

'I-I don't know. He convulsed, and the room exploded. Now he's unconscious.'

Blaise tried to wake him, but it was no use. He pulled back Varian's eyelids to see that his eyes were now as red as the blood flowing from his nose. Cursing, Blaise held his hand to Varian's neck to check for a pulse. 'He's not simply unconscious. He's in a coma.'

This couldn't be happening to him ... 'What do we do?'

Blaise's eyes were filled with sympathy. 'I don't know. I can't get the powers that be to answer.'

'What?' she asked incredulously.

'Merlin and Nimue are ignoring me.'

She looked down at Varian as her heart shattered, and grief overwhelmed her. Was he going to die?

But what set the fire inside her was the fact that no one seemed to care. Not even his aunt. His own flesh and blood ... After all he'd done to protect the Lords of Avalon and all he'd suffered, this was to be his fate?

And as those thoughts went through her, her rage built.

This was wrong. *So* wrong. How dare they turn their backs on him when he needed them.

261

'Merlin!' she shouted. 'Answer me now!'

To her surprise, he did. His voice echoed through the room. 'I know what you want, and there's nothing we can do. One sorcerer can't undo the spell of another.'

Merewyn made a sound of absolute disgust. 'He's to die then?'

'His life is in the hands of Damé Fortune.'

She seethed at the mention of the ancient entity who controlled the fate of them all. Tall and handsome, he was a capricious evil beast who only seemed to find joy by tormenting others. The handful of times she'd seen him in Camelot, he'd been indifferent to the pleas of those who begged him for mercy.

He'd been indifferent to her own pleas. However, she was willing to plead with him again for a chance to help Varian. Anything was better than seeing him suffer like this.

'Then can I summon him?'

Merlin laughed. 'You can try, but I assure you he won't come here. He never has and never will. There's nothing for him in this realm.'

Frustrated, she wanted to choke them all for this. How could they be so cold?

She looked up at Blaise. 'Varian said a sorcerer could mitigate the magick of another. Is there some way to mitigate this?'

His expression was sad and troubled. 'If there is, I don't know it. Since it's a power restriction spell, mitigating it could kill him.'

His words made her ill. 'So the only person who can remove this is his mother or Damé Fortune?'

'Yes.'

Merewyn wanted to curse at the irony and injustice of that. Her fury roiling, she brushed her hand through

Varian's damp hair. The heat from his fever radiated to such a state, she wasn't even sure how it hadn't killed him already.

And as her gaze fell to the scar of his father's symbol that had been burned into his shoulder, her resolve shattered.

She couldn't let him die or suffer. No matter what she had to promise or who she had to barter with, she was going to get him out of this.

Chapter Seventeen

Blaise stayed with Varian while Merewyn excused herself to attend to her needs. Honestly, he felt every bit as ill about this as Merewyn did.

Poor bastard. First Varian had been caught between Narishka and Lancelot, then Morgen and Aquila Penmerlin, and now this.

Even though Varian was unconscious, Blaise knew he was in pain. Blaise had only had his powers constricted once, as a boy. Emrys Penmerlin had done it to show him why it was so important to make sure that no one put a binding spell on him.

It was a lesson he'd never forgotten.

Blaise's powers were nominal compared to Varian's, which meant Blaise's experience had been very mild comparatively speaking. When someone as powerful as Varian was bound, it had to be excruciating. The more power that was withheld, the more pain. And with someone like Varian, it could very easily leave him permanently damaged.

That bit of information Blaise had kept from Merewyn since there was nothing they could do. He figured Varian only had another day or two like this. After that, Varian would most likely never recover.

He'd be in a vegetive state forever. Maybe that had been Narishka's intent from the beginning. She'd probably assumed Varian would strike any bargain with her to keep from degenerating into a zombie.

It only showed how little she knew of her own son.

But the worst part was that, as a comatose zombie, his magick could be funneled and used by someone else. It wouldn't be as strong as if he were directing it himself. Still, someone like his mother could use it to enhance her own powers. From where Narishka had stood either option had probably been a win for her. Either she got her son on her side or she got a portion of his magick to use for her purposes.

And Blaise had foolishly thought his own mother was callous. Her worst crime had been abandoning him because of his albinism. She'd never actively tried to kill him. Much.

Blaise let out a tired breath. 'I know you can hear me, V. I'm sorry we didn't break the spell in time.' The two of them had talked only yesterday about what would happen in the event of Varian's magick revolting. Varian must have known this was coming. 'Don't worry. I'll keep my word. No harm will come to Merewyn. I'll protect her for you.'

As expected, there was no response.

Sitting there, he could feel Varian fighting this. He could sense it rippling against his own powers.

He also knew it was hopeless. Not even Varian was that strong. How he wished he'd taken time to get to know the man better before now. Like so many others, he'd allowed Varian to push him away and hadn't given much thought to the sorcerer who preferred solitude to company.

What Blaise had found over the last few days was a friend he'd learned to value. Varian duFey might have been hellspawned, but he'd grown into something else. And the man didn't deserve this kind of bullshit.

Blaise felt someone behind him. Turning his head, he saw Beau hovering in the doorway.

'Beau brought water for the master.'

Blaise smiled at the small gargoyle as he moved forward with the bowl. Much of it sloshed out from his jarring gait, but nonetheless, it was a touching sight. 'Thanks, Beau. I'm sure Varian appreciates it.'

The gargoyle set the bowl down by the bed. He cast a grieving look at Varian before he turned back to Blaise. 'My lady cries, and it makes Beau sad, too. Can the master not tell her not to cry?'

How he wished it were the easy. 'No, Beau, he can't. He's sick.'

That seemed to make him feel better. 'Then Beau will make him well.'

'I'm afraid you can't.'

But he wasn't to be deterred. 'Yes Beau can. Gargoyle spit is curative.'

'Yes, but not for this. If Varian could be cured by something like gargoyle spit, I could have cured him with my powers.'

'Oh.' Even though he was made of stone, Beau seemed to deflate as a dark sadness settled over him. 'My lady loves the master. Every night, she whispers her prayers when she goes to bed, and she always prays for him. She says he needs someone to watch over and care for him. Tell him he must get up. Otherwise, my lady will always cry.'

'I wish I could, Beau, but it's not that easy.'

'Why is it not easy? Beau doesn't understand.'

'It just isn't. It's like you trying to fly before you had wings.'

Shaking his head, Beau dipped a cloth into the

water, but his hands were so large that he couldn't pick it back up. Blaise stepped forward to get it. He wrung the cloth out, then placed it to Varian's brow.

That seemed to please the gargoyle. 'The master will be better now. The water will repair him, and he will get up so that my lady won't cry anymore.'

How Blaise wished he had the gargoyle's naivete. But he knew better. Varian would most likely die in the coming days, and there was nothing more to be done for him.

Merewyn knelt on the floor of her room with her emotions churning. It was done. Varian would probably hate her from now on, but at least she'd saved his life.

At what cost?

'It doesn't matter,' she whispered. Because she knew the truth.

She loved him. From the moment he'd picked her up and run with her when anyone else would have left her to her own means, she'd been his.

She only hoped that one day he could forgive her for the bargain she'd just made. Rising to her feet, she left her room solemnly and headed for where he lay unconscious while Beau and Blaise watched over him.

'Lady,' Beau whispered as she entered the room behind them. He indicated the cloth on Varian's brow. 'Beau made the master better for you.'

Tears welled in her eyes at the gargoyle's kindness. 'Thank you, Beau.'

She didn't look at Blaise as she headed for Varian's cot. She didn't dare for fear that she would regret her actions and try to change them.

But this . . . this was for the best of all involved.

Without a word to Blaise, she reached for Varian's wrist.

'What are you doing?'

Merewyn couldn't answer. Instead, she pulled at the bracelet as hard as she could. *'Lyra daludité,'* she whispered, repeating the fey words over and over. *Freedom is only an illusion ...*

She felt heat suffuse her body. It radiated through her like lava as it surged toward her hands. And just as she was certain her hands would explode from it, the bracelet shattered. Sparks flew into the air, and something forceful knocked her back.

Beau ran to her as Blaise cursed. Merewyn sat up, watching Varian as his eyes slowly fluttered open.

Joy rushed through her. She'd done it.

Varian couldn't move for several heartbeats as his head swam. He was completely aware of everything, but more than that, he could feel his powers again. They surged through him, radiating every molecule. It felt like lightning skipping through his body.

He felt for the bracelet only to find it gone. How?

Varian glanced at Blaise to see him staring at Merewyn in disbelief. He followed the line of Blaise's vision to find Merewyn on the floor with a small smile hovering at the corner of her mouth.

'What happened?' Varian asked.

Blaise shook his head. 'Hell if I know.'

He waited for Merewyn to respond.

She didn't. Instead, she opened her mouth as if she would, but no sound came out. She patted at her throat, then mouthed the words, 'I can't speak.'

Varian frowned at her as he pushed himself up from the cot. 'What?'

He didn't miss the look of 'oh shit' on Blaise's face.

'Do you know what's going on?' he asked the mandrake.

'Not a clue. But I have a feeling the two of you need

to talk.' And before Varian could blink, Blaise was out of the room with Beau right behind him.

A sense of dread went through him as he saw the fear that tainted the joy in Merewyn's gaze. Ignoring the fact he was naked, he left the cot to kneel on the floor beside her.

'What did you do?'

Tears welled in her eyes as she reached one gentle hand up to touch his lips. She fingered them before her gaze dropped to the scar beside his ear. She trailed her fingers to it and ran them up until her hand was buried in his hair.

'Merewyn?'

She answered him with a tender kiss.

Varian groaned at the taste of her and at the unexpected heat that flooded his body. Every part of him wanted her, but he didn't dare until he understood what was going on here.

Reluctantly, he pulled back. He tried to use his powers to read her thoughts, but something had him blocked. She wouldn't have that ability . . .

A tremor of betrayal went through him. There was only one person she could have bargained with.

His mother.

'What did you promise her?'

She shook her head in response to his question.

'Merewyn!'

Merewyn wanted to tell him what she'd done, but if she did, the spell would return with one more stipulation. This time it wouldn't just restrict his powers . . .

It would kill him.

Terrified of that, she bent her head down and tucked it under his chin as she kept her hand buried in his hair. She only wanted to feel his strength. His comfort. She needed it more than she needed to breathe.

Closing her eyes, she listened to his heart beating. Never had she heard a better sound. His body was back to a normal temperature.

Varian closed his arms around her as he felt her trembling. What had she done? He wanted to be angry, but how could he? Whatever bargain she'd made, she made for his life and powers. Only an absolute cad would condemn her for such a thing.

'It'll be all right, Merewyn,' he whispered against her hair as he tightened his arms around her.

She pulled back to look up at him and he offered her a gentle smile. 'Are you angry?' she mouthed.

He cupped her face in his hands and hoped that the sincerity he felt showed. 'No.'

Merewyn wanted to shout in relief. She'd been terrified that he would hate her for her actions. As it was, she only wanted to be closer to him. She pulled his lips to hers so that she could taste the warmth of his mouth. She ran her hands over the bare skin of his back, delighting in the feel of him.

Growling, he pulled her closer to him as he nibbled and teased her lips. Merewyn gave a silent laugh at his eagerness. But the truth was, she wanted him as badly as he wanted her.

She felt him lifting the hem of her skirt so that he could skim his hand along her thigh. Her entire body heated in sweet expectation. But before he could touch her, the door to his room crashed open.

Merewyn pulled back with a gasp to see Merlin and Nimue standing there. Black armor instantly appeared on Varian's body as he released her.

'What have you done?' Merlin demanded, his eyes blazing red.

Varian knew better than to answer until Merlin explained his anger. 'What?'

270

'Morgen has an army marching across the moat, heading into the valley.'

'What?'

Merlin's anger was only matched by Nimue's as she stepped forward. 'You heard him. Someone has betrayed us.'

He felt Merewyn stiffen, and suddenly he knew what she'd traded for his life. He placed a comforting hand on her as he kept her behind him, away from the two who would kill her if they ever learned the truth.

'I will deal with her,' Varian said.

'How?'

'She wants me, remember? I'll take care of it.'

Merlin curled his lip at him. 'You damn well better.' The two of them vanished immediately.

Varian stood and turned to help Merewyn to her feet. 'Woman, what have you done?'

Anger glared in her eyes.

'It's all right,' he tried to soothe her. He led her from the room to where Blaise and Beau were waiting. 'I'm sending the three of you over to Avalon.'

Blaise arched a brow at that. 'What about you?'

'I've got something to do.'

Merewyn grabbed his arm and shook her head no.

He covered her hand with his. 'I have to. Merlin will kill you if he finds out what you've done, and I can't risk Morgen or my mother capturing you again.' He gently pushed her toward Blaise. 'Take her to Merlin and tell her that I'll be over as soon as I can.'

'And if you don't make it back?'

'I'll make it back.'

There was no denying the skepticism in Blaise's gaze. But Varian didn't have time for it. Before anyone else could protest, he shot all of them into the next realm.

And then he laughed as he felt his powers coursing through him. Oh yeah. It was good to him. Good to be a Merlin . . .

Now he had a bit of a debt to pay.

Leaning his head back, he extended his arms and took a deep breath to channel the elements around him. Elemental power flowed through him like hot wine.

'You can't face her alone.'

He jerked at the deep, heavily accented voice. Reaching for the hilt of his sword, he spun to find a lean man dressed all in brown leather, who wore a cowl pulled low over his head. He stood with his legs wide apart and his arms folded over his chest. He was dressed as an archer, complete with a quiver of arrows and carved longbow crossed over his back. And over his left shoulder he wore a thin, black leather baldric that held a plain, foot soldier's sword.

All Varian could see of the stranger's face was his brown goatee and a bit of chiseled cheek. He had no idea of the man's features or age, but something about him seemed ancient. Wise.

Formidable.

Which meant he was most likely foe. 'Who the hell are you?'

'I'm called Faran.'

Varian frowned at the name that in Old English meant traveler. 'What are you doing here?'

A deep laugh rolled out from him. 'Hiding from Emrys. He'd be rather peeved to find me here in his domain.'

Varian narrowed his gaze as something in the stranger's voice sounded eerily familiar. 'Do I know you?'

'Doubtful. I don't even know myself most days.'

What a strange individual. But that was neither here nor there. 'Look, I don't—'

'Have time to deal with the likes of me. I know. You're about to head off to commit suicide. God forbid I should intervene with that, huh?'

Varian scowled at the playful note in the man's voice. 'Who *are* you?'

'Like you, I'm just another hemorrhoid on Morgen's ass. And if you're going to irritate her, then I think I should join ranks with you.'

Varian wasn't sure if he could trust this man or not, but he strangely liked his outlook on life. 'Why would you help me?'

'Because you need it. Even a champion needs someone to lend him a hand from time to time. Trust me. That was the hardest lesson I had to learn in my life.'

Again he had the strangest sensation of familiarity. He tried to peer under the cowl, but the man stepped back and lowered his head. 'We have to move quickly to head them off. Right now, Morgen doesn't know Nimue and Merlin are alive, but if her envoy makes it past Sagremor, she will.'

'How can she not know?'

'Good question. Wish I had an answer for it. I don't know why her informant withheld that bit. Maybe to play both sides, or maybe the informant felt like he owed Merlin something.'

A shiver went down his spine at what Faran was telling him. Did he know the informant was a she or was the man testing him to see if he knew the answer? 'Do you know who the informant is?'

'The real question, Varian, is do you?'

'How do you know me?'

He gave a light laugh. 'I make it a point to know all

273

of Morgen's hemorrhoids by name. Gives me something to do on a Sunday night rather than watch bad TV reruns.'

Varian scowled. 'You're not going to answer a straight question, are you?'

'Lesson two, there's no such thing as a straight question – just as there's no such thing as a simple answer. The more simple it seems on the surface, the more complicated it is on the bottom. Now are we going to turn back the tide of unholy goons or should we stand here philosophizing until they come knocking on the door?'

'Let's go turn them back.' He gestured toward the door. 'After you.'

Faran laughed. 'Good man. Trust no one at your back.'

'Lesson three?'

'No, I came out of the womb with that one already in place.'

'And yet you're trusting me?'

Faran's answer came as a bright flash. One moment they were inside the cottage and in the next they were on the bridge where Sagremor had confronted Varian only days before.

Varian noted that he wasn't at Faran's back. He was at his side. Shaking his head, he pulled his sword. 'How long ...'

He didn't even get to finish the question before the small band of Adoni broke through the woods.

Varian cursed. 'Where's Sagremor?'

'He can't manifest until they touch the bridge. Besides, we don't want him here if we can help it. His mist will only blind us from our targets.'

Good point.

The Adoni split apart, literally. In a bright flash of

light, the four men became eight, then sixteen, then thirty-two. It was a good trick that came from a spell of Morgen's, and it was one she'd used to her advantage against the knights of the Round Table at Camlann.

This was going to get ugly.

Faran pulled the longbow from his back and nocked two arrows into place. 'They'll think you're still bound, so we have a slight advantage.'

'"Slight" being the key word, right?'

Faran laughed.

'Have we missed the action?'

Varian jerked around to find Merrick, Derrick, and Erik. 'What are you doing here?'

'Merlin sent out a call to everyone to get ready in case we're invaded. We figured you'd be here to hold the line.'

'Is anyone else coming?' Faran asked.

Derrick shook his head. 'Merlin's counting on Varian to win; otherwise, Merlin's going to blast him.'

'Into pieces,' Merrick added.

'Oh goodie.' Varian left every ounce of his sarcasm in his voice.

'Varian duFey!' a dark-haired Adoni shouted. 'Surrender to us, and no one will be harmed.'

Varian snorted. 'I daresay *I* would be harmed in that action.'

'But your companions will go free.'

'Screw them. If they can't beat your rotten asses, they deserve to die.'

'Hey!' Merrick snapped. 'I resent that.'

Derrick pulled his sword. 'Yeah, but it's true.'

Varian frowned at Derrick's actions. 'I thought you were a lover and not a fighter.'

'Yeah well, sometimes you have to fight for love, or

in this case, life. They come across this bridge, and there won't be enough left of me to seduce anyone.'

He had a point.

Varian summoned his magick as he watched the Adoni pull their swords and mount their assault.

Faran let fly his arrows. Like the Adoni, they split apart as soon as they left the bow and formed a dozen arrows that took out seven of the Adoni. Five of them dissolved, proving that they weren't real, while two hit the ground and rolled in agony. Erik howled in victory.

Varian sent out a blast while Faran reached for more arrows. Unfortunately, that blast was ineffectual against Morgen's magick.

Faran let fly more arrows. They embedded into the Adoni, but those who weren't hit merely split apart into even more attackers.

Varian cursed.

'We'll have to burn the bridge,' Faran said as he launched more arrows.

Varian was completely aghast. 'What?'

Faran lowered the bow, and even though Varian couldn't see Faran's face, he could tell the man was giving him a penetrating glare. 'Morgen won the last battle fought here. Let's keep history from repeating itself. Burn her to the ground.'

'What about Sagremor?'

'It'll free his soul. It's the best thing for him.'

Merrick frowned. 'What about the forest? No one will be able to cross into the valley. When Morgen banishes her lovers, they'll be trapped with the Sylphs.'

Faran showed no mercy there. 'When you bed with the devil, you should expect to suffer in hell.'

'As one of those people in hell, I resent that.'

'Resent later,' Faran snapped. 'Right now we're

276

about to be overrun.' He fired more arrows, then took off running toward the Adoni.

Merrick's gaze bored into Varian. 'You're not really going to burn it, are you?'

'We have to protect Merlin and the others. You guys cross to the back, and I'll take care of it from the front.' Varian turned to leave and the instant he did, a bad feeling went through him.

Two seconds later, he knew what had caused it.

Merrick raised his sword and lunged. He angled the blade so that it slid up beneath Varian's hauberk.

Varian hissed as the sword stroke laid open his back. His ears buzzing, he could hear Erik cheering his brother on.

'What are you doing?' Derrick demanded.

Merrick twisted the blade and shoved it even deeper into Varian's body. 'We're getting back into Morgen's good graces. All we have to do is deliver him to her and she'll give Erik back his body and we can go free.'

Varian wanted to call out and warn Faran, who was already engaging the Adoni, but the wound had collapsed his lung. All he could manage was a short, sharp breath as he tasted his own blood. So much for trusting anyone at his back ...

'Morgen!' Merrick called out. 'We're—' His words broke off as Derrick struck him hard.

Varian was thrown forward as Merrick's fall jerked the sword out of his body.

Derrick head-butted his brother before he came to Varian's side and put Varian's arm around his shoulders. 'Come on, let's get you off the bridge so we can burn it.'

Erik ran at Derrick and bit him. Derrick kicked his brother back. 'I'm not betraying you, you idiot. I'm saving your life.'

Still, Erik screamed, while Derrick helped Varian off the ground. Faran was doing a remarkable job, but not even he could hold back the multiplying Adoni.

As they reached the edge of the bridge, Merrick shoved Derrick forward. Derrick let go, and Varian slid to the ground. He was too injured even to stand. All he could feel was the excruciating pain and a strange numbness.

'Give us him.'

'No.'

Merrick attacked.

Derrick grabbed him in a headlock. 'Fire the bridge.'

Varian could barely focus on the bridge as his sight dimmed. He cursed as he coughed up blood. Even so, he forced himself to summon his magick. His body charging, he sent a blast straight at the wood. It immediately ignited.

The fire spread over the bridge like waves over a shore. And as it burned, he saw the image of Sagremor. The knight stood in the center with his sword drawn. He stared at the flames as if he couldn't believe it, then, with a peaceful look on his face, he saluted Varian with the sword before he vanished into the smoke.

Still the brothers fought.

Varian heard someone approaching him. He rolled over, trying to get to his feet to fight them off.

He struggled for his sword. Looking up, he glimpsed . . .

No, it couldn't be.

And the next thing he knew, everything went black.

Chapter Eighteen

Varian came awake slowly. He waited for the pain to return, but it didn't. Instead, he felt a gentle hand in his hair and smelled the scent of rosemary and lavender.

Opening his eyes, he didn't see the grayness of the forest or hear the sounds of battle. He saw sunlight spilling in through an open window. And he was lying on the floor in Aquila Penmerlin's chambers.

'Feeling better?' Merlin asked as she stared at him with her head cocked.

Varian frowned until he saw Merewyn and Blaise behind her. Merewyn offered him a smile, which he returned before he spoke to Blaise. 'You healed me?'

Blaise nodded. 'Couldn't leave you to bleed all over the floor. You were making an awful mess. Glad I don't have to clean it up.'

Merewyn rolled her eyes at the mandrake before she withdrew her hand.

Varian frowned as he noted who was missing from their group. 'Where's Faran?'

'Faran?' Blaise asked.

'He had to leave,' Merlin explained.

Blaise duplicated Varian's scowl. 'Who's Faran?'

'A friend.' Merlin stepped back as Varian rolled to his feet. 'How are you feeling?'

'I have to say I'm getting really tired of being stabbed and bespelled.'

Merlin looked past him to where Merewyn was rising. 'I have to say I think Merewyn is getting as sick of it as you are.'

He could just imagine since the poor woman seemed to be the only one to tend him whenever he was down. But that didn't explain what'd happened.

If Merewyn hadn't sold out their location to break his spell . . .

The brothers?

'Where are the triplets?' he asked Blaise.

'Derrick is in the TV room fixated on *Lost* reruns. Merrick and Erik are cooling their heels downstairs in lockup.'

They got off rather easy, and something in that went against his grain. 'You should have turned them over to Emrys.'

'I thought about it. But my father would have killed them, and Derrick would have felt guilty that he'd saved your life by sacrificing theirs. This way he gets to be a good guy with no regrets.'

The mandrake was a lot wiser than he appeared. 'Where's Beau?'

'Off with Garafyn, and that's a mighty scary thought, huh? God help us if he picks up any of Garafyn's personality. We'll have to make gravel out of him.'

Varian had to agree with that. Garafyn was an acquired taste – like drinking formaldehyde.

Varian turned back toward Merlin. 'Has Merewyn told you the good news?'

'What news?'

'She knows the identity of our traitor.'

Merlin's eyes widened. 'Is she sure?'

Merewyn nodded.

'She knows him by sight,' Varian explained. 'But not by name.'

'Then we will have to take care and keep her hidden until she can find him. If he sees her first, he'll probably try to kill her.'

'Don't worry. I won't let her out of my sight.'

Blaise cleared his throat. 'Well, while it's amazingly fun to watch you two make goo-goo eyes at each other – and please note the sarcasm in my voice, I think I'm going to go bug Seren and Kerrigan for a bit. Check in on the baby and all that. See you later.' He vanished out of the room.

Merlin laughed at his departure. 'He's so glad to have his powers back. What about you?'

'You have to ask?'

Merlin started away from them, then paused as if something painful went through her.

Varian steadied her with his hand. 'Are you all right?'

Her face was terribly pale. 'Morgen is summoning me.'

'Summoning you how?'

She held her hand out, and a small crystal globe flew from the table beside Varian, toward her. It hung in the air, spinning until an iridescent red light emanated from the center of it. The light cast a spooky glow all over them as it formed the face of Morgen.

She stared at the three of them as if they were the lowest of life-forms. That was something amusing coming from the Queen Bitch.

Morgen glared at Merlin. 'You have something that belongs to me.'

'I really don't think so.'

'Oh yes. You do.'

'And what, pray tell do you lay claim to?'

'Merewyn of Mercia.'

Varian took Merewyn's hand in his as he put himself between her and the globe. 'Like hell.'

'Watch your mouth, Varian,' Narishka snapped from the background. 'I taught you better than that.'

'Of course you did, mum, but I have two ladies here with me, and I don't want to offend them with the language I learned from you.'

An evil laugh rippled out of Morgen's throat. 'That's no way to soften her up, Varian.' Her gaze went to Merlin. 'The chit is our property. We demand her back.'

Varian ground his teeth in anger. 'Over my dead body.'

'Those terms are acceptable to us.'

Varian wanted to reach through the orb and kill them both. If only he could.

'Either Varian or Merewyn must return to us within the half hour or else . . .'

'Or else what?' Merlin asked.

'Merewyn dies on the spot.' Morgen turned over an hourglass that was filled with black sand. 'If the last grain falls and no one is here in my hall, she will draw her last breath.'

Varian shattered the ball with his powers as his fury exploded.

Merlin took his rage in stride.

'I won't let my mother have her.'

'We don't have a choice. You know why *you* can't go there again.'

Varian shook his head as Merewyn moved to the table where Merlin had left pen and paper. Frowning, he watched as she scribbled something, then brought it over to him.

And as he read the words, his heart shattered.

You told me that your mother would force you to this and that when the time came you would sacrifice me to her. It is the way of it.

'No!' he snarled, balling the paper up in his fist. 'I will not allow you back there.' He looked to Merlin for help. 'Merewyn knows the traitor. I don't. She can give him to you.'

'Your mother will kill you if you go back there.'

Probably so. But he was going back with his powers intact. If they wanted to take him on, let them. 'Let her try.'

Merewyn was terrified as she listened to Varian rail. She couldn't let him go back to Camelot. She'd made her deal already, and there was nothing to be done for it.

But first she had to find some way to make Varian see the light. She placed one finger over his mouth as he started to argue more with Merlin. How strange that he who'd told her he would die for nothing would now be willing to give his life for hers.

No one had ever given her so much.

She only wished that she could tell him what she felt. Tell him why she had to do this. Tell him that she loved him.

But instead all she could do was show him how much he meant to her.

As if Merlin understood, she pulled back. 'I have to go check on ... something.' An instant later, she vanished.

Varian let out a sound of disgust. 'Merlin! You can't get out of this that easily.'

As he started for the door, Merewyn took his arm

283

and pulled his lips to hers. The taste of him made her silently gasp. Honestly, this was all she wanted. To stay with him and hold him forever.

But they'd never been destined to be together. All she could do was distract him. And with that thought in mind, she dipped her hand down and slid it under his armor.

Varian couldn't think straight as Merewyn's hand brushed the skin of his stomach. Wanting more of it, he melted his armor to his leather jerkin and breeches.

She immediately slid her hand down until she cupped him. His body swelled instantly. He deepened their kiss as her hand stroked him from tip to hilt.

And when she pushed his breeches down below his hips to expose him, all rational thoughts evaporated. All he could focus on was her.

She pulled back from his lips, then sank down in front of him. His lids heavy, he held his breath as he watched her. She stroked his sac with the back of her soft hands an instant before she took the tip of him into her mouth. He hissed as she took him in deeper and deeper still while her tongue gently stroked him.

Merewyn moaned at the taste of his body. If she'd learned anything in Morgen's court, it was that men were slaves to their hormones. This was their weakness.

But, unlike Morgen and Narishka, she wasn't about to use it to hurt him. She wanted only to protect him, which meant she had precious little time.

Varian's heart pounded as she tongued him so sweetly. But this wasn't what he wanted.

He pulled away before he lifted her from the floor.

Merewyn held her breath, afraid she might have angered him. But there was no anger in his eyes, only desire. His breathing ragged, he lifted her to the table before he lifted her skirt to pool at her waist, baring her to his gaze.

She bit her lip as he dipped his hand to stroke her. Spreading her legs wider, she leaned her head back. He bent over to kiss her throat an instant before he thrust inside her.

He made love to her furiously, driving himself into her deeper with every stroke. Merewyn held him close.

But their time was getting perilously short.

Her body on fire, she wanted more of him.

Varian quickened his strokes as he pressed himself deep inside her. He couldn't remember wanting any woman as badly as he wanted her.

She buried her hands in his hair and held tight an instant before he felt her climax. Her soundless cries of pleasure delighted him, urging him on until he joined her.

His body convulsing, he held her close and wished he could take her somewhere and spend the rest of the day naked in her arms.

But his mother wouldn't allow them that peace. She would allow him nothing.

Resigned to the truth, he withdrew from her.

Merewyn panicked as he pulled his breeches up and fastened them. She didn't know what to do. Her plan had been to seduce him, and instead he'd rattled her own senses.

She had to think of some way to keep him here, away from Morgen. Unfortunately, there was only one other way she knew.

When he started away from her, she seized a wooden mallet from the table and struck him hard on his head. He turned toward her with an accusing look an instant before he sank to the floor.

'*Narishka!*' she shouted at the woman in her head. '*I am yours. Come get me.*'

She'd no more thought the words than she was snatched from Avalon, back to the colorless drab world of Camelot.

Merewyn cringed at the horror of it, especially as she saw Morgen and Narishka waiting for her.

'How disappointing,' Morgen pouted. 'I was so hoping Varian would come in your stead.'

Narishka laughed. 'He has.'

Morgen frowned in deep consternation. 'What are you talking about?'

Narishka pulled Merewyn to her, then turned her to face Morgen. 'Are your powers slipping, my queen? Can you not feel his powers inside her?'

What were they talking about?

Morgen's interest sparked. 'Why you little slut. You're pregnant.'

Merewyn shook her head in denial. She couldn't be pregnant . . . could she?

Well, of course she *could* be. At least in theory. But how would they know that?

Narishka grabbed her by the hair and jerked her head back. 'And she's been with him recently. Her body is still marked by his touch.' Narishka ran her hand over the spot where Varian had suckled her neck. 'There's no way he won't come for his whore and child. We have him right where we want him.'

No! The word radiated inside her. This wasn't what was supposed to happen. Varian was supposed to be safe. And all she'd done by trying to protect him was drag him deeper into this.

Dear Lord, what had she done?

Varian came awake slowly to someone patting his

back. Expecting it to Merewyn, he was stunned to find Beau standing over him.

And no sooner did he focus on the gargoyle than he remembered what'd happened. Merewyn had struck him on the head with a hammer.

'Where is my lady?' Beau asked quietly.

'In trouble, I'm sure.'

'In trouble how?'

Varian didn't answer. Instead, he rose to his feet fully intent on reclaiming her. The only problem was that when he tried to flash himself to Camelot, he stayed in Merlin's chambers.

'Merlin,' he snapped.

She appeared instantly before him.

'Free my powers.'

'I can't. I'm not the one who's restricting them.'

'Excuse me?'

She held her hands up in surrender. 'I swear I'm not the one doing it.'

'Send me to Camelot.'

'I can't do that. You might not be able to return, and there's no way I'll be responsible for your death.'

'Like you care. Now send me over.'

'I do care, Varian.'

He cursed at her words. 'I have to protect Merewyn.'

'And she is trying to protect you.'

'I don't need protection. What I need is . . .'

She arched a brow at his words. 'Is?'

He'd wanted to say that he needed a way to Camelot, but those words stuck in his throat as he thought of Merewyn being hurt. Grief, raw and unimaginable, seized him. Crippled him. The thought of her in his mother's hands made him sick on a level he'd never known existed.

'I need Merewyn,' he said simply. 'And I won't live knowing that my life was bought at the expense of hers. Ever.'

Disembodied applause filled the room.

Varian frowned. What the hell was that?

The thought had barely finished in his mind before Damé appeared beside Merlin. Tall and well muscled, the ancient god looked more like a god of war than one of fate. The only thing missing was armor, but Damé never wore armor. He'd once told Varian the reason for that was because it chafed.

The god was dressed in a simple tunic and breeches. He had his dark blond hair tied back at the nape of his neck with a small leather cord. 'Well put, Varian. But I have to say it shocks me. Never thought I'd hear something like that from the likes of you.'

'I don't have time for your bullshit, Damé. I have a serious problem.'

'Yes, you do, and neither of you realize just how dire it is.'

Merlin frowned. 'What do you mean?'

'Well far be it from me ever to play sides, but right now, old mommykins and Morgen have a tool in their hands that could give them exactly what they want.'

Merlin went pale. 'They've found the grail.'

'Not yet. But they have in their possession one who could.'

Varian went cold. 'They've found another grail knight.'

Damé nodded.

'Who?' Merlin asked. 'They're all accounted for.'

'Yes, but one knight has fallen, and so another will be chosen to replace him.'

Varian exchanged a puzzled stare with Merlin. 'It has to be someone with a Merlin's line... Oh jeez, don't tell me it's Arador,' he said, using the name of the new king of Camelot, who was a Merlin in his own right.

Damé shook his head. 'Think closer to home. More to the point, think of you, yourself putting that tool in your mother's hands.'

'What are you talking about?'

'Merewyn's pregnant,' Merlin whispered.

Varian's breath left his body as if he'd been delivered a staggering blow. In fact, he felt like someone had landed a sledgehammer right in his stomach.

Merewyn pregnant?

'I have to go to her.'

Damé's cold steel gaze bit into him. 'You do, and it's over for you. Your mother has finally found the one noose to hang you with.'

'I don't care. I won't leave her there to face my mother's wrath.'

'So are you willing to make the ultimate sacrifice for her?'

'What do you think?'

One corner of Damé's mouth quirked up. 'I think words are cheap.'

Two seconds later, Varian was alone in Camelot.

He summoned his armor, including his helm. Unwilling to take a single chance, he unsheathed his sword and used his powers to locate Merewyn.

He paused as he found her, and a wave of disgust filled him. She was with the MODs of course. Where else would his mother have put her?

Bracing himself for the fight to come, he flashed himself down to their hole. As he materialized, it took a second to get his bearings. He was in Bracken's chambers, but the MOD leader was nowhere to be found.

However Merewyn was. She sat on the floor, chained by her neck to an iron chair.

She looked up at his approach with eyes filled with terror. The sight of it froze him to the center of his being as rage took hold of him. How dare they subjugate her like this.

The instant he pulled the helm from his head, her fear melted. At least for a few heartbeats. Then it returned even stronger than before. '*You have to leave.*' Her words were silent, but he understood.

'I will . . . as soon as I have you.'

She shook her head fiercely as she gestured for the door.

'You take her from here, and I'll kill her.'

Varian paused at the sound of his mother's voice. Turning, he saw her and Bracken standing in the center of the large room. 'You wouldn't dare.'

'Don't bet on it, boy.'

Had it been anyone other than his mother making that threat, he might have. As it was, he knew she wasn't lying. Looks like they'd have to play another round of *Let's Make a Deal*. 'What do you want, mum?'

'World domination. Bloodshed. War. Not much really. But I'll start with you delivering to me the grail knights.'

'I can't do that.'

'Then you'll have to die.'

'What? No more trying to convert me?'

'Not really. I'm tried of wasting my time with you. But I wonder how strong you would be while I tortured your plaything in front of you?'

Varian shot out a blast at his mother. It caught her and Bracken and knocked them off their feet. He turned to free Merewyn only to learn that his magick was useless against her chain.

His mother laughed. 'You didn't think I'd make this easy on you? The bitch belongs here with us. She made a deal with me, and hell will freeze before I release her.'

'Hmm ... it appears Lucifer's munching icicles.'

Varian looked past his mother to find Damé standing with his arms crossed over his chest.

Narishka pushed herself to her feet. 'What are you doing here?'

He snapped his fingers, and Merewyn let out an audible gasp as the chain fell from her throat. 'Collecting *my* property.'

'What?' Narishka breathed. 'You can't do that. I have a contract with her.'

'Yes for one moon cycle and that ended while she was in the valley. Technically, Merewyn is free. At least she was until she sold her life to me for Varian's.'

Varian's jaw went slack as he stared in disbelief.

'She wasn't allowed to tell you,' Damé explained. 'I wanted to see if you were worth the price of her life or not. Lucky for her, you stood by her side even when it appeared she'd betrayed you and Emrys. Good man. Now, her life belongs to me.'

Narishka shrieked in outrage. 'You can't take her. I won't allow it.'

'You can't stop me.'

As Damé started toward them, Narishka lashed her hands out.

Varian had no idea what his mother was throwing at Merewyn, but he didn't care. Without hesitation, he threw himself over her to protect her.

The shot went through him like a blast of painful lightning.

Merewyn cringed as she felt Varian shaking. She

wasn't sure what to expect, but when their eyes met, all she could do was stare in horror.

Gone was the beautiful dark-haired knight who'd stolen her heart. In his place, was an old, twisted man.

Damé cursed at Narishka, who showed no remorse.

Instead, she laughed. 'Well, I'd planned to make the chit hideous again. But this will do. You take her for your own, Damé, and Varian can live knowing no one else will ever touch him while you get to screw his plaything. Poetic really.'

Cursing, Damé sent his own blast at Narishka. It struck her hard, knocking her against the wall and singeing her hair. Bracken took a step forward, then cowed back as Damé gave him an arch stare.

Damé turned to face them, and in the next breath, they were back in Avalon.

Merewyn was still holding Varian against her.

'Come, Merewyn,' Damé said. 'Time for us to leave.'

She shook her head. 'I can't leave him. Not like this.'

'You made a deal with me.'

'Please,' she begged, as tears suffused her eyes. 'You don't know what it's like to be deformed and hated. I can't abandon him to that cruelty.'

'Go,' Varian breathed, trying to push her away. 'I'll be fine. Besides I'm used to it.'

'No,' she breathed, as her tears started to fall. 'You don't deserve this.'

Damé cocked his head as he stared at her. 'So what are you saying, Merewyn? Do you love this man?'

'Yes.'

'Truly? You would rather spend the rest of eternity locked to an old, twisted man when you could spend it with me?'

292

She looked at Damé, who was truly the epitome of male beauty. His face and body were flawless. His power absolute.

Even so, Merewyn didn't hesitate with her answer. 'Only if that man is Varian.'

'Look at him when you say that.'

She did. His skin was gray and pockmarked. His fingers twisted. But his eyes were still that clear, beautiful green.

'Do you still want to stay with that? To marry him?'

'Yes.'

Damé stepped forward. 'Think about what you're saying, Merewyn. Think about what it means.'

Before she could respond, she saw a clear image of Varian's twisted form making love to her. Of his gnarled, warted hands on her body.

It should disgust her, but for some reason she wasn't repelled, and for the first time she understood what Varian had meant in the valley when she'd been ugly.

'I don't care what he looks like.'

'Hmm ... well then, prove it to me, and I'll rescind our agreement.'

A wave of fear went through her. 'Prove it how?'

'Kiss him.'

'Is that all?'

Damé laughed. 'Isn't it enough?'

Varian cringed as Merewyn faced him. If he looked half as bad as he suspected, he wouldn't have blamed her had she run for the door. 'You don't have to do this.'

She stepped into his arms. 'Yes, Varian, I do.' She brushed the matted hair back from his face. 'I don't care what you look like. It's you I love, not your looks. Your humor, your kindness, even that little snuffle snore you make when you sleep.'

293

'I don't snore.'

She laughed. 'Yes, you do.' And with that she pulled his lips to hers. Merewyn wrapped her arms around his shoulders as Varian nipped and teased her mouth with his crooked teeth.

'Ahhh, yuck, that's disgusting,' Damé railed. 'People get a room.' He shivered in revulsion. 'Fine, you win. I release you from our bargain. Now stop kissing the toad. I'm going blind.'

Merewyn pulled back, but only so that she could place a kiss on Varian's hand.

And as she did so, a strange orange glow appeared on his knuckle. It spread slowly over his body and as it did so, he returned to himself.

Merewyn blinked in confusion. Until she realized what Damé had done. 'Thank you.'

'Don't thank me. I had nothing to do with this.'

'What do you mean?'

'I didn't break Narishka's spell. You did, just like Varian broke it in the valley. Instead of glamour, this is the spell of aversion. The only way to break it is to find someone who can see through it.'

'But I thought one sorcerer couldn't break the spell of another.'

'One can't,' Varian explained. 'At least not with magick. But a human heart can shatter anything.' He looked at Damé. 'I should have thought of that.'

'Ah, you had other things on your mind. Now kids, I have more people to piss off. Have a nice life.' And with that, he left them alone.

Varian turned his hands over to see them as they'd always been. Then he met Merewyn's happy gaze. 'Thank you.'

'No, thank you for coming for me. But why did you do that?'

'Isn't it obvious?'

'That you're insane? Yes. Don't ever do something like that again.'

He pulled her into his arms. 'I'm not crazy, Merewyn. And I will always do something stupid and insane if you're in danger.'

'Why?'

'Because that's what a man does when he loves a woman. And I would give my life for you. Always.'

Those words tore through her. They were words she'd never hoped to hear, especially not from a man like Varian. 'I love you, too.'

And this time when they kissed, Varian felt the one thing he'd never felt before. Not just her love, but for the first time in his life, he had faith. Faith in her and, most of all, faith in their future.

Epilogue

One month later . . .

Merewyn still couldn't believe that Varian's mother hadn't found some way to punish them. Every morning, she woke up with a lump of fear in her stomach. But so far, Narishka had done nothing.

And as every day passed, Merewyn loved Varian more. She treasured every moment spent with him. Every conversation, every stolen and freely given kiss.

There was nothing she wouldn't do for him.

After their quick marriage in the small chapel at Avalon, the others there had begun to treat him with more regard and more kindly. It was as if having her by his side made them see him more as a man than a demon.

Best of all, she'd found something in Avalon she'd never really had before. A friend in Kerrigan's wife, Seren. The petite blonde had been a poor weaver's apprentice until fate had found her to be one of the missing Merlins in charge of the loom of Caswallen.

Seren had been the one to save Kerrigan from Morgen's clutches, and now the two of them, along with their infant daughter, made Avalon home.

Seren was with her now even though Merewyn was

suffering greatly with a bout of illness from her pregnancy. She wasn't sure who'd named it morning sickness when it seemed to strike without warning at any time of day.

They'd just returned to sit in the hall and continue their conversation. Holding her baby, Seren was smiling kindly as Merewyn picked up her small sewing frame.

'Does this ever end?'

Seren laughed. 'The illness, yes. Fear for your child, no. But don't worry. You're birthing a Merlin. If you think this is bad, wait until the baby's powers start surging through you. The little darlings can be quite demanding. There are times when you feel completely out of control.'

Oh joy. Merewyn couldn't wait for that experience. 'Does that pass?'

Seren adjusted her daughter Alethea on her lap so that the baby could sleep more comfortably. 'After their birth. I think, though, it's why women who carry Merlins have so few children. It's actually frightening when those powers are brewing. But don't worry. You have me and Merlin and countless others who will help you through it.'

Merewyn smiled at her. 'Thank you.' And as she watched the infant sucking on her tiny fist, she couldn't wait to hold her own baby.

Laughter broke out as a group of men entered the hall across the room from them. Merewyn glanced up from her embroidery, thinking it was Varian returning from Merlin's latest assignment.

It wasn't.

It was the man Varian had gone to find. The traitor. Merewyn's blood went cold at the sight of him making merry with his group.

Terrified, she leaned forward to speak in a low tone. 'Seren? Who is that man speaking to Bors? The short one?'

Seren glanced over and frowned. 'Ademar, why?'

Merewyn didn't answer. She was too afraid even to speak for fear it would draw his notice. Because she could identify the traitor, they had all been careful to tell no one she was from Camelot. Instead, they'd said she'd met Varian, Blaise, and the brothers in the valley.

Ademar turned toward her.

Merewyn instantly dropped her gaze to her lap, hoping he hadn't seen her watching him.

The man strode across the room until he stood before them. 'Greetings, Lady Seren. I trust you are well?'

Poor Seren had no idea who the man was. 'I am, thank you, Lord Ademar. I trust the same of you.'

'I couldn't be better.' His gaze went to Merewyn. 'You are new to our company, my lady. I've never seen you here before.'

'She's Varian's new wife,' Bors said from behind him.

Hatred flared in his eyes at the mention of her husband's name.

'I'd heard he'd taken a wife. Who knew she would be so lovely.'

Strange, he hadn't been this kind the last time they'd met. Rather he'd insulted and degraded her before he shoved her out of his way and spat on her.

He gave her what she was sure he thought a charming smile. 'So tell me, my lady, where are you from?'

Before she could answer, Seren gasped. 'Oh my goodness, Merewyn. Note the time. We have to leave and meet with Kerrigan.'

Merewyn started to frown since she had no idea

what Seren was talking about, but then she caught the look in her friend's eye. 'Oh yes. I completely forgot. He'll be waiting for us.'

'Yes, he will.' Seren stood up. 'Forgive us, gentlemen.'

She stood up first, then helped Seren rise. By the time they'd left the hall, Merewyn thought her heart would burst from her panic.

'How did you know to leave?' Merewyn asked as soon as they were away from the men.

Seren winked at her. 'The look on your face. I could tell you would rather be anywhere than there with him. Care to tell me why Ademar made you so uncomfortable?'

She didn't answer. 'We need to get to Merlin.'

'You're starting to scare me.'

'I'm sorry, but we have to hurry.'

They'd barely neared the end of the hallway when all of a sudden Ademar appeared before them. His face stern, he made no move to let them pass.

'Is there a problem, Ademar?' Seren asked.

He narrowed his eyes on Merewyn. 'I know you, don't I?'

That was a question she could answer honestly. 'No. You don't.' He'd never bothered to learn anything about her.

He allowed Seren to walk past him, but when Merewyn tried, he grabbed her arm. 'You and I aren't through talking.'

'Oh yes we are.' She head-butted him hard and wrested her arm free. 'Run, Seren!'

Merewyn tried to run with her, but Ademar recovered himself and grabbed her again.

This time, Seren blasted him. It knocked him back, but not before he returned her hit.

Scared it would hit Seren and make her drop the baby, Merewyn threw herself in front of it. It went through her with a jolt and knocked her to the ground. She lay there, her limbs shaking as she struggled to breathe.

She wanted to tell Seren to run again, but she couldn't speak from the pain.

But luckily, Seren vanished and left her alone with Ademar. He sauntered over to her and pulled her up by the front of her gown. 'Now who are you?'

'She's my wife.' Varian's voice rang out angrily an instant before Ademar went flying. He landed in a heap a few feet from her.

Varian appeared, then seized him. He backhanded Ademar so hard, he rebounded off the wall. Still he wasn't appeased. He struck him again and again, never allowing him even a chance to recover or defend himself.

Suddenly, Merlin appeared. And her face rivaled Varian's for rage. 'Varian, stop!'

Varian did, but not before he locked his arm around Ademar's neck. The man's eyes bulged as he tried to breathe.

'Varian?' Merlin chided.

His answer was simple. 'He hit Merewyn. I'm going to kill him.'

'Varian . . .'

He locked gazes with her, and the look in his eyes made Merewyn's blood run cold. She'd never seen such from him before, and for the first time, she fully understood the depth of her husband's ruthlessness.

'No one hurts *my* wife.'

Before Merlin could act, Merewyn stood up. 'He's your traitor, Merlin. Ademar is the one I saw with Morgen.'

Ademar sputtered as Varian's eyes flamed even more.

'Are you sure about this?' Merlin asked.

'Yes. We've met several times.'

The compassion and kindness melted from Merlin's face. She turned to Varian. Her tone and demeanor were every bit as cold as Varian's. 'Before you kill him, we need to ask him a few questions.'

Varian inclined his head before he vanished with Ademar.

'What are you going to do with him?' Merewyn asked.

'I will merely find out what all he's told to Morgen.'

'And then?'

She shrugged. 'He threatened you, Seren, and Alethea. Therefore, his fate will be up to Kerrigan and Varian. And given the brutal death of Tarynce, whatever they decide to do with him is fine by me, and I'm sure it will be far kinder than what Tarynce suffered.' She hesitated. 'Then again, it is Kerrigan and Varian . . . so maybe not.'

Varian had warned her that Merlin wasn't quite as benevolent as she appeared. Now Merewyn understood. When it came to the Lords of Avalon, their Merlin could be as severe as any man.

Varian returned to address Merlin. 'He's waiting for you.'

Inclining her head to him, Merlin dissolved.

'Are you all right?' Varian asked, searching Merewyn's body with his gaze.

'A little shaken, but fine.'

He wrapped his arms around her and held her close. 'I thought I'd die with worry when I heard Seren calling to me that you needed me. She didn't say what was wrong. Only that you were in trouble.'

'I thought she went for Merlin.'

'No.'

Merewyn smiled and shook her head. 'I'm just glad we found him finally. Now you can stay home.'

'I wish, but there are more of them out there. More traitors yet to find. More battles to come. You know Morgen and my mother. They won't give up.'

She leaned back to look up at him. 'No, but then neither shall we.'

A slow smile spread across his face. 'No, we won't.'

The Legend

In a world of magic and betrayal, one king rose to unite a land divided and to bring unto his people a time of unprecedented peace. A time when might no longer made right. When one man with a dream created a world of chivalry and honor.

Guided by his Merlin, this man's destiny was to be the Pendragon – High King of Power. But Arthur was a man who had many enemies, and none of them greater than his own sister, Morgen. Queen of the fey, she was ruled by her own jealousies and by her desire to rule as Pendragon in her brother's stead.

It is a story that has been told for centuries. The rise and fall of the great King Arthur, the betrayal that led to the destruction of the Round Table.

But what happened the day after the battle of Camlann? Arthur is mortally wounded and taken to the isle of Avalon. The sacred objects of Camelot that gave him his power have been scattered to protect them from evil. The Round Table is fractured. The good guys have retreated to Avalon to serve their fallen king and the surviving Penmerlin, who came forward after Arthur's Merlin mysteriously vanished.

Camelot has now fallen into the hands of Morgen

and her comrades. No longer the place of peace and prosperity, it is now the land of the unholy. Demons, mandrakes, and darklings make up the brotherhood of the new table, and another Pendragon has stepped forward to take Arthur's place.

Once human, he is now something else entirely. A demon with one single mission: to reunite the Round Table and to claim the sacred objects. With those under his control, there will be nothing to stop him from making the world into whatever he chooses.

The only hope mankind has is those who still remain from Arthur's company. No longer the knights of the Round Table, they are now the Lords of Avalon. And they will do whatever is necessary to stop the Pendragon from succeeding.

The line between good and evil has become blurred. It is a realm of chaos and of champions. Of wizards and warriors who struggle to right the balance that was upset when one man put his trust into the wrong person.

Welcome to a realm that exists out of time. Welcome to a world where nothing is ever as it seems. It's a battle that ranges from the Dark Age moors of Arthur well into the future, where the one true king and Mordred may one day fight again.

Theirs is a world without boundary. A place without borders. But in this power struggle, there can only be one winner . . .

And winning has never been more fun.

The Thirteen Sacred Objects

These were the sacred objects that the Lenmerlin Emrys, entrusted to Arthur Pendragon so that he could rule the land peacefully without contestation. But once Camelot fell to evil and the king vanished, the new Penmerlin entrusted the sacred objects into the hands of their Waremerlins. They were scattered and hidden in the realm of man and of fey so that they would never fall into the hands of evil.

It is now a race to reclaim and reunite the lost objects.

1. **Excalibur**
   Sword created by the fey for good. The one who wields it cannot be killed, nor can he bleed so long as he holds the scabbard that sheaths it.

2. **Hamper of Garanhir**
   Created in order to feed the Pendragon's army while at war. Put in food for one, and out will appear food for one hundred.

3. **Horn of Bran**
   Given as a companion for the hamper, this horn is

a never–ending cup that will provide wine and water for any to drink from it.

4. **Saddle of Morrigan**
A gift to the Penmerlin from the goddess Morrigan, this will enable a person to go instantly wherever he desires. It was created so that the Pendragon would be able to oversee his kingdom with ease. No distance or time is too great. It can move a person from one continent to another or from one time period to another.

5. **Halter of Epona**
Given by the goddess Epona, the halter, if hung on a bedpost at night, will grant the one who possesses it whatever horse he desires in the morning.

6. **Loom of Caswallan**
A gift from the war god. Any cloth produced from this loom will be stronger than any armor forged by a mortal's hand. No mortal weapon will ever be able to penetrate the cloth.

7. **Round Table**
Table of power that was created by the Penmerlin. When all people are seated and the objects are in place, it is the ultimate in power. Whoever rules the table rules the earth.

8. **Stone of Taranis**
A gift from the god of thunder. Should a knight sharpen his sword with this stone, it will coat the blade with a poison so potent that even a tiny scratch from the blade will bring instant death.

9. Mantle of Arthur

A gift from the Penmerlin, this will enable the wearer to become invisible to everyone around him.

10. Orb of Sirona

Created by the goddess of astronomy, this will enable the person who holds it in his hand to see clearly on even the darkest night.

11. Shield of Dagda

Whoever holds the shield of Dagda will be possessed of superhuman strength, and so long as the shield is held in place, he cannot be wounded.

12. Caliburn

A sword of the fey, this is the evil sword that balances out Excalibur. It is said that this one sword carries even more power and that it can destroy the other sacred objects.

13. Holy Grail

No one is quite sure what it is or where it came from. It is the greatest object of all for it can bring the dead back to life.

Vocabulary

Adoni—a beautiful race of elflike creatures. They are tall and slender and capable of complete cruelty.

Grayling—as ugly as the Adoni are beautiful, they are essentially servants in Camelot.

Mandrake—a race of beings who have the ability to become dragons or human. They have magical abilities, but are currently enslaved as a race to Morgen.

Merlin—magical advisor.

Miren—a magical being who can sing a song so beautiful that it will kill whoever hears it.

MODs—minions of death. Interesting creatures who will be around in many future tales.

Pendragon—the High King of Camelot.

Penmerlin—the High Merlin of Camelot.

Sharoc—shadow fey.

Stone Legion—cursed race, the Stone Legion is under the command of Garafyn. By daylight, they are ugly gargoyles who are forced to sit as stone (they can only move if they are commanded by the one who bears their emblem), but at night, they can move about freely, and under the light of a full moon, they can again take the form of handsome warriors and knights – but only so long as the full moon touches them. Should they leave its light, they will immediately return to their gargoyle state. There are those who say there may be a way yet to lift their curse, but so far all those who have tried have met with failure and death.

Terre derrière le voile—land behind the veil. A term for both Avalon and Camelot since they exist outside of time and place.

Val Sans Retour—Valley of no return. An area outside Camelot where the damned wander in eternal misery.

Waremerlin—term for any Merlin.

Sherrilyn Kenyon's award-winning paranormal romances have topped the *New York Times* bestseller charts, offering readers a world full of dark and dangerous heroes, feisty heroines and a richly imagined mythology. Sexy, fun and utterly addictive, this series is best described as *Buffy the Vampire Slayer* meets *Sex and the City*.

First in Sherrilyn Kenyon's Lords of Avalon *series of historical paranormal romance, also available from Piatkus Books*:

Sword of Darkness

Sherrilyn Kenyon writing as Kinley MacGregor
Welcome to the dark side of Camelot ...
King Arthur is dead and his arch enemy, Morgen le Fey, has placed the ruthless Kerrigan on the throne of Camelot. Kerrigan, a Lord of Darkness, is feared throughout the land, and will stop at nothing to claim the powerful Round Table of legend.

From the refuge of Avalon, the remaining Knights of the Round Table have only one hope for the future. Seren, a young apprentice weaver, dreams of breaking free from her life of drudgery, and becoming her own woman. But destiny has chosen Seren for a higher purpose ...

Praise for Sherrilyn Kenyon:
'Kenyon gives readers scrumptious heroes – still with a dark edge and dangerous powers ... she creates a world full of depth and intelligent details ... and gives her stories an underpinning and a foundation in authenticity without sacrificing the breathless pace of her plots – no small feat!'
Romantic Times

Also by Sherrilyn Kenyon, available now from Piatkus Books:

Upon the Midnight Clear

Ever think Scrooge had it right before the ghosts ruined his life? Meet Aidan O'Conner. At one time he was a world-renowned celebrity who gave freely of himself and his money without wanting anything in return ... until those around him took without asking. Now Aidan wants nothing of the world – or anyone who's a part of it.

When a stranger appears at his doorstep, Aidan knows he's seen her before ... in his dreams. Born on Olympus as a goddess, Leta knows nothing of the human world. But a ruthless enemy has driven her from the world of dreams and into the home of the only man who can help her: Aidan. Her immortal powers are derived from human emotions – and his anger is just the fuel she needs to defend herself ...

One cold winter's night will change their lives forever ... Trapped together in a brutal winter storm, Aidan and Leta must turn to the only power capable of saving them – or destroying them both: trust.

Devil May Cry

Ever since that moment his status as a god was revoked by Artemis, Sin has done nothing but plot his revenge. He kidnaps a woman he believes to be the goddess, but she is Artemis' servant, Katra. And instead of imprisoning her, Katra captures him and refuses to release him until he promises not to seek vengeance on her mistress. Despite himself, Sin finds himself intrigued by Katra, who is nothing like the goddess she serves. She's fierce, true, but she's also compassionate and loyal.

However, Sin is not the only enemy Artemis has and it quickly becomes apparent that he must help Katra save her mistress or the world as we know it will end. What's a wannabe god to do?

The Dark-Hunter Companion

'We are Darkness. We are Shadow. We are the Rulers of the Night. We, alone, stand between mankind and those who would see mankind destroyed. We are the guardians. The Souless Keepers. Our souls were cast out so that we would not forewarn the Daimons we pursue. By the time they see us coming, it's too late. The Daimons and Apollites know us. They fear us. We are death to all those who prey upon the humans. Neither Human, nor Apollite, we exist beyond the realm of the Living, beyond the realm of the Dead. We are the Dark-Hunters. And we are eternal.'

The *Dark-Hunter* Creed

Sherrilyn Kenyon's Dark-Hunter Companion is essential reading for anyone who has recently made that once-in-a-life-time deal with Artemis. Packed with insider knowledge and secrets mankind are rarely privy to, it's also a valuable guide to the Dark-Hunter series for lesser mortals. It includes a Dark-Hunter directory, a handy reference guide to Dark-Hunter and Greek mythology, useful tips on dealing with daimons and squires, lessons in conversational Greek and Atlantean; there's even a section on how to handle unexpected visits from ancient gods...The companion also includes a brand new short story from every Dark-Hunter's favourite writer Sherrilyn Kenyon.

The Dark-Hunter Companion is a must-have book for every Dark-Hunter and Sherrilyn Kenyon fan!